Ekani's Journey

By

RANDALL PROBERT

Ekani's Journey
by Randall Probert

www.randallprobertbooks.net
email: randentr@megalink.net

Photography credits:
Cover photographs ~ iStockPhoto
Author's photograph-p.248 ~ Patricia Gott

Disclaimer

I was unable to find the name of Shivaji Maharaj's wife, so I created a name for her. Also in all of the research of the Maratha Empire I was not able to determine if Shivaji had any daughters; only sons were listed, so I created Princess Katarikari for the story. I also created the characters Gopal Das and Chapal.

I never believed Benedict Arnold was a traitor and after researching his history, I am now more convinced than before that Arnold was a hero and not a traitor.

I created the character Will Roberts to explain some of the history of the Andersonville prisoner of war compound in Georgia and the atrocities associated with the prison.

Most of Kyler Pardy's character is fictional as is his time in Vietnam.

ISBN: 978-0-9852872-9-0

Printed in the United States of America

Published by
Randall Enterprises
P.O. Box 862
Bethel, Maine 04217

Ekani's Journey

Prelude

India is a diverse and enchanting land. It is full of enticing and strange wonders and ideas. It is as mysterious as it is beautiful, with its rich farmland, jungles, the Deccan Plateau, the Punjab desert. Each year the rivers bring silt and nutrient rich soil down out of the high Himalayan Mountains to fertilize the farm lands and fields.

The country is full of exotic herbs and spices not easily found anywhere else. The women wear brightly colored silk clothing, where most of the world wears rather drab clothing. And most all of India is steeped in culture and traditions.

India is a collection of cultures, religions, ideas and languages. India has been invaded by the Hyperboreans of Africa, the Turks, the Greeks, the Aryans from the north (The Mongolia Empire), the Afghans, the Portuguese and the English; with each invasion they brought new ideas and culture with them. The Sanskrit language was formed. Names of cities and villages were changed. Even some words were changed to suit the new invaders. Some were looking for the unique riches that were so common in India, while others only wanted to dominate the people and control the land with ruthless power.

When Genghis Khan came out of the north and invaded Afghanistan, he found favor with the Muslim people, their traditions and culture. So when he finally returned to Mongolia he brought with him many Islamic ideas. He had also left behind many descendants, one of whom was Akbar the Great, son of Babar the first Mughal conqueror.

Often times sons would kill their father to gain control of an empire or kill their own brothers to maintain this control. Grandsons would kill grandfathers, all in the name and purpose of power.

Babur invaded India in 1526 and established the Mughal Empire. The Empire extended to western India near the limits of the Punjab Desert, the foothills along the Himalayan Mountains to Bengal in the east. And for a brief period in history the Mughals controlled most of the Kashmir.

Most of the sub-continent and the Deccan Plateau was controlled by the Maratha Empire.

The Mughal Empire in India surely flourished until their demise in about 1707. The Mughals brought with them economic advances and religious harmony—as long as you were Muslim. The Mughals opened wider markets and agriculture also began to flourish and farmers were improving their crops and income. And of course this meant more taxes could be collected to support the empire.

Towards the end of Akbar's reign, his eldest son Jahangir took over most of Akbar's duties. Akbar and his son Jahangir became followers of a new religion called Deen-i-Ilahi.

During the reign of the Mughals fifth emperor, Shah Jahan, India or the Mughal Empire began to experience a golden culture and times. Shan Jahan built many monuments. The most elaborate and famous is the Taj Mahal at Agra. He also built the Moti Masjid, Agra, The Red Fort, The Juma Masjid, Nelhi and The Fort at Lahore.

Under Shah Jahan's rule the Mughal Empire was beginning to experience a brief time of peace and contentment. Shah Jahan had slowed his expansion desires. Partly because of his frail health.

His third and younger son Aurangzeb confined his father

at the Agra Fort and although he could not yet declare himself the sixth and new Emperor of the Mughal Empire in India, he did assume most of the control and decision making.

This infuriated his two older brothers and Aurangzeb ordered the execution of his brother Prince Dara Shikoh, who he claimed had assumed too many of the Hindu ways. But in all actuality it was probably more for political power. For he then had his other brother Prince Murad Bakhsh arrested for murder and executed.

In 1666 Aurangzeb's father Shah Jahan died, and Aurangzeb became the new and sixth Emperor of the Mughal Empire. Now he could rule as he saw fit and wanted, without family influence.

He was strictly Muslim and he would not tolerate any Hindu prejudices. He ordered that anyone found not wearing the typical Islamic clothing to be punished.

He ordered the governors of all districts to demolish all non-Muslim schools and temples.

Aurangzeb's biggest worry and his greatest threat was the Maratha Empire and Hinduism to the east and south. The Deccan Plateau. Where the Muslims were ruthless and aggressive, the Hindus were more passive and only wanted to protect their land and their precious way of life, which totally describes what Hinduism truly is. A way of life.

Muhammad is Islam's greatest prophet, although they do accept Abraham and Moses as prophets also. They believe in the oneness of God. The Quran is their bible and they live strictly by what is laid out in the verses.

The Marathas which controlled the Deccan Plateau of India, and most of India follow the teachings of Hinduism. The Marathas were not interested in expanding their Empire, only defending it against the Afghan Muslims and preserving their beliefs and way of life.

In Islam the Muslims have one God, and of the three prophets, Muhammad was unquestioningly the greatest.

In Hinduism the Hindus had three deities. Brahma the creator, Vishnu the protector, and Shiva the judge.

Hinduism, although is a way of life, it is also accepted as a religion. Rather than being based on strict rules and guidelines as Islam, Hinduism is more a collection of philosophical ideas.

Hinduism is often considered to be the world's longest surviving religion or way of life.

There doesn't seem to be a known person who established Hinduism. The practitioners have always accepted it as gospel and the devoted follower works to achieve Moksha in this lifetime. The liberation of soul from having to reincarnate again and again. And they achieve this consciousness through honesty, self-discipline, kindness to all living creatures and a pure heart. Which is called Eternal Law.

Hinduism can be defined as obtaining Moksha by living the right way, through vast traditional and intuitional philosophies.

And this eternal way of life was Aurangzeb's, the Mughal Emperor's, greatest obstacle in expanding the Mughal Empire to include all of India and Bengal.

While the Muslim movement was aggressive, working towards expanding their empire, the Maratha's and Hindus were more passive trying to protect their land and liberty. Their "Eternal Way."

Chapter 1

1656 Maratha Empire

In 1647 the Marathas, under the leadership of Shivaji Bhonsle, had defeated the Mughals and had captured forts at Purandar, Raigad and Torna and now had complete control of Pune. The citizens were relieved when Shivaji had finally driven the Mughals out and off their land. Manufacturing of textiles and agriculture were now prospering. But half of what the farmers earned from the sale of their crops and hand woven silk and cotton cloth was paid to the Empire as taxes to afford the Maratha legions to fight the Mughals.

Aamir and Carma Mukul had three sons and one daughter. And the daughter would be wed soon and Aamir did not have much for a dowry; he could no longer afford to feed his family with the heavy taxes paid to the Empire each year.

Aamir said goodbye to his wife one spring morning and said, "I will return in two days."

"Where are you going, my husband?"

"Business with the Maharaj Shivaji in Satara."

Carma honored her place in the family and knew not to ask her husband what business he had with the Maharaj. The evening meal was eaten and the house cleaned and she worked by candlelight late into the night weaving silk thread on her loom.

It was after midnight when Carma finally finished work with her loom. When she went to bed Aamir was still awake. Knowing what he had to do to feed his family kept him awake all night. He lay on his back all night trying to think of another way to support his family.

By daylight he did not have an answer and he got up and fixed himself a cup of tea and ate some bread. When he left the house he didn't say goodbye to his wife or children. He was too overcome with guilt with what he knew he had to do.

While he harnessed a mule to a cart, Carma lay in bed, worried about what business her husband was involved in that would require him to council with the Maharaj Shivaji. She had no idea what her husband was doing.

It was a hot day in the middle of May and the road was dusty. Sometimes Aamir would walk beside his mule to give it a rest.

He hadn't thought to bring any food or water with him. But he wasn't sure he could eat anything if he had. When he was thirsty he would drink from the streams that he passed along the way to Satara.

The mule was old and slow. It was late afternoon before he reached Satara and then he had to wait in line to see the Maharaj. Two hours later.

When their meeting was finished Aamir was taken downstairs to meet the palace chief of staff. "I am called Canda. I take care of all the house servants."

"I will return in three days."

"I'll show you the servant entrance when you come back. Knock on the door and someone will assist you."

"Thank you, Canda."

On the trip back he just traveled at a slow pace, looking for a grassy place to bed down for the night and where the mule would have grass to eat and water. He still wasn't hungry. He wasn't at all happy about the deal he had made with the Maharaj. It would be a long time before he would be able to forgive himself.

He was exhausted and he did manage to sleep, but pitifully. By daylight the next morning he was hungry and wanted something to eat. But he had not brought any food, nor did he have any means to purchase any. So he harnessed the mule and continued his journey home.

He dreaded having to tell Carma what he had done. He knew she would burst into wailing and a flood of tears. "But I must support my family and I don't have a choice," he said out loud. He wished he could put off telling her, but he had told the chief of staff he would return in now two more days.

Even though he had traveled some the day before and the fact that he was not in any hurry, he didn't reach home until time for the evening meal.

"You look tired, husband. Are you feeling okay?" Carma asked.

"I'm hungry. I forgot to bring along any food. And I didn't have any money to buy some food. After we eat I must talk with you."

Aamir and Carma's three children sat down with them for the evening meal and there was very little conversation while they ate. When Aamir had finished he went outside while Carma and his daughter cleaned up and put the food away. Aamir sat down under a tree and leaned back against it.

The sun was just above the horizon when Carma came outside to join her husband. She sat down beside him and leaned against the big tree also. "What is wrong, Aamir? Why do you have such a long face for days? And what is on your mind so much that you can't sleep or forget to take food with you for a two day trip? What is so wrong, my husband?" she pleaded.

Aamir cleared his throat before answering. "We are starving, Carma, and at the end of the summer our daughter is to wed and all I have for her dowry is one goat. What kind of a dowry is that? What kind of a father am I? Half of what we make we have to pay in taxes.

"Even when Varsh leaves I still cannot afford to feed us

and three sons, and pay taxes each year," Aamir paused.

"So my husband, what have you done?"

Aamir was silent for a long time before answering. "Aamir, what have you done?" she pleaded again.

Finally he said, "I sold our youngest son, Ekani, to the Maharaj yesterday."

Just like Aamir knew would happen Carma started wailing and crying. "Why? Why did you sell him into slavery?"

"He is too young to do much work on the farm, unlike his two older brothers. I just can't afford to feed him if he can't work. Varsh helped with the household and the silk loom. We won't have that money now. I had no choice Carma. I don't like this any more than you. It's done and I'm the man of the house. It's my responsibility to provide for my family."

"But why slavery?" she wailed some more.

"Because the Bhonsle family will be able to care better for Ekani than I will ever be able to care for him. He will live in the palace, wear new clothes and always have food to eat. Yes he'll be a slave, but he will be well taken care of."

"How much were you paid for my son?" she was angry now.

"The Maharaj gave me twenty silver rupees and no taxes for a year."

Carma kept wailing and there just wasn't any more tears to be cried. She had stopped talking to her husband.

* * * *

The next morning Aamir and Carma were up early. Neither of them had slept much. Aamir awoke Ekani and said, "You must get up now, Ekani, and dress. Do not awaken your sister or brothers."

Ekani got up being careful not to awaken the others. He folded his one blanket and sleeping mat and put them away.

He looked at his mother and father and wondered why

they were not speaking to each other. They all ate bread, cheese and strong tea. Then Carma got up and put up a lunch of bread and cheese and a flask of water. Aamir had gone out to harness the mule to the cart.

When Carma turned to look at her son she was crying. "Why do you cry mother?" Ekani asked.

"Your father is taking you to the Maharaj Palace, my son, and I will never see you again." She hugged her son and crying with remorseful pain in her heart.

Ekani could not understand this—how could he? He was six years old. So he said nothing. He hugged his mother.

"Your father will explain while you are on the road for Satara. I love you, son."

She was wailing so loudly now the rest of the family had awakened and were picking up their sleeping mats.

"Get in the cart, son. I must speak with your mother."

Aamir closed the door to their bedroom. Carma turned to face him and said, "I will hate you for the rest of my life for what you are doing. As your wife, and mother to the three children who you did not sell, I will cook, clean and keep house. But I will always hate you!"

"Carma—this decision wasn't easy for me to make. I don't like the idea of selling our son into slavery for the rest of his life. But he will be better cared for with the Maharaj family. Life is all about making choices, Carma. You should understand this. The Hindu Way of Life. It's a choice I had to make, Carma." With that said he left the house and sat in the cart beside his son.

As they were leaving Ekani started to turn around and look back. Aamir put out his arm and stopped him. "Don't look back, Son. Never look back. Your life is always in front of you."

"Where am I going, Father?"

"I am taking you to live at the big palace in Satara. You will live and work for the Maharaj family."

"You say, Father, I will live at the palace?" Ekani seemed to be excited about this.

"Why me, Father, and not one of my older brothers?"

"Because you are so young, you can't do much work to help put food in our bellies or rupees to pay taxes."

"Then you do not love me any more, Father?" Ekani was deadly serious and Aamir could hear it in the tone of his voice.

Aamir stopped the mule and hugged his son. "No, Son, this does not mean I no longer love you. I will always love you. You are my son. I just cannot take care of you any more."

Ekani was silent then for quite a while. Then he asked, "What will I do at the palace, Father?"

"You will be a servant to the Maharaj's young daughter. She is the same age as you."

Again Ekani was silent while he thought about this. Aamir noticed that he didn't seem to be as troubled now about where or why he was going.

Ekani was beginning to enjoy the trip now. Much of his anxieties now gone or for the moment forgotten. He knew he was seeing things that he had never dreamed of seeing before.

"I feel sorry, Father, for Varsh, Chaga and Sumir."

"Why is that, Son?" Aamir was both surprised and shocked.

"None of us have ever seen what I am now seeing, and to think I'll be living in a palace."

Ekani's next question really surprised his father. "Father, when I was born, do you suppose it was my destiny to live at the palace as a slave to a little girl?"

Aamir was quiet for a long time, thinking how to answer. "Every time we reincarnate into this world son, we bring with us certain things that we must do. Things that we must experience. I like to think that by you being a slave in this life you won't have to go through it again in your next life and that your next life will be easier. Do you understand, Ekani?"

"I think so, Father. There is nothing as a real coincidence then, is there, Father?"

"I'm proud of you, Son, for understanding."

Aamir along with Ekani was feeling much better about what was happening.

They stopped for lunch when the sun was directly overhead. They both were hungry and they ate their fill and drank water. The mule ate grass beside the road and rested.

With both of their spirits lifted, the rest of the trip to Satara was not as gloomy or heartrending. When they arrived at the staff worker entrance and they were met by Canda. "Is this the boy you are leaving with us?" she asked.

"Yes. This is my son, Ekani."

"Hello," Ekani said.

"My, he is a polite one, and I am surprised he is not crying," Canda said.

"We had a long talk while on the road here."

"I'll leave you two here alone to say your goodbyes. I'll be back shortly," and Canda left father and son.

Aamir hugged his son and his eyes were filled with tears. "Remember this, Son, I will always love you. As will your mother, sister and brothers. Remember, Son, this is not happening by any coincidence. You—for whatever reason—are meant to be here. As long as you remember this, life here will be what you make of it." Aamir hugged his son again.

"Father, tell Mother I understand and I will be fine. Tell her I love her. And Varsh, Chaga and Sumir."

"I feel your destiny, Son, will take you to places that I cannot even imagine. All you have to do, Son, is make the right choices."

There was no more he could say to comfort Ekani or himself. "Always remember, I love you, Son," and he turned and walked away.

"Goodbye, Father."

Chapter 2

"Ekani," Canda said, "you'll have to come with me. I must get you out of those rags you're wearing and give you a proper scrubbing.

"How old are you, Ekani?"

"I'm six."

"You're so small you don't look like six. We'll have to fatten you up."

Ekani followed Canda into a room with a wash basin. "Now take your clothes off."

When he hesitated taking his clothes off in front of Canda, she said, "Now, or I'll take them off for you."

Ekani took his clothes off and Canda balled them up and threw them away. "Get in the wash basin." The water was warm and it felt good to his skin. Canda put some soap in the water that had a little fragrance with it. He had never bathed like this before.

"You sit and soak a while. I'll go and find you some new clean clothes."

She was gone for so long the water was no longer warm. The door opened and Canda had her arms full of new clothes. She put these down and picked up a brush and began scrubbing Ekani all over. He didn't know if he would have any skin left or not.

When Canda finished scrubbing Ekani she said, "You can

get out now and dry yourself off with this towel." She handed it to him.

"I noticed when you took your clothes off you were not wearing anything under them. From now on you will wrap this loincloth around you and then this mundu (a sheet-like wrap that goes around the waist down to the ankles) and you are to wear this shirt on your top. Do you understand?"

"Yes."

"Good, then get dressed. There is much I must inform you about your duties. Now make it quick. And put these sandals on your feet."

When Ekani was fully dressed with sandals he said, "I have never worn new clothes before and such nice clothes, too." Canda actually smiled, thinking back when she first became a servant when she, too, was so young and wearing fresh new clothes for the first time.

"Now follow me. At all times you must walk behind your charge, the Princess. You are not her equal therefore you cannot walk beside her or in front of her. Do you understand this?"

"Yes."

Canda left the wash room and walked down the long corridor to another room that looked like a meeting room of sorts. There were many wooden chairs all in rows. "Take a seat in the front row, Ekani."

After he was seated, Canda stood leaning against a table in front. "There are a few things I must go over with you.

"Each morning, for a while until you are used to the routine, someone will awaken you shortly after the sun rises. You will dress and report to the staff dining room. As soon as you have eaten you will return to your room which will be next to the Princess' room. You clean and straighten your room. While the Princess is eating you will empty her chamber pot; you will have one also that will need to be emptied each morning. I will show you where you are to empty them. Then you are required to wash them out every morning. Do you understand?"

17

"Yes."

"You are not the Princess' equal. So you are only allowed to talk with her when she speaks to you. You are to call her Princess or Princess Katarikari. Do you understand?"

"Yes."

"You are expected to do anything the Princess asks of you or the entire Maharaj family. Do you understand?"

"Yes."

"You cannot go to sleep until the Princess has turned in for the night. Do you understand?"

"Yes."

"Do you think you'll have any trouble remembering everything so far?"

"I think I can remember it all, Canda."

"I think this will be all of the instructions for today. It is getting late and you have had a long day."

"Yes, Canda."

"I will now take you where you will eat your evening meal, then I'll take you upstairs and show you to your room. You will not meet Princess Katarikari until after more instructions tomorrow."

As Ekani followed Canda to the servants' dining room his head was all-a-blur trying to remember everything Canda had said to him.

He ate rice, pumpkin and fish. And he was allowed to eat all he wanted. He had never before been allowed to eat until his stomach was full. When he had finished, Canda showed him to his room. "The next door down the hall is the Princess' room. You will meet her tomorrow. As I said earlier someone will wake you after sunrise tomorrow.

As Canda turned to leave Ekani said, "Thank you, Canda." That was quite a surprise. A six-year-old sold into slavery, and now he thanks her. She was beginning to form a favorable opinion about Ekani.

* * * *

The next morning Ekani was already awake when another servant came to wake him. "It is time." That's all that was said and Ekani got up and dressed and picked up his bedding and stored it. After eating, another servant told him where to empty the chamber pots. "When the Princess has left her room to eat, then you can enter her room and empty her chamber pot," the servant said. "Then you are to go downstairs to the same room you were in yesterday for more instructions with Canda."

"Yes," that's all Ekani could say. He emptied his chamber pot and washed it and returned to his room. The Princess was walking down the long corridor for her morning meal.

The door was open to the Princess' room and Ekani hesitated before walking in. He moved forward in a state of wonder. He had never seen anything of such extravagance. She had a bed not just a sleeping mat on the floor. There were thick silk blankets on the bed, and a pretty rug on the floor next to the bed. Everything in the room was so luxurious. Then he remembered he was at the palace of the Maharaj. And that he was only a servant and he had chores to do. Above everything else he must remember he was a slave. Servant for the Princess.

When he returned with the chamber pot, Canda was waiting near the Princess' room. She even smiled when she saw Ekani walking briskly toward her. "For one so young, Ekani, you show great responsibility and possibilities. Put the chamber pot back in her room and we will continue your indoctrination."

Ekani remembered to follow Canda, even though she too was only a servant, until he would be considered her equal. For someone so young Ekani seemed to have a greater understanding of things than a lot of people older in years than himself.

"Mistakes happen, Ekani. But if the same mistake is made repeatedly, or if you conduct yourself outside the realm of your status or do some willful act, you will be punished. Sometimes severely depending on the seriousness of your act.

If you run away and are caught you will be tied to a rail and whipped almost to death. You do understand this?"

"Yes, Canda, I do."

In the afternoon when the indoctrination had ended, Canda said, "Now I will give you a tour of the palace. The palace is so huge the tour will take most of the afternoon."

Ekani followed Canda. The floors everywhere were made of polished marble and there were servants who were busy cleaning each stone. "Unless on personal business, you will accompany the Princess wherever she goes. You are as much a protector as you are her servant. This will all come to you as you go along. Whatever she asks you to do you must do it.

"She is only a child and I know she will be excited and happy to show you around the palace, too."

At the far end of the palace there was a red line across the floor from one wall to the other. "Unless you are directed to do so, you and all servants are not allowed to go beyond this line—only the personal servants of the Maharaj and his wife. This is the Maharaj and his wife's personal quarters and also the political arena of the Maratha Empire.

Ekani really enjoyed his tour of the palace. He would never have imagined that someday he would walk the corridors of the palace and work within its walls. Even if he was only a servant. So far he was enjoying the experience.

Canda was impressed with Ekani's genuine interest and his attention to everything she was telling him and his excitement about the palace itself. And more importantly he had not displayed any sadness of having been sold into slavery or abandonment by his family. In Canda's opinion, young Ekani was certainly an exceptional young boy.

Having eaten the evening meal Canda escorted Ekani to Princess Katarikari's room. She stopped and knocked on the door casing before entering. Ekani observed and made a point not to forget.

"Princess Katarikari, this is Ekani Mukul, your personal

servant," Canda said.

"If you have any questions about anything, Ekani, you can ask Princess Katarikari or myself. I'll leave you now in the Princess' charge," and Canda left.

"Are you scared, Ekani?" Katarikari asked. She had a nice voice, Ekani noticed.

"No, your Princess."

"You are so small. You are no bigger than me."

"You have a rope that goes through the wall and I have a rattle in my room," Ekani said.

"Yes, if I want you, I pull this rope and when you hear the rattle you are to come here.

"Are you nervous, Ekani?"

"Yes, Princess Ka-ta-ri-kari," he had difficulty saying her name.

"Why are you nervous, Ekani?"

"You are the daughter of the Maharaj, a Princess, and I am only your servant."

"I can understand this, Ekani. But you do not have to be nervous. Would you like to sit down?"

"Yes, Princess, I would. I am tired." And when he started to sit on the floor Katarikari laughed and said, "No silly, not the floor. Sit in that chair."

Ekani sat in the chair, but he wasn't feeling comfortable. "Ekani, you act like you are afraid of me."

"I'm not sure how I should act in your presence, Princess Ka-ta-ri-kari."

"Do you have a problem saying my name, Katarikari?" When she said her own name it was like music to Ekani.

"Yes—some."

"Then call me Kari. I like that better. Except around the Maharaj and my mother you must never call me Kari. It will have to be Katarikari."

"I can do that, Princess Kari."

"That is better. Now you sound like a friend."

21

"Princess Kari."

"Yes."

"You aren't anything like I imagined you would be."

"How do you mean?"

"Because you are a Princess that means you are royal, and I am only a servant and I come from a very poor family. My father sold me to your father. I was worried that you might be a mean person."

"I don't have anybody to play with my age. I have older sisters that have their own families and all my older brothers are off somewhere fighting the Mughals who are trying to control all of India. So I get bored and lonely sometimes."

They talked for a long time and Ekani had almost forgotten that he was Katarikari's servant and not her playmate. "After I eat tomorrow, Ekani, I will give you my tour of the palace and show you things Canda did not.

"Now Ekani, it is time for you to return to your room."

"Yes Princess," and Ekani left and closed her door.

He laid on his sleeping mat for a long time that night thinking everything he had been instructed to do or not to do. The grandiose palace and his position as servant to the Princess. He had a room and bed all to himself, new and clean clothes to wear and he was never hungry.

Maybe his father had done a good thing by selling him to the Maharaj. He started missing his family then and he suddenly snapped himself out of the sad emotions. He could hear his father saying, "Never look back son. Always look at what is in front of you."

But still, he hoped his family would be okay. He swept all thoughts from his mind and fell into a deep sleep. It seemed no sooner had he fallen asleep and he was being awakened the next morning to start his chores.

* * * *

"Your Highness Chira, you asked to see me?" Canda asked, not looking directly at her Highness.

"Yes, Canda, come in and sit down with me. Would you like some tea?"

Canda sat down at the table and replied, "Yes, Your Highness, I would like tea."

Chira stood up and filled two cups with tea and sat down across from Canda. "Tell me, Canda, how is the new boy servant adjusting?"

"It is strange, Your Highness."

"How so, Canda?"

"He does not show any sadness that he has been sold to serve your daughter as her servant. He is in fact, I think, happy to be here and he remembers everything I have instructed. He is an exceptional young boy. When his father left him he did not cry.

"I also believe Ekani will be good for your daughter, Highness. They are of the same age and he is only slightly bigger than Princess Katarikari. This will help to give her some responsibility. She will now have someone her own age to talk with."

"You approve of this Ekani, I can tell by the way your eyes light up when you speak of him. You can tell my daughter that I wish she bring him to me, so I may meet the boy.

"Any problems with any of the other staff, Canda?"

"Only the two men who go out after firewood. They seem to take too long when I question them about it, I'm sure they have to travel further now for the wood."

* * * *

Canda knocked on Katarikari's door and then opened it. Ekani was sitting in a chair and the Princess on her bed. "Your Princess, your mother has informed me that she wishes you to escort young Ekani to her room today."

"Why? Did she say, Canda?"

"Yes Princess, she wishes to meet your new servant."

"We can go now. Come on, Ekani," Katarikari said.

Canda watched them leave, to see if Ekani would follow her as he was instructed. He was, and Canda returned to her duties.

When Katarikari crossed the red line, Ekani stopped. Katarikari knew under ordinary circumstances no staff servants were allowed beyond this point. "It is okay, Ekani, you are with me."

He was still hesitant, but he followed Katarikari. Shortly after entering this section there was another corridor to the left where Her Highness had her quarters. Katarikari stopped and knocked and waited for an answer.

"Come in." Ekani followed Katarikari into the spacious beautiful room.

Katarikari walked with Ekani and stood in front of her mother.

"Mother, this is my new servant, Ekani. Ekani, this is Highness Chira."

Ekani waited for Her Highness to speak. "Hello, Ekani. What is the rest of your name?"

"Hello, Your Highness. Ekani Mukul."

"I have been well informed and I approve of your manners. Canda speaks well of you and I now can see why."

"Thank you, Your Highness."

"Do you miss your family, Ekani?"

"I love my family, but my father said never to look back, to always look ahead. My destiny is here."

"So well spoken and so wise for someone so young. I understand now why Canda finds favor with you."

"Thank you, Your Highness."

When their visit was over, Katarikari said, "I'll show you the palace where I know Canda would not have taken you."

She explained not even she was allowed in where her father the Maharaj conducts his business. "Usually there are a lot of high ranking army officials coming and going. But yesterday they all left anticipating a battle near Bijapur. Do you know where that is, Ekani?"

"No, I have never heard of it."

"It is to the south and east of here controlled by the Aurangzeb's force, the Mughal army. They are trying to control all of India."

"Why are the two armies fighting?" Ekani asked.

"The Mughals are Muslim and are trying to control all of India. In the Maratha Empire we are Hindu and my father is trying to protect our land, our homes and our eternal way of life, our religion."

Katarikari took him into closets with hidden passages that some led downstairs to the next level and three closets with passages that converged into a central passage that led outside on the backside of the palace. "These passages are for escape, if we are ever attacked here by the enemy.

"Come, Ekani, let's walk along the path; it follows out through a beautiful park. No one ever uses it and I was comfortable coming here by myself. Now I have you," and she ran off and Ekani ran after her, being careful to stay behind her.

They were out of sight of the palace and Katarikari stopped running. "Out here, Ekani, when no one can see us, you can walk beside me. It is easier to talk with you."

Ekani was hesitant at first. "Come on, Ekani, it is okay."

"Okay, Ka-ta-ri-kari, I just don't want to be punished."

"You won't and since you seem to have a problem saying my name, call me Kari. I like it better."

"Kari," he said. "I like it too."

"When Canda or my mother and father are near you should call me Princess Katarikari."

"Okay."

They spent half the day walking around the park. Kari picked a bouquet of flowers for her room. "We should return to the palace now, Ekani."

Chapter 3

Katarikari's father, Shivaji Maharaj, had been concerned for a long time now about the closeness of the Mughals at Bijapur to the south and east of Satara. The Mughal sultan at Bijapur periodically kept attacking the Maratha army. They were never able to gain any ground and always retreated from a battle. But the constant attacks were wearing on the Maharaj's nerves and the battles were costing the empire in soldier lives as well as rupees.

So with his own small army he left Satara and marched towards Bijapur to council with his commanders to figure out a way to permanently stop the Mughal army.

Bijapur was located on the Deccan Plateau between the two Ghats Mountain Ranges. Shivaji Maharaj and his small army of two hundred men were a week traveling to the Maratha territorial combat headquarters. Still several days travel to Bijapur.

When Shivaji arrived he asked for the General Commander to come to his tent as soon as possible. General Parsaji Bhosale and the two direct subordinates entered Shivaji's tent two hours later.

"Yes, Maharaj, we came as soon as I received your request," Bhosale said.

"Men, we have been fighting the Mughals at Bijapur for too long without any advances and the battles are getting expensive in soldiers and rupees. We have always fought the Mughals on their terms. I think we need to change our tactics.

"Every time they attack they always take the route to the right."

"Yes Sir, that's true."

"They always bring up the heavy cannons with elephants and then their soldiers."

"Yes."

"Well, we need to start guerilla fighting. When the battle starts, send two squads to flank their main body and come in behind them. Hit and run. Dig elephant pits and sharpen stakes that'll kill the elephants when they fall into the pits. Cover the pits with strong enough material so that the foot soldiers and horse mounted swordsmen can ride over, then trap the elephants with the heavy cannons once the soldiers have cleared. These are suggestions, men. You work on them and expand the ideas and I want some results or I will replace you.

"Tomorrow morning I return to Satara. Work among you and decide what will work best."

* * * *

During his trip back to Satara, Shivaji began to think about the Mughals stronghold on Surat, a shipping port. Ever since Aurangzeb's army took control of that port city, he had been afraid Aurangzeb would make a two-pronged attack against the Marathas.

With the new guerilla tactics soon to be implemented near Bijapur, he hoped he would be able to send a few more men from Bijapur to fight at Surat. But because of the distances, he knew this could not happen overnight.

He wished he could drive the Mughals—the Afghan Muslims—from his empire and all of India. The cost of fighting the Muslims was hard financially for everyone. Then he thought of Aamir Mukul having to sell his son into slavery so he could feed his family. That surely was not what Hinduism was all about. The Eternal Way of Life.

* * * *

When Shivaji Maharaj returned to the palace he summoned a courier. "Take this scroll to Commanding General Dwijesh at the Pune Fort. Then wait and return with him."

He wanted the Port at Surat badly and he knew by acquiring Surat it would seriously hamper Aurangzeb's army. He also understood that neither Surat or Bijapur would be a quick battle. He expected each battle could take a few years.

Five days later the courier and General Dwijesh arrived at the palace. The courier excused himself and General Dwijesh walked down the corridor to Shivaji's headquarters. "Come in, General Dwijesh. I have some strong tea ready.

"General, I have recently traveled to Bijapur and talked with General Bhosale. In two years time I want both Surat and Bijapur captured and the Muslims run out of the Empire. I have advised Bhosale to start using guerilla tactics.

"I want you to select four of your most confident men and send them to Surat as spies. Send them one at a time so each one will not know of the others. They must be in Muslim attire and must observe Muslim customs. Aurangzeb is punishing all people found not wearing proper Muslim clothing or practicing Muslim customs.

"We, you and I, Dwijesh, need to know their strength, when and where they plan to attack your troops. Their weaknesses as well as their strengths. What they have for heavy artillery. I think you get the picture of things, Dwijesh?"

"Yes Sir, I do."

"Good. Surat is very important to both the Mughal Empire and mine. I must have that port. I want patrols sent out patrolling about Pune, and watch for Mughal patrols. But most of all, discover their weaknesses and planned attacks against us.

"It wouldn't surprise me, General, if there was a Mughal spy in your troops. Find out, and if you can. use him to provide disinformation to Aurangzeb's army. And do this promptly, because I don't want any information getting back to Aurangzeb about you developing guerilla tactics.

"If you cannot accomplish all of this, General Dwijesh, I will replace you with someone who can. Make it happen and I want to take Surat before Bijapur. Is that understood, General?"

"Yes, Maharaj Shivaji," Dwijesh replied.

After General Dwijesh left Shivaji relaxed on his settee thinking he needed to secure the Port of Surat soon to cut off the Mughal army. If it was to become necessary he would take command of General Dwijesh's army himself.

Once he had Surat under the Empire's control he would take Gujarat across the bay. With all of his attention on protecting the Maratha Empire he had no idea of the status at the palace. He had left that to his wife, Chira.

He was exhausted. To him it seemed the welfare of Hinduism rested on his shoulders. He leaned back and before he drifted off to sleep, he started thinking how tragic life would be in the Empire if the Muslims were ever able to push through and take control. The Hindu Eternal Way of Life would come to an end.

Chapter 4

A few months had passed now since Ekani's introduction to the Maharaj Palace. He had been able to stop thinking about his past and his family. He was too busy with his present life and making sure he did not forget his place or chores.

Canda had stopped watching Ekani as closely. She could find no fault with his performance. Princess Katarikari had accepted Ekani as a friend, but at the same time his demeanor around Katarikari was flawless.

She did notice that when the two were alone, Ekani called her Kari at Katarikari's suggestion. Apparently Ekani had a difficult time pronouncing the proper name. Canda overlooked it as he always used her proper title and name when in the presence of someone else.

Ekani had become more than Katarikari's personal servant. He had become the Princess' playmate. And as far as Canda was concerned this was alright also. After all, Ekani was the only other person of Katarikari's age. And any child needs friends to play with. As long as they were discreet with their friendship. And she saw no need to say anything to Her Highness about their friendship. She very seldom came to this end of the palace anyway.

Ekani had slowly felt more comfortable and not as shy around Katarikari. But he also was aware that he had to demonstrate a servant's respect towards his charge and this also became a game for the two. They never talked socially around other people, not even other servants. These times were kept in check, and cherished when they were alone.

Once Her Highness did come to see Katarikari in her room and Ekani was there and standing very erect in a corner, as if waiting for an instruction from his mistress. "Katarikari?" Her Highness asked, "Why do you spend so much time, even in this hot weather, walking in the park behind the palace?"

"I like being in the park, Mother. I enjoy being outside even if it is hot. Ekani is always with me and nothing is going to happen to me. There is very little to do cooped up inside here. I don't go out when it is raining or too windy."

"I think maybe I can understand that. I was a little girl once. It won't be long though and I'll have to start instructing you about your duties as a Princess. And as soon as this heatwave has passed, you will attend school here in the palace, so you'll learn to read and write. This will be very important for you in your position."

Ekani had spent enough time around Katarikari for him to realize that she was a special person, not just a little pretty girl or princess. There was more to her than being a pretty little girl. There was a knowingness and understanding about her that he had noticed in few adults.

Even though she was mistress, she was never hateful or bossy towards Ekani. She was as happy to have Ekani as her personal servant as Ekani was to be her servant. Ekani was young, but he couldn't have imagined his life being any better than now, before he came to the palace. He actually considered himself to be very fortunate, even though he was a servant.

One day while they were in the park and out of sight of others, Katarikari started running and Ekani ran after her. Even though during these times he never tried to better Kari or out-run her. This was something that he had decided on and Kari never teased him that she always won or that she ran faster. They both understood their positions in life and they didn't want anything to ruin their friendship.

The foot race ended at a clear cool stream only a few inches deep. They kicked off their sandals and went wadding. The cool water felt good on their feet. They started laughing and Kari pushed Ekani over backwards and he fell in the water. Instead of being cross or pushing Kari over he sat in the water and began to laugh even harder. Kari laughed along with him. He knew Kari should not get completely wet. There would be too many questions to answer.

Even though Ekani's clothes were wet they still stayed out in the park to play and away from people.

Canda met them back inside the palace and, "Why are your clothes all wet, Ekani?"

Katarikari started to say something and since Canda had been speaking to him, Ekani answered and cut Katarikari off.

"I was wading in the stream and slipped."

Katarikari looked sheepishly at Ekani and smiled ever so slightly.

Chapter 5

Two months had passed since Shivaji had summoned General Gwijesh to the palace in Satara. Now with a small escort of soldiers, he had returned to speak with the Maharaj.

"Come in, General Dwijesh. You are just in time for some hot tea."

"Thank you Sir; we traveled hard and fast from Pune and my throat is parched."

Shivaji's personal servant poured their tea and set a tray with sweet cakes on the table and then he was dismissed. "Try these cakes, General, they are quite good."

When they had finished the tea and sweet cakes, Shivaji asked, "Now, General, what information do you have for me?"

"You were correct, Maharaj. There was a spy in my ranks. Once I counseled my officers about the possibility, it was no problem to discover who. The entire fort was being watched and one night one soldier left after midnight and he was traveling in the direction of Surat in a straight course. My men followed and waited until he was some distance from Pune before apprehending him. He was brought directly to me and after some extensive interrogations we were able to extract some useful information.

"The Afghan Muslims are planning to attack the Fort at Pune before the monsoon season starts. A month before the start of the rains, a ship is supposed to arrive with many fresh soldiers, food and fighting equipment. That was all we were able to obtain from him," Dwijesh said.

"And what did you do with him, General?"

"He was executed."

"Good," Shivaji replied. "And what information have your own spies brought you?"

"When I left to come here only two men had come back with any information. The other two may have returned by now though. The Mughal spy was right. Aurangzeb's general at Surat is planning an attack mid-May. And the ships are bringing five hundred fresh soldiers that will be replacing some of the older and wounded men. They are bringing food and each ship will have a cache of new rifles and gunpowder."

"Well, I'll want to attack before the arrival of the first ship. Have you seen the fort there?"

"Yes, before Aurangzeb's troops took control of it."

"Will it burn?"

"Most of it. The inside is constructed mostly of wood at the east walls. The west wall is thick rock, to withstand cannonading from ships. What have you in mind, Sir?"

"We must know where their guards are positioned during the night, and how many.

"We send in selected men to take care of each guard. Then other men bring up highly flammable oil and set fires throughout the interior. Once the fort is ablaze we move in with our troops and take the fort. The fire should cause so much chaos and confusion our troops should have an easy time subduing the entire fort and peninsula in one fierce attack. Then we train their heavy cannons on the arriving ships.

"While you're working on the details, General, I will— how many soldiers do you have at Pune?"

"I have two hundred, Sir."

"I'll find you another five hundred before then. When you move on Surat, move at night so the enemy will not discover you are coming. And when I have the five hundred troops, I'll move them to Pune under the cover of darkness and I will accompany them.

"Do you know what you must do until—let's say by April first, I'll have the extra troops a mile from Pune and will send a courier to you. I think these troops should stay there until we make our move to Surat."

"I have been taking notes, Maharaj Shivaji. I and my men will be ready when you arrive.

"Where will you find the five hundred soldiers, Sir?"

"There is a large garrison at the Fort in Rairi. If I need any more I'll get those from the local villages around. They won't be as well trained, but they'll have to do. We both have much work ahead of us. I suggest you get started for Pune immediately, General."

"Yes Sir. At once." General Dwijesh took his leave.

Shivaji poured another cup of tea and relaxed in his big cushion chair and thought about the plans to take Surat. He knew Surat would fall, and once the Mughal ships were sunk he would take Gujarat and then Bijapur and then he would be rid of Aurangzeb and his Mughal army.

Shivaji leaned back and closed his eyes. He slept for an hour then got up and walked down to his daughter's quarters. He had not talked with her for quite some time now.

Canda met him in the corridor and asked, "Are you looking for the Princess, Maharaj Shivaji?"

"Yes, Canda, is she in her room?"

"No Sir, about every day at this time she goes for a walk in the park."

"She should not be alone, Canda. She is only a little girl."

"She is not alone, Sir. Her servant Ekani always accompanies the Princess."

"But he is only a boy himself, Canda."

"Yes Sir, but he is beyond his years, as is Princess Katarikari."

"How is Ekani doing? Are there any problems?"

"On the contrary, Sir. He has accepted his duties here very well. I cannot fault him at all. He appears to be happy at the palace, Sir.

"He has been good for the Princess, Sir. If you will remember, before Ekani arrived, Princess Katarikari was never happy, she seldom talked to anyone and she stayed in her room most of the time. She has completely changed and I have a better understanding of her now and I think it is all because of Ekani. Because of him, she now has become responsible for someone besides herself. She talks and laughs and is a pleasure to be around. I have discovered that for a little girl she like Ekani is wise beyond her years also, Sir."

"Thank you, Canda. I must get back to work. Do tell Katarikari that I was here asking about her."

"Yes Sir."

* * * *

Shivaji Maharaj returned to his quarters and sat down at his desk and buried his head in his hands. The whole Maratha Empire was at risk if he should fail at Surat. If he did fail, the idea of capturing Bijapur would only be a dream.

He didn't sleep much that night. He was so worried he wouldn't be able to succeed at Surat. The next day he summoned the Commander at Surat. "Commander, I want a small detail to accompany me to Rairi and I want to leave this evening."

"Yes Sir. Immediately."

Shivaji poured a cup of tea with some figs and cheese. It was the end of December and he had only three months to put his regiment together with equipment and food and meet General Dwijesh April first.

Traveling from twilight to sunrise Shivaji and his detail were four days traveling to Rairi. The moon was in full phase that week which made travel at night possible.

Shivaji waited for darkness before entering the gates to

the high top fortress at Rairi. Commander Kashi was surprised when Maharaj Shivaji appeared in his quarters after dark.

Maharaj Shivaji and Commander Kashi talked most of the night. Kashi wanted to be part of the invasion troop at Surat, but Shivaji said, "I appreciate you want to be there, Kashi, but I need you here rather than at Surat, the palace in my absence. I am leaving the palace's garrison there, intact, to protect my family and I have all the confidence with your abilities, Kashi.

"I want you to have five hundred of your best soldiers, accompanied by you, at the palace March first."

"We'll be there, Sir."

"Good. I'll need a place to sleep today and I'll leave at dusk in the evening."

Shivaji did not have to remind Kashi to bring extra ammunitions and gunpowder. He had all the confidence with Commander Kashi. Kashi wanted a battalion of his own and a garrison. He was young, but in time Kashi would have all that.

* * * *

There was a grand celebration with the new year with fireworks display all night at the palace. And this was the only occasion when the lower class of people, the townspeople and country farmers, were allowed inside the palace on tours.

Ekani watched for his family with little doubt they would travel so far. He had extra duty that Canda had him working with the kitchen staff, making sure there was always plenty of food and drink at the banquet tables.

Princess Katarikari, though, as young as she was, was giving tours of the palace. Whenever she was close to Ekani, she would look his way and smile. He would smile back. Canda saw this exchange and decided to say nothing.

When the celebration was over, Ekani had to help clean up. He was okay with that. The next day everything was back to routine.

Shivaji had earlier sent a courier to General Parsaji Bhosale requesting him to travel to Satara as soon as possible. He arrived at the palace five days later.

Shivaji briefed the general about his plans to invade and secure the port and fort at Surat. And then the Gujarat Peninsula. "Once I have Gujarat and Surat firmly under the Empire's control, we'll turn our attention to Bijapur. When we secure Bijapur then the Marathas will control all of the Deccan Plateau. And the subcontinent of India and Hindus will not have to worry again."

* * * *

"Ekani, when you have your morning chores done, come down to see me. We need to talk."

Ekani had no idea what Canda wanted. "Come in, Ekani, and close the door. Is there anything going on between you and Princess Katarikari?"

"I am her servant, Canda, and we have become friends."

"As long as you remember the Princess is your mistress and you are her servant. You must at all times conduct yourself accordingly. That's all I want to say. You can go back to work."

* * * *

The extra soldiers from Rairi would be leaving soon for Satara and Shivaji Maharaj hoped he had not overlooked anything. He went over his notes again and again to make sure. Nothing must go wrong with this campaign or the Empire would be doomed.

A courier arrived at the palace a day ahead of the rest of the column. "My aide will show you where to bivouac the soldiers. And advise Commander Kashi to stay with the troops until he is requested."

Shivaji had lost weight and he wasn't sleeping much at night. He was that worried if things should go wrong with this campaign. There was much riding on his success. Failure meant Muslim rule and probably the end of Hinduism.

The troops arrived on March first and Shivaji Maharaj left the palace with his usual pack. When he arrived at the encampment the soldiers already had their tents up and the camels and horses corralled and all weapons secured.

"Commander Kashi, walk with me please." Shivaji strolled leisurely with Commander Kashi beyond the encampment so no one would overhear them.

"Commander, when we have finished talking I wish you to return to the palace and safeguard it, until my return. I may be absent for several months, Commander. If you need any assistance my second in command is there and my wife Chira will be of great assistance to you.

"Chira and Canda see to the operations of the palace, so you'll be free for politics.

"When you depart I don't want the soldiers to know where you are going. General Dwijesh at Pune found a spy in his ranks. This campaign must go off without a hitch, Commander."

"You can trust me, Maharaja," Kashi assured and left.

* * * *

For some reason Shivaji slept well that night and awoke early the next morning refreshed and alert. "Jitesh, come to my tent please. Sit." Shivaji poured two cups of tea before he spoke. "Commander Kashi has been assigned to another detail. He spoke highly of your abilities and I am promoting you to Commander. Now I must inform you about what we are doing. Our destination and time table you will not disclose to any of your men.

"You'll need to keep your men busy while we are here. Have them clean all of their weapons and make sure each archer has plenty of arrows.

"Tomorrow I am taking a small detail on a fast trek to

General Bhosale's encampment near Bijapur. I'll only be gone four days, five at the most."

Two days later Shivaji arrived at Bhosale's encampment and went directly to his tent. They talked for hours about the preparations for invading Bijapur. The elephant pits were all dug and covered over enough to support soldiers walking over them, but too weak to support elephants.

"Dwijesh found a spy in his ranks, so I want you to take precautions and if possible send two of your own men to Bijapur to gather information. They need to be dressed as Muslims."

Shivaji was pleased with Bhosale's preparations. He did get two hours of rest before heading back to Satara.

* * * *

"Ekani, when I have finished eating this morning I want to find my father. He has not visited for a long time," the Princess said.

Ekani waited patiently while Katarikari ate. He was not allowed to watch her eat, so he waited in the corridor, leaning against the wall.

When she came out she said, "Okay, Ekani, let's find my father."

They walked to the other end of the palace and Ekani stopped at the red line. "I'll wait here, Princess Katarikari."

"No, it'll be alright."

"I think I should stay."

"Okay," and she went to her father's quarters. There was no one there. On her way back she met a strange man who asked, "Who are you and what are you doing here?"

Real indignant, she replied, "I am Princess Katarikari and I am looking for my father. And who are you, may I ask?"

"My apologies, Princess. I am Commander Kashi from Rairi. I'm here while your father is away on business."

"Where has he gone, Commander?"

"I cannot say, Princess. His orders."

Katarikari turned around and walked off without answering Kashi. "Come, Ekani, Father is not here. Maybe Mother knows where he is." Ekani followed her down the corridor to her mother's quarters, always at the proper distance behind her.

Ekani waited outside of her mother's personal room. "Mother, where is Father?" Katarikari asked. "I was just informed by a Commander Kashi that he was replacing Father in his absence and he wouldn't tell me where Father has gone."

"Commander Kashi has been here for a week and while your father is away, as he says, on business, Kashi is in charge here at the palace.

"Where is your servant, Katarikari?"

"He is waiting in the corridor until we have finished."

"You have trained him well, daughter."

Katarikari and Ekani returned to her own quarters and then outside to walk in the park. When they were out of view from the palace Ekani walked beside Katarikari. "I wonder where Father has gone and what he is doing."

"No one seems to know, Kari, even your mother."

The weather was ideal this time of year for activities out in the park and Kari and Ekani took advantage of the nice weather. They spent the rest of that day walking the paths or sitting on the stream bank talking. It didn't matter what they talked about, they each were simply enjoying the other's company.

* * * *

While Commander Jitesh drilled his soldiers, Shivaji found a moment to relax in his tent with a cup of tea. Bhosale was doing a fine job preparing for that campaign later on and he had no doubt Dwijesh was doing as fine a job. If all went as planned, the Deccan Plateau and most of the sub-continent of India would once again be under Maratha's control.

Two days later Shivaji summoned Commander Jitesh to

his tent again. "Commander, in three days we must move out. And it will be at night in the darkness to cover our move. You will need to send out scouts to find places to bivouac away from the road. Our movement must be in secret."

"Yes Sir, I understand and I already have found good scouts."

"Sir, the soldiers know that they are heading to battle, but no one knows who we will be fighting. They are getting edgy. Actually they are wanting to do battle to break the boredom."

"We must keep secret where we are going. I can't risk any information about the campaign leaking out."

"Yes Sir."

During the daylight hours of the eve when they would leave, Jitesh ordered his men to pack everything for departure at dark, then to lay down in some shade and sleep or at least rest. "It will be a long night, men, and we have a great distance to travel."

Shivaji Maharaj also packed his gear and found shade in amongst some bushes and he laid down to rest. He knew sleep would be impossible.

Having eaten a hearty meal and drinking plenty of water, the column of five hundred men started north toward Surat, shadowing the western Ghat Mountains.

Two scouts had already left four hours earlier to find a secluded place to camp during the daylight hours.

Everyone was full of energy and glad to be finally on the move. They were making good speed. Shivaji expected they would make twenty-five miles that first night.

When they finally stopped the next morning they all were too tired to bother setting up their tents. They ate, took care of the animals and went to sleep. Even Shivaji fell easily to sleep.

They traveled like this for two and a half weeks before reaching General Dwijesh's encampment. There were now 2,500 men all willing to lay down their lives to preserve their Eternal Way of Life.

"April first, Maharaj Shivaji. Just as you said. Come, you must be tired. I have hot tea and food in my tent," Dwijesh said.

The next day Dwijesh and Shivaji talked at length with the four spies who had been in Surat. "They are not prepared for any kind of battle at the fort. They have been lounging all winter," one spy said.

"I learned that the Marathas wouldn't dare attack them. And they are fat and lazy," another said.

"But we must attack before the first ship arrives, before the monsoon rains begin. There is plenty of powder and ball for the cannons," another said.

"There are six guards at night. Two walking around the fort and four on the ground. The four on the ground are stationary at posts. Two on the west side towards the sea and the other two on the east side. They are equipped with rifles and scimitars and each carries a sharp dagger. The guards are posted 6pm to 6am and a change of guards at midnight," the fourth spy said.

"The interior of the fort is made up mostly of wood. There is some stone work though. The timbers are dry and should blaze quick."

"Sketch the interior of the fort for us," Dwijesh asked.

"I have already done that General," and he removed a scroll from inside of his blouse.

"Where inside is the most timber?" Shivaji asked.

"Here and here. The soldier's quarters and the mess hall."

"Where are the officers' quarters?" Dwijesh asked.

"Here, off this corridor on the same end as the Commander's office."

Shivaji Maharaj and General Dwijesh studied the hand drawn sketch with interest. "That was fine work, men. You all brought back valuable information. You may go now," Dwijesh said.

"How do you want to attack, Shivaji?" Dwijesh asked.

"We take out the six guards at 10pm. They'll be tired and their relief won't be out yet. Then we send men in with oil to set fire to the interior and create a confusion. Then our main body moves in and attacks. The details, General, and which men take out the guards and those that set the fires I leave to you. You are an excellent strategist. Now what about the fire weapon—*agneyastra*?"

"I have pine pitch mixed with turpentine mixed with coal oil."

"Do you have enough, Dwijesh?"

"Yes Sir, there is plenty."

"How many soldiers are there, Dwijesh?"

"Including officers, about two thousand."

"We have now twenty-five hundred. A surprise attack... there shouldn't be a problem," Shivaji said.

"May I make a suggestion, Maharaj?" Shivaji nodded his head to continue, "You look exhausted. Why don't you see if you can sleep? I have everything in hand."

Shivaji Maharaj retired to his own tent and lay on his cot and was instantly asleep. He slept through to the next morning.

* * * *

"General Dwijesh, I have a suggestion. Since we out-number the Muslim soldiers, I think it might be prudent if you detail a hundred men to make sure that no one leaves Surat to warn Aurangzeb or his army. I want those ships to feel safe when they arrive. Any word about the battle and Aurangzeb will more than likely not send the ships."

"That is a good idea. I will make it so."

They had three and a half weeks to wait for only a sliver of a moon to shine—first week of May. This sliver of light would be enough light for the soldiers to make their way on foot to Surat. But the problem was getting the regiment within striking distance without alarming those in the fort.

It was decided to take only enough mules to carry what equipment they would need, besides what each man would be expected to carry on his back. Elephants and horses would need too much food and water and they were noisy.

General Dwijesh had decided that since the four spies who knew more about the fort would escort the six men to take out the six guards and then dress in Muslim attire to enter the fort and set the fires.

Since the battle would be close quarters, the weapon of choice was the sword. There would also be archers. The British-made flintlock muskets would be more of a hindrance than any possible good.

After the fires were set General Dwijesh had decided to have a squad of five hundred men at each of the two main entrances, another five hundred surrounding the fort and the rest would enter the fort.

The fort was situated on the peninsula away from the city. It was built here to protect the harbor from invasion. Then cannons were mounted on high ground at the very edge of the embankment. Provided they were not discovered beforehand, General Dwijesh was sure the acquisition of the fort, the city and the harbor would be accomplished without too many casualties.

There were only a few of the soldiers who knew and understood what this campaign was about. Shivaji Maharaj had said early on that he didn't want the troops to know, so to keep the threat of information from leaking outside the company of soldiers. Although there were many who suspected what their goal was, but at the same time were too afraid to talk openly about it to others.

* * * *

The first of May had arrived and one night of only a sliver of moonlight to guide them, General Dwijesh ordered his soldiers to equip themselves and move out. Ahead of the column were two scouts, followed by a detail of six guardsmen and then General Dwijesh and the Maharaj Shivaji. There was a standing order that no one was supposed to talk or make any unnecessary noise at all. Even the mules were quiet as the column stole through the night.

It was an eerie procession of twenty-five hundred men. If looked upon from above, the column would have resembled a giant anaconda snake slithering through the underbrush.

The scouts had found an ideal place to stop for the day. There was some low lying wet land with heavy vegetation that would conceal the entire column. "How close are we to the fort?" Dwijesh asked.

"About two hours, General," one scout replied.

"That's perfect."

Dwijesh called for all of his officers to a meeting and for them to make sure their men knew what to do. That they must take Surat. Then he said, "This close to our target there will be no fires, no talking. If you have to talk, do so only in a whisper, and no noise. Your men will have to eat cold rations as the Maharaj and I will do. Then tell them to get some sleep. They will need it."

All was quiet in the camp that day. So quiet the birds and a few of the smaller jungle animals were not concerned about their presence.

Shivaji and Dwijesh only catnapped, but they remained quiet and resting. There was just so much going through their minds to relax enough to sleep. There was so much that could go wrong.

At late afternoon Dwijesh told his officers to tell their soldiers to eat, that they would have to leave their food there, so they would not be encumbered with any unnecessary baggage or weight. But to take a flask of water. "Tomorrow, men, after sunrise we will feast on the spoils of battle."

* * * *

"The time is right, Shivaji Maharaj," General Dwijesh said.

Shivaji only nodded his head. The six soldiers who would take out the six guards at the fort were dressed in Muslim clothes and they led the column silently to the fort. It was dark and the sliver of the moon had not yet risen above the horizon, which was good.

When they were close enough to see the profile of the fort, without any audible command. The six Muslim-dressed men advanced on the fort. The rest of Dwijesh's soldiers remained where they were. Fifteen minutes later the men with fire weapons followed the first six soldiers. At the same time the squad of a hundred broke off and circled the fort to prevent escapes across the Tapi River and into Surat.

These men were so well trained, no order had to be given. Shivaji was pleased with Dwijesh's thoroughness.

The attacking body waited. Their only signal would be when they saw flames erupting from the fort.

Dwijesh waited patiently for the flames above the fort. Shivaji was not so patient. An hour had passed and he looked at Dwijesh and nodded his head. They moved out towards the fort silently, still not wanting to be discovered. Once the fires had been set there should be too much confusion for the Mughal army to arm themselves. Especially when they only saw the flames and no Maratha soldiers.

Dwijesh stopped the column and had a drink of water. His throat was parched. So did many of the others.

Then precisely at 10pm flames shot up above the fort. Dwijesh knew there would be total confusion and disorder among the ranks of the Mughals as most would have been awakened from sleep. Dwijesh said with keeping his voice low, "Okay, men, you know what you must do. Let's go!"

As they closed in toward the fort without any signal, half of the squad broke off to circle around to the other exit. Even though the Mughal soldiers had not seen any enemy inside the fort, many were armed with scimitars. But because of the fire and total disarray they were not much of a deterrent. They fought as well as they could.

Never had the Maratha Army attacked during the night and now that they had set fire to their fort while they slept was beyond comprehension. There was no leadership among the officers. It was a battle of self reliance.

The Maratha soldiers who had come through the entrance at the officer's quarters of the fort found little resistance from the officers. They all surrendered without a fight. "Disarm them and six men corral them into a room and hold them there," Shivaji Maharaj said. Then he led the others into the thick of the fighting. When the *agneyastra* (fire weapon) had burned out, the timbers were smoking but little damage had been done to the structure and the fire had burned itself out, and the smoke was also beginning to clear.

Because of the total confusion inside of the fort it was a quick battle. Two hours after the first flames were visible over the fort, the Maratha Army had secured the fort and corralled the soldiers separate from the officers.

"Maharaj Shivaji what do we do with the prisoners? Dwijesh asked.

"The officers will be executed after we learn all we can from them. The troops, for taking up arms against the Empire will spend ten years in prison camps. On work farms. Some go to the jungle harvesting timber, some to the mines, some to the rice farms and quarries. I'll take care of that; you're in charge of interrogating the officers.

"Our men are hungry so detail someone, Dwijesh, to organize a staff to start preparing food immediately," Shivaji commanded, then he left.

The soldiers guarding the river had captured twenty men who were trying to escape.

* * * *

When the news broke in Surat that the Mughal fort had fallen to the Maratha Army the citizens ran off the few Muslims who were living there.

Dwijesh obtained very little new information that his spies did not already have. On the third day of occupation the officers were executed and the Mughal soldiers marched off to prison camps where they would work for ten years to pay back their debt to the Empire.

The fort was opened up and cleaned thoroughly. The charred timbers were scraped clean and the rest was washed several times before the stink of the smoke was gone. It was actually a very nicely built fort, and Shivaji intended to put it to good use.

The cannons, gunpowder and shot were inspected. They would be used soon, when the Mughal ships arrived.

Shivaji sent details into the countryside to obtain food from farmers. They were all paid with written guarantees to be paid, and not silver rupees. Herds of sheep and goats and flocks of chickens and wagon loads of rice and other vegetables. Bought with the same guarantee to be paid.

General Dwijesh was busy planning how best to attack the ships when they arrived and he had sent out at Shivaji's request spies to Gujarat for information.

One day about three weeks after securing the Surat Fort, a soldier cleaning one of the heavy cannons spotted sails in the distance. He sent another soldier to inform Shivaji Maharaj and General Dwijesh that a ship had been seen coming towards the harbor.

Dwijesh already had an excellent artillery squad and they prepared the four big guns. A smaller cannon was used to signal the approaching ship, as was the custom. The ship replied with their own single shot.

As the ship came closer, everyone at the cannon parapet began waving enthusiastically. Those on deck waved back. The gunnery Lieutenant waited until the ship was broadside and then he signaled two gunners to fire. Both heavy balls hit the ship, one in the forecastle and one just below the bridge. Then Dwijesh ordered, "Put one across her bow." This was another signal requesting their surrender.

The skipper knew when he was out gunned and he raised a white flag, surrendering.

The ship was brought into port up river and the sailors were taken into custody. There were fifteen seaman and forty soldiers, and an abundance of food.

Dwijesh learned that two more ships were scheduled to arrive in three days and then a fourth, two days after that.

* * * *

When the next two ships arrived it was almost a repeat performance. The gunnery Lieutenant waited until both ships were broadside before firing all of the heavy cannons. This time there was a few casualties and both skippers raised the white flag. Each ship was carrying two hundred men and provisions.

When the fourth and final ship arrived, it was again a repeat performance. This ship was carrying one hundred men, munitions and food.

"General Dwijesh, that was some brilliant strategy taking all four ships, crew, soldiers and provisions. How soon can two of these be made sailable?"

"A week at the most, Sir. What do you have planned?"

"I was thinking about sending two into the fort at Bhavnagar. A skeleton crew, only enough to keep the ships moving head-on towards the harbor. These ships will only be a decoy, while our army comes in from behind. It should be an easy conquest. We secure the Gujarat Peninsula, we secure the Maratha Empire.

* * * *

With the officers, crews and soldiers from the four ships taken care of, the food and munitions and the two ships repaired enough to act as decoys, the Gujarat campaign was almost ready to begin.

"General Dwijesh, did you find any able-bodied men who can sail the two ships?" Shivaji asked.

"Yes Sir, six men per ship should be able to handle it," Dwijesh said.

"How many days will it take for our army of two thousand men to travel around the bay and come in from the back to Bhavnagar?" Shivaji asked.

"We would use a good road to Vadodara then cross-country to Bhavnagar. If we allowed a week before the ships approach Bhavnagar, I think we would be okay" Dwijesh replied.

All preparations were made. Leaving a regiment of soldiers at Surat was a good idea. But everyone wanted to be at Bhavnagar. They lusted for battle, now that they had so easily defeated the Mughals twice already.

Dwijesh planned to have the troops positioned behind the fort at Bhavnagar waiting for the arrival of the two ships. Each ship was carrying a small cannon up forward and when they fired on the fort this would be Dwijesh's signal to attack, while hopefully the Mughals would be concentrated on the two ships.

The soldiers were anxious for another battle with the Mughals. During the two battles the Maratha Army had lost ten men. They were as eager as Maharaj Shivaji to drive them out of India.

There were no more preparations that were needed and Dwijesh and Shivaji with their army set off on the road to Vadodara. Their time table of the ships were to leave Surat Port in one week in the morning.

The days were increasingly warm and the road was dusty, but this did little to dampen their spirits.

Once they had left Vadodara and the dusty road behind

they were quite often in the shade of tall bushes and trees. After all the marching the soldiers had been doing since leaving Satara, the men were not tired. In fact they were eager, because they knew once this was over and the Gujarat Peninsula was once again under Maratha control, they would be heading home.

* * * *

On the day the two ships were due to arrive in front of the fort at Bhavnagar, Shivaji Maharaj and his army were well camouflaged in the bush about a quarter of a mile behind the fort. They had been there since before daylight, waiting patiently for the signal to advance.

The two ships had set sail at dawn and at 8:30am with a favorable tide, they were in front of the fort and both ships fired a cannon shot at the fort. This was no signal. They reloaded the cannons and fired again. All four shots hit the fort and now the Mughals were aiming their cannons at the two ships, but a head on shot was not so easy. The first volley of shots were way short.

Before they could reload General Dwijesh and his soldiers had entered the fort and had taken control of that and now there was a furious hand to hand battle between the fort and the shoreline. Men on both sides were killed, but far more Mughals. Their commander saw the futility of continuing the fight and he ordered a surrender.

Dwijesh had lost fifteen men while the Mughals had lost four times as many.

With Surat and the Gujarat Peninsula now under control of the Maratha Empire, and the enemy soldiers sent to work camps for ten years, Maharaj Shivaji promoted General Dwijesh to Viceroy of the Gujarat District. And Shivaji and his five hundred soldiers were on the way home to Satara.

Shivaji Maharaj offered an option how they could return. They could walk back. Or five hundred men could squeeze into two of the confiscated ships and ride the waves to River Vashisht and the Maratha Fort, Arjnavel, across the river from the old Mughal port Dabhol which stands in ruins.

To a man they all chose to ride the waves to the Arjnavel Fort and from there Satara was almost directly east. There was a lower mountain range they would have to cross. The Western Ghat Mountains.

Not being use to the rolling seas, many of the men were seasick the entire trip and were wishing they had taken the long route home, over land.

After only three days at sea the two ships tied up at Fort Arjnavel. Everyone was in a rush to stand on solid ground. It was mid-morning and they left Arjnavel immediately for the pass over the Ghat Mountains.

They were in a hurry and two days later they walked into the palace at Satara.

Chapter 6

Katarikari heard her father was back from wherever he had been and she said to Ekani, "Come, Ekani, I want to go see my father."

He followed the Princess down the long corridor, mindful to keep a proper distance behind her. It had been more than seven months since Katarikari had seen her father. Her mother Chira was already there in his quarters.

"Come in, daughter. How is the Princess?" he asked. He hugged her and kissed the top of her head.

Then he told his wife and daughter all about his campaign to secure Surat and the Gujarat Peninsula. "Are you home for a while now, Father?" Katarikari asked.

"For a few weeks and then there is another matter that needs my attention.

"You have changed much, Katarikari, since I have been away on the campaign. You have come out of your shell and you are more happy now than I remember."

"I am happy, Father. Thank you for noticing."

"How is your young servant doing?"

"He is doing just fine. He waits for me at the 'red line'. He tries very hard to please me and not to make any errors," Katarikari said.

The three talked and visited for a long time. Ekani stayed seated behind the red line awaiting the Princess' return.

It was the height of the monsoon season and Shivaji knew it would be useless to try to eliminate the Afghan Mughal threat at Bijapur. There was a break in the weather a week after returning and he sent the five hundred soldiers on to General Parsaji Bhosale's camp near Bijapur. "Tell General Bhosale I will be at his camp September first and he is to have all preparations done by then," Shivaji said.

Shivaji saw his daughter walking toward the park with her servant walking behind her and noticed the boy had put on some weight and filled out. He wasn't a runt anymore. At first he had had his doubts about the boy. But it looks as if Ekani has proven him wrong.

Shivaji enjoyed being home, but he had an empire to oversee and sometimes that took him away from his family. "How long will you be staying home, my husband, before you're off on another campaign?"

"This is for your ears only, Chira. I must meet General Bhosale at his camp September first, and I don't know how long I'll be gone. And no one is to know," he added.

* * * *

Shivaji Maharaj enjoyed being home with his family, but all of his time now was administrative. Although he knew that most of the administrative work had accumulated while he was away fighting the Mughals, it now had to be done. There were many bills that had to be paid, let alone wages for all the soldiers, etc. But deep down he wished he could escape now and leave for General Bhosale's encampment.

He watched his daughter almost daily as she and her servant walked away from the palace through the park. He thought, *Maybe Ekani is helping my daughter to come out of her shell that she had put up herself.* He was pleased to see the change. But he also had difficulty giving a servant, a slave, credit for anything.

He was relieved when the day finally came, and he and a small detail left the palace for Bhosale's camp. They traveled much faster than he had a year ago.

At Bhosale's camp the General asked, "Shivaji Maharaj, would you accompany me in my tent?"

When they were seated, the General's aide brought in a tray of hot tea, figs and sweet cakes.

"Bring me up to date, General," Shivaji said.

"I have had two spies in and around Bijapur, and Sultan Adilshah is very much aware of this camp, but he does not know of the preparations we have been making.

"I decided it would be a mistake to attack Adilshah in Bijapur. We bring him to us," Bhosale said.

"How do we do that?" Shivaji asked.

"My spies in Bijapur will leak information that once we receive reinforcements, we will attack Bijapur in October. Once Adilshah learns of this he will try to attack before October."

"Okay, tell me about your preparations General."

Bhosale unwrapped a sketch of his preparations. "Adilshah always attacks first with three field cannons, transported by elephants. Then behind the elephants are horsemen with scimitars, then foot soldiers with rifles and scimitars.

Bhosale pointed to the sketch, "Here, there is a road that passes through here and here," he pointed again, "is a passageway that runs through a heavily wooded area. There are three elephant pits, like you had asked. In a V pattern.

"Adilshah's elephants travel abreast and the passage is wide enough to allow them to pass side by each. When the elephant in the middle breaks through the pit on the apex the other two will travel only a little ways forward before they stop. Then they will be in their pits.

"Back here," and he pointed to a spider web, "are buried powder kegs covered with stones and the sand to match the surrounding landscape. We don't detonate these until the foot soldiers are in the middle of the spider web.

"The rear-most kegs will detonate last as the Mughal soldiers are retreating. We should be able to get their horsemen as well as their foot soldiers.

"My men will be split up into three squads. One on each side of the passage and well hidden in the trees. A third squad will circle to their rear.

"My soldiers will carry both rifles and scimitars. Once we have Adilshah's army secured, then we move onto Bijapur with our cannons. Most of his soldiers he would have sent against us, so that would leave only a skeleton crew to defend the fort."

"You make it sound so easy."

"Well Sultan Adilshah is a creature of habit. He always attacks using the same methods and weapons. In the past we have always fought our battles on the open field. Two enemy forces lining up and facing off against each other. These new warfare tactics of yours, Shivaji Maharaj, will intentionally confuse him and he won't know how to respond. That's when we attack from both sides and the rear. I am certain he'll have more men than we have, but because of these new tactics, I don't worry about being outnumbered."

"General, how will you detonate the powder kegs?"

"I'm glad you asked. I had forgotten to explain that. We have bamboo filled with gun powder to each powder keg. We have four ignition points, in case one fails. And they are not set to detonate all at the same time.

"It is my guess that when the powder kegs are detonated they will think it is only cannon fire and not land mines."

"When do you send your spies to Bijapur to leak the information?" Shivaji asked.

"Now that you are here, tomorrow morning. Then in two days we set up and wait. I don't think we'll have long to wait. Especially once Adilshah learns about our fake plans of attack."

* * * *

The next day General Bhosale briefed the two spies what they were to do. As soon as they had changed into Muslim clothes they headed for Bijapur.

The soldiers in camp were making their last preparations. Along with their weapons each man was to bring three days supplies of rations and water.

On the morning of the second day General Bhosale along with Shivaji Maharaj left camp. By late afternoon they arrived at the ambush passage. There was not a word said. The prearranged three squads separated and took up their rightful positions. General Bhosale and Shivaji Maharaj stayed with the squad on the west side of passage. They had a better view from there.

The two spies of course would have been able to travel much faster than the Maratha Army and Shivaji was anticipating that Sultan Adilshah would be putting together his army and making plans to attack.

The next day there was no sign of Adilshah or his army. They were not expected to show this early. Adilshah's army didn't arrive the second day either, nor the third. But at mid-morning on the fourth day they could hear the elephants trumpeting and a faint cloud of dust rise behind them.

Shivaji was hoping that all of Bhosale's preparations and hard work would be enough to stop the Mughal Army. He turned to look at General Bhosale. No visible concern at all. His face was like a mask of stone.

Adilshah did not have any forward scouts. If he had, there was nothing to see or hear.

The elephants were coming just as Bhosale had said they would and then behind them were the soldiers. The elephants had passed through the spider web of mines and were approaching the covered-over elephant pits. The foot soldiers were far enough back so they would be mostly beyond the first series of mines. The elephants had only a hundred yards now before reaching the first pit. They were each harnessed to a heavy cannon.

When the middle elephant went crashing through the first pit the elephant trumpeted a shrill alarm. This spooked the other two into running straight ahead and they both charged into the other pits and each trumpeting a high pitch alarm and then all the elephants were quiet, as the sharpened stakes in the bottom of the pits had done their job. The foot soldiers had stopped in confusion and they were not quite at the position for the fuses to be lit.

Their Commander was shouting at his men to move on. Just before the soldiers reached the outer limit of the spider web, the four fuses were lit.

Suddenly there was an explosion and the stones covering the powder keg went flying through the air with more damage to the foot soldiers than the flintlock rifles could have caused. There was a pause after the first explosion. The Mughal soldiers started running. Then came a rapid detonation of the powder kegs that sounded like rapid fire artillery. The ground was littered with dead and wounded bodies. The passage was now littered with potholes, rocks and bodies. Two thirds of Adilshah's Army had been subdued in the spider web mine field. His elephants and heavy artillery were gone and now after the last powder keg mines detonated General Bhosale's soldiers moved in and surrounded the enemy. There was some resistance. But what little there was, was futile.

In less than three hours after the elephants had first been seen, the battle was over. General Bhosale had not lost a man and there were only a few soldiers that received wounds, although none would be fatal.

A small squad was left to secure all the prisoners and they were made to look after their own wounded comrades. "When you have everything secured here, Lieutenant, bring the wounded to Bijapur," General Bhosale said.

"Yes Sir," the Lieutenant replied.

This part of the Bijapur campaign was finished. Shivaji wasn't sure how much resistance they would face at the fort. He along with General Bhosale hoped Adilshah had deployed all of his men, leaving only a skeleton force at the fort. Shivaji was disappointed that the Sultan had not been with his army. Both he and Bhosale had looked extensively for him. Even among the dead.

On the march to Bijapur General Bhosale was thinking that before Maharaj Shivaji had ordered that they fight the guerilla war, the close quarter battles in the past, even those he had won, he had lost too many men. Fighting like that was senseless and terribly costly in human lives. Fighting a guerilla war, he had not had a single fatality. But they still had the fort to secure.

At the fort a squad entered each entrance and the entire fort was ringed with Maratha soldiers, in case anyone tried to escape. There was an underground level and three above ground. Each level was searched simultaneously.

Adilshah was located in the underground level and six aides and only a dozen more Mughal soldiers in the entire fort. Adilshah didn't offer any resistance, "But how did you do it so quickly?" he asked.

The wounded were soon brought in and their wounds were attended to and then all Mughal prisoners were held in a secured level of the fort.

"Sir, what do you wish I do with these prisoners?" Bhosale asked.

"There was no resistance, so ten years in work camps. Officers as well as the soldiers."

The next day while eating their noon meal Shivaji Maharaj said, "I am impressed with your military skills, General. You have proven that you are also a good organizer. Do you have anyone in your ranks who could effectively replace you?"

General Parsaji Bhosale didn't have to stop and think about his answer, he said, "Yes Sir, I do. My second in command, Gangel Sudhir."

"Are you absolutely sure about Gangel. No reservations at all?"

"No reservations, Sir."

"Good, then promote him to General in Bijapur District, and as of this moment you are the Viceroy."

"Thank you, Sir. I will not disappoint you."

"Parsaji," Shivaji started laughing, "Parsaji I didn't think that would be possible with you, I have complete confidence with you, General."

* * * *

Maharaj Shivaji was very pleased with the securing of the Deccan Plateau and the sub-continent of India. Even though the Afghan Mughals would always be a nuisance to the Maratha Empire, Shivaji doubted very much if they would ever again be a serious threat. It seemed that Sultan Aurangzeb's dynasty was slowly collapsing around him.

Aurangzeb had accomplished some good and positive progress and built many fabulous temples. But he never allowed the freedom of an individual to follow whatever religion they chose. He wanted his empire to be Muslim only.

Shivaji returned to Satara and his home, satisfied now that the Maratha people could live, work and worship in peace.

Shivaji Maharaj did have one concern however. Viceroy Ishwar Raman of the Rajasthan District in the capital city of Jaisalmer on the eastern edge of the great desert that separated India and Pakistan, the eastern edge of the Mughal Empire. For the last two years Shivaji had been noticing some dissension and he had to do something to quiet and pacify Raman's discord. And the only way to do that would be a trip to Jaisalmer. And since he had quelled the Mughal's push across the Deccan Plateau he felt it safe for his wife to join him. He would leave Katarikari in the capable hands of Canda.

Chapter 7

1659

Maharaj Shivaji and his wife Chira were away from Satara for six months at Jaisalmer talking with Ishwar Raman trying to dissolve any apprehension Raman might have had.

To strengthen the alliance with Viceroy Raman and the Rajasthan District, Shivaji made the proposal that his daughter Katarikari marry Raman's son Adheer. When she turned seventeen he and his wife Chira had promised to deliver their daughter to the Raman family. That way Shivaji knew he would always have Raman's loyalty.

Chira wasn't at all happy, but she also knew she had no right to object.

* * * *

Two years had passed since Shivaji had left the palace to start his campaign to drive the Afghan Mughals from the Maratha Empire.

Katarikari had grown and although she was only nine years old she looked to be somewhat older. It may have been because of her grace and although she was only taught to read, write and basic numbers, she had knowledge and wisdom far beyond her age. And Ekani was growing physically as well as consciously in her presence. She was the fire that consumed his every thought. She was leading him to his illumination.

At night when the others had gone to sleep and the palace was quiet, Ekani would go to Katarikari's room and she would teach him how to read, write and his numbers. A whole new world had opened for them both.

Katarikari and Ekani had managed to keep their friendship a secret from everyone in the palace except for Canda. Canda understood that both the Princess and Ekani were very special young people. Only once in a while would she remind Ekani of his position in the palace. Being a servant herself for most of her life, she understood there was no future for the two of them together, so she saw no harm with their friendship. After all, Ekani had been good for the Princess.

One day while walking in the park behind the palace— it was the middle of May and the grass was a little wet with dewdrops—Katarikari had knelt on the grass to pick some flowers when Ekani saw a cobra snake about to strike at her leg. Without thinking, he pushed Katarikari out of the way and laid down on the grass, half on top of her and shielding her from the snake.

The cobra struck and bit Ekani in the muscle of his lower right leg. "Aah!"

Katarikari felt his body go rigid. "What is it Ekani? Why did you push me? And why are you lying on top of me?"

"A cobra raised its head and was going to strike at you, Kari," he said in between bouts of pain. "The cobra bit me, Kari."

"Oh my God! No, Ekani!" There was real emotion in her voice. She rolled out from under him and rolled him over so she could see the wound. The cobra had already disappeared. She tore a strip of cloth from her silk sari and tied it around his leg above the wound. She tied the strip as tight as she could and then she helped him to stand. "I must get you back to the palace as fast as you can walk, Ekani." She put her arm around and under his arms to support him and help him walk. He put his arm around her shoulders to take weight off his injured leg.

"How are you, Ekani?" She was real concerned as his face was covered with sweat.

"My leg is tightening like a piece of stone and hurts really bad, Kari."

Canda saw them coming up the park path, with their arms wrapped around each other. This was too much display of their friendship and she rushed out to meet them and put a stop to it before Chira or Shivaji saw them together.

Before Canda could say a word, Katarikari said, "Canda, help me! A cobra has bitten Ekani!" There was definitely command in her voice and Canda supported Ekani from his other side and the two more or less carried him. He could no longer use is injured leg.

They literally had to carry him up stairs. When Katarikari turned to go to her room Canda said, "No, Princess, we must take him to his own room."

In a clear and commanding voice that Canda never had assumed of the Princess before, Katarikari said quite clearly, "No, Canda! Ekani saved my life. We are not going to lay him on the floor. We will put Ekani in my bed and I will take care of him."

There was no need to say anymore for either of them. Canda did as she was told and helped Ekani into Katarikari's bed. "We must remove his clothing, Princess," Canda said. They left his loincloth on and then pulled the covers up over him.

"Canda, go find the doctor," as simple as that.

Canda left immediately, running down the corridor. Katarikari washed his face with a piece of cloth and cool water. Then his whole body. He was sweating so much and he was becoming delirious, moving his head back and forth and mumbling words she could not understand.

When the doctor arrived, he pulled the bed covers back and saw the cloth strip tied around his leg. "Princess, you probably saved his life by tying this cloth on his leg. I'll leave it on for now. But in two hours you should remove it." Then he put some pine pitch on the snake bite and wrapped a cloth bandage around it to hold it in place.

"The pine pitch will help draw the venom back out and kill any bacteria. You did a fine job, Princess. Where did you learn to tie this cloth on his leg?"

"I just knew, Doctor. Will Ekani be okay?" Both Canda and the doctor noticed the concern in her voice.

"Only about 6% of cobra victims die. He is young and strong, so my guess is he'll be fine in a week. How long was the cobra, Princess?"

"I don't know. I never saw it. Ekani pushed me out of the way and protected me with his body. His leg was between me and the cobra. He saved my life, Doctor."

"He'll have periods of chills, when you will have to keep him warm. Then he'll sweat and he'll need cool compresses on his face, neck and chest. The next two days will be his roughest. If he survives the two days, then he'll live.

"I'll send an *ayah* (nurse) to see to him."

"That won't be necessary, Doctor. I will take care of him." Then she looked directly at the doctor and then Canda and said, "He saved my life." That's all that was necessary to be said.

Canda watched as the Princess bathed Ekani's body with cool water. She was so gentle and tender. Then Canda understood. Katarikari's and Ekani's relationship was more than friendship. They were in love with each other. Why hadn't she seen it before now?

"Princess Katarikari, you look as if you have everything under control. I must get back to my duties."

She went to her own room and sat down in a chair, thinking how strange it was. *Two people from completely different walks of life, a Princess and a slave, falling in love with each other.* She had not believed in coincidences. She had always believed that everything had a purpose. Aamir selling his son Ekani to the Maharaj Shivaji for his daughter was no coincidence. There was a reason—a reason far greater than Aamir needing a few rupees.

Where would their love take them? she wondered. She did know that Ekani, sometime in his life, would have to face the greatest sadness that she could imagine.

She had a mother's fondness for Ekani ever since he came to the palace. And she didn't want to see him hurt so badly that it could destroy him. But there again, she didn't want to deny him the love that she herself had always wanted and knew she could never have. "I will not interfere. But I will try to protect them," she said aloud.

Katarikari bathed his body with cool water, then removed the bandage and pine pitch poultice, she bathed the injury with warm soap and water. The muscle had swollen some and had turned black and blue around the bite marks. She heated some water and held a hot compress over the wound to draw out the poison. She kept thinking how nice it felt when Ekani had put his arm around her and her arm around him. She sat on the bedside all that night bathing him with cool water and then tenderly drying his skin with a cloth.

She had dozed off once and had lain across him, until he started shivering with the chills. This awoke her and she pulled the bed covers up over him.

In the morning Canda brought a tray of food for Katarikari. "I'm not hungry, Canda, but thank you."

"You must eat something, Princess, to keep up your strength so you can take care of Ekani." Katarikari not aware of the concern in Canda's voice.

"I will eat something, if you will bathe Ekani with cool water."

"How is he, Princess?"

"I had to put hot compresses on the wound during the night. His leg was becoming infected. It looks much better now."

When Canda had finished bathing Ekani she said, "Princess I must leave now and finish my duties. When I have finished I will return, so you can get some sleep, while I take care of Ekani." Katarikari looked at Canda and nodded her head.

Katarikari awoke two hours later and there was no change with Ekani. But his leg did look better. "I must return to my duties now, Princess. I will bring you more food later."

"Thank you, Canda."

"Ekani, I know you have traveled in your spirit body to a far off beautiful land. It should be me laying there and not you."

Later during the afternoon Canda brought Katarikari some more food. "Any change, Princess?" She was really concerned.

"No change. But he isn't getting any worse, so I suppose that is good."

"Let me see his leg, Princess."

Katarikari folded back the covers. The black and blue was gone. There was only redness around the bite marks. "His leg is looking much better. Remember what the doctor said, Princess. If he survives this night then he has a good chance of living," Canda said.

"Ekani will survive the night, Canda. He will live."

Somehow Canda knew the Princess wouldn't let him die. There was something special about Princess Katarikari. She left and closed the door.

Katarikari was happy to be caring for Ekani, but she felt guilty with Ekani laying unconscious from a cobra's bite. Protecting her. She took a clean cloth and dabbed it in the water and parted his lips and squeezed a few drops of water in his mouth. He did not respond and he didn't swallow. He had lost so much water while sweating.

The sun had set and the interior of the palace was quiet. Katarikari was tired and sleepy and slowly she slumped over Ekani's stomach, asleep.

She awoke when he started shivering again with the chills. She brought the bed covers up again and rubbed his hands and arms to warm them.

The chills were gone now and he started sweating and she put more cool compresses on his head and chest.

It was well after midnight and Ekani was still unconscious. Katarikari put another cool compress on his forehead then dried her hands and placed them lightly on his chest and went deep inside herself as spirit, and began to chant softly the word *Aum*. *Aaa Uuu Mmm*, like she had been taught. This chanting would produce a harmonious vibration which would take spirit to the highest of the three inner worlds of Hinduism.

Katarikari had gone so deep within that she was not at all aware of her physical surroundings. After daylight there were the usual noises within the palace and Katarikari was once again back in the physical reality.

Just as she was opening her eyes she felt Ekani move. It was only a slight movement, but she knew he was coming back to his conscious mind. She rubbed his hands, his cheeks. She was excited and she leaned over him and kissed him on his lips so tenderly. Ekani responded and kissed her back, moving his lips with hers.

Katarikari pulled back and sat up and said, "Ekani, Ekani, open your eyes."

He did, very slowly and when he recognized Katarikari he smiled and said, "I was dreaming about you, Kari."

"Where am I, Kari?" Then he looked around and realized he was in her bed. "Oh my God!" and he started to get out but his leg still hurt.

"It's okay, Ekani, it's okay. Do you remember the cobra snake biting you?"

"Yes."

"That is why your leg hurts. You saved my life, Ekani."

"But I'm in your bed."

"You saved my life, Ekani. I was not going to have you lay on the floor. And you'll stay here until you are better."

"How long have I been here, Kari?"

"The cobra bit you three days ago. Are you thirsty?"

68

"Yes I am. And I'm hungry."

"Here is some water first. I'll have Canda bring our breakfast to us. You stay in bed. I'll find Canda."

Just then there was a knock on the door. "Come in, Canda," Katarikari said.

Canda opened the door and came in and asked, "How did you know it was me, Princess?"

"Who else would it be?" she answered.

Canda walked over to the bed and surprised to see Ekani awake and feeling better. "I'll be. You said yesterday, Princess, that Ekani would survive the night, that you would take care of him. You healed Ekani, didn't you, Princess?"

Katarikari didn't answer her. Instead she said. "He still can't get out of bed. His leg is too painful. So for now he stays in my bed. And Canda, we both would like breakfast and hot tea brought up for us." And then she added, "Please."

This 'please' surprised Canda as much as anything. She knew something very special had taken place during the night. She would like to know, but she would never ask.

"At once, Princess," and as she was leaving Katarikari said, "Thank you."

This was the first time she had ever heard the Princess say 'please and thank you'. Something happened during the night. But she could not imagine what. Ekani was brought back from the edge of darkness and the Princess saying please and thank you, and both Ekani and the Princess seem so happy. She didn't know nor could she even imagine what had come to pass during the night. But she was positive about one thing. Because of Ekani a great weight had been lifted from Princess Katarikari.

* * * *

Ekani's leg was healing from hour to hour and the day after he had awaken and realized he was in Katarikari's bed he managed to get out of bed and stand. "You don't have to leave my bed, Ekani," Katarikari said.

"Yes I do. And you know that as well as I do. It doesn't matter how we feel about each other Kari—inside the palace I am only your servant. And it is not right that I remain in your bed any longer. I am only thinking of you, Kari."

"I know, but I have grown used to caring for you, Ekani. I enjoyed the time—the time alone with you."

Shivaji Maharaj and his wife Chira were never told the whole story about Ekani, the Princess and the cobra. Only that Ekani had pushed Katarikari away from the cobra and had been bitten himself. That after three days he had recovered and was now performing his duties as servant. Nothing was ever said to anyone that Princess Katarikari had nursed Ekani back to health while in her bed. Outside Canda and a few servants no one else knew the entire story and Canda threatened the other few servants with death if they were ever to say anything.

Now whenever the two would walk in the park, they no longer chased each other like children or played games. They walked holding hands and sometimes with their arms around each other. Their favorite place was a new bench or seat Katarikari had one of the ground servants make and put in the garden of many splendid and unique flowers. The little cool stream ran through it. They would sit there for hours talking. Sometimes they would lay on the grass and look up at the clear blue sky. And always watchful for any more cobras. Away from the palace and prying eyes, Ekani and Katarikari were lovers, and with each passing day their love for each other was growing. But around the palace, servants and nobility they were mistress and servant.

Chapter 8

1662

Three more years now have passed and Aurangzeb's Mughal Afghans were only making nuisance raids at a few of the close border forts, trying desperately to push the Maratha Army back and reclaim some of the ground he had lost during the last six years. But his control and empire in India was slowly disintegrating.

In two years Shivaji Maharaj was going to move his family and his governing base to the Raigad Fort. Years prior he had employed Ankur Kumer, a well reputed architect and a company of carpenters and masons to rebuild the fort to his specifications.

The fort at Raigad, before it was seized by Shivaji Maharaj, was called Rairi. The fort rises 2,700 feet above the sea in the Sahyadri Mountain Range and only one main entrance. 1703 steps to the main entrance called the Nagarkhana Darwaja. Shivaji Maharaj had a secondary entrance built which he used. He also had the architect install the capability of hearing sounds from the main entrance to Shivaji's quarters.

The fort was originally built by Candraaro Mores in 1030.

"Ankur, I want running water piped through the new palace and I want a bathroom in each bedroom. A reservoir can be constructed between the building and the two high peaks. Rebuild the dam and increase the depth of water, so there will always be sufficient water flow throughout the palace.

"I want the bushes pulled up by the roots, and trees, grass and flowers planted. I want Raigad to become my home and palace, and then the capital of the Maratha Empire. If you need more workers you can keep some of Commander Kashi's troops. I am moving him to Satara and his soldiers to Bijapur and Surat.

"I know you won't have everything completed in two years, but I am moving in regardless and your workers will have to work around us. I am paying you well, Ankur Kumar, and I expect perfection," Shivaji Maharaj said.

"And you shall have it, Sir," Ankur replied.

* * * *

"Ekani have you heard that we'll be moving to a new palace Father is having built at the old city of Rairi? He has renamed it Raigad. It sits high up in the mountains. He says where Brahma, The Creator himself, sits. He says in the morning right after sunrise there is a layer of clouds between the palace and the city below. He says it's like being in the Land of Brahma."

"I have heard the rumors, Kari."

"Father says that in the evenings as the sun is setting it illuminates his empire just like the World of Brahma. He says the sea becomes calm, so calm that the sun's golden rays as it sets reflect off the water, making the water look like a sheet of pure gold.

"Just think, Ekani, we will have a new palace to explore and the lake behind the palace, Lake Ganga Sagar.

"Oh, Ekani, it'll be so much fun exploring Raigad." She hugged him and they kissed passionately and then walked back to the palace, their lives as lovers, now again as mistress and servant.

"Kari, wait a minute please." Katarikari stopped and

turned to face him. "Kari, three years ago when the cobra bit me and I was unconscious, I was still aware what was happening around me. Although I still was in some far off land filled with beautiful lights, I was lying in your bed and I was dying. I know this. But that night, somehow, you brought me back from the dead. You, Kari, healed me. How Kari? How did you heal me?"

Katarikari smiled at Ekani and said, "I didn't, Ekani. I only became an open channel for Brahma, and He healed you."

"Will you teach me this, Kari?"

"Yes we will start tomorrow."

The next day was raining so Katarikari and Ekani stayed in her room with the door open and they talked all day about their Eternal Way of Life, Hinduism. Ekani could remember some from his father, but Katarikari seemed to know so much more.

"How do you know all this, Kari? I am with you almost all day every day and I have never known anyone to teach you this."

"I don't know, Ekani, how I know. I only know that I do. I cannot explain it beyond that."

"Coming from anyone else, Kari, I would not believe it. But I do believe you. You are very special, Kari."

1664

Shivaji Maharaj ordered the move to Raigad begin.[1] He also sent couriers to all of the districts within the Maratha Empire that once the move to Raigad was complete he would be announcing that he would be assuming the position of the entire Empire—that he would declare himself Emperor. He also invited all the District Viceroys and their families to attend the coronation and celebration. And if any of the District Viceroys

---

1   This event actually took place in 1674. I had to change it to 1664 to fit the storyline.

objected they were to come and see him before September first. This gave them four months notice.

Most of the work at Raigad had been completed and the constant interruptions of the move to the new palace was slowing the builders down. But they would make do.

There was so much to be taken from Satara to Raigad and all they had were small carts and wagons. Not only the family were moving, but the entire household staff of servants, the political cabinets and their offices and supplies. Food, bedding and there would be a hundred soldiers housed at the new palace and all of their gear and equipment.

Ekani was asked to help out with the move and he was separated from the Princess for days at a time that summer.

The last to move to Raigad were Chira and Katarikari and the household staff servants. Everything else had already been transported to Raigad. Ekani of course was required to assist Princess Katarikari. He was to walk beside her as she was carried in a wicker woven palanquin chair by four servants. His job was to keep the insects away from her and fan her when she was too hot and fetch her water when she thirsted. For Ekani this was an act of love not a slave's duty.

Once everybody and everything was at Raigad it took another two weeks to get everything in order.

Guests from the Empire Districts were already beginning to arrive and daily tours were given of the new palace.

Aurangzeb of the Mughal Empire also heard the rumors that Shivaji Maharaj had re-established his palace at Raigad and he was already studying for a way to capture it. He had been terribly embarrassed losing so much to the Maratha Army.

On the day of the coronation: "Ekani, I will be need your help today, serving food and kitchen duty," Canda said.

After breakfast, Ekani was only able to talk with Katarikari for a few minutes. "I have to work with the kitchen staff and food servers today, Kari. At least I will be able to see you at the coronation. You look so beautiful. I have never seen anything so beautiful, Kari." She was wearing a maroon silk sari embroidered with gold, and she wore gold colored silk slippers.

Katarikari smiled and even dared to kiss him on his cheek.

Tables and chairs were already set up in the grand ballroom and the kitchen crew began bringing out the food and setting up dishes on the tables. Ekani was so busy he didn't have time to look for the Princess. There was so much, the visitors were directed to take a seat and Maharaj Shivaji, his wife Chira, sons Sambhaji, Rajaram and Katarikari. Shivaji's personal aide called for silence and when the room was quiet Shivaji stood up and addressed his guests.

"I would like to thank all of you for making a long trip to Raigad to help celebrate a new era and a new beginning for our people, now that we have driven the Afghan Mughals from our land. Now our commerce and agricultural industries have already begun to expand and flourish. This will lower the taxes on the poor farmers and workers. We are once again free to worship our three Deities: Brahma, Vishnu and Shiva without fear of being punished.

"We still have work to do to insure this way of life that we so desire. In the future there may be small battles to be fought, but not to the extent of these last ten years. Many lives were lost and we should never forget those who have fallen.

"Today I am declaring myself Chhatrapati Shri Shivaji Maharaj[2] of the Maratha Empire and the sub-continent of India. And from this day forward I am also declaring that Raigad is now the Capital City of the Maratha Empire.

"Now enough of me boring you with talk. There are fine sweet cakes and tea and enjoy the celebration. Thank you all for coming."

Once in a while Ekani could catch Katarikari's attention and she would smile at him and then quickly turn away before anyone noticed.

2   King

The celebration lasted long into the night. As much food as had been eaten, there was still enough left, Ekani thought, to feed many of the poor villagers. Before the celebration and feasting was over, Princess Katarikari excused herself from the head table and kissed her father on his cheek and said, "Goodnight, Father. I am going to my room now and sleep. I can no longer stay awake."

Ekani excused himself also. It was his duty to escort the Princess wherever she went. He followed the proper distance behind her as she walked the length of the long corridor to the other end.

The next morning Ekani had to help the kitchen staff pick up everything and clean the grand ballroom. And much to Ekani's surprise, Shri Shivaji Maharaj had ordered all the leftover food be distributed to the villagers below.

Some of the guests had already left to return to their own Districts and a few more would be leaving the next day. Some of the Viceroys had urgent matters to discuss with Shri Shivaji.

Three days after the celebration Princess Katarikari was summoned to her mother's quarters. "Come in daughter and close the door and sit down. We need to talk about your future." Ekani stood outside and he could not hear what was being said. "I was hoping that Adheer Raman, Viceroy Ishwar Raman's eldest son, would have accompanied him. You see, daughter, when I traveled with your father to Kumbhalgash Fort in Rajasthan, your father arranged for you to wed Adheer when you are seventeen."

"Mother! How could you? You want me to wed someone I don't even know! What about my feelings, Mother?" Katarikari was crying now.

"I had nothing to do with this arrangement, Katarikari. Your father thought it would strengthen the relations between here and Rajasthan and the Empire."

"But I don't love him, Mother! I don't even know him!" she screamed.

"It isn't all that bad. Once the shock of it wears off. My marriage to your father was arranged. I had nothing to say about it. When you are royalty, Katarikari, this sort of thing is expected. And you are expected to comply and adjust. As women in nobility in India, Katarikari, we have no control about whom we wed."

"That doesn't make it right, Mother."

"No, daughter, that is true. That is just how it is. You must remember you are nobility and this alliance with the Ramans will be good for the Empire. It is time, Princess Katarikari, that you grew up and accepted your responsibilities to your father and the Empire."

Katarikari started crying again and rushed out of her mother's room and slammed the door and ran down the corridor crying. Ekani had to run to keep up with her. And he could not ask what the problem was. Not until they were alone.

Katarikari ran into her room and laid face down on her bed crying. Ekani came in right behind her. "Close the door, Ekani, please."

He closed the door and he wanted to sit on the edge of the bed beside her and console her. But he knew what the punishment would be if someone came in and found a servant sitting on the mistress' bed.

"Kari, what is wrong? Why do you cry? I have never seen you cry before."

Katarikari kept crying, until there were no more tears to cry. She rolled over and sat on the edge of the bed and looked at Ekani. There was so much warmth and concern in his voice and on his face, she began to cry all over again.

She stood up and Ekani walked over to her and hugged her. She pressed her face into his neck and hugged him back. He could feel her trembling. He gently stroked her hair. "Kari, talk to me please. What is the problem?" he pleaded.

She held him close. Ekani was feeling so much compassion for Katarikari at the moment and there was nothing he could do. She was too distraught to put into words how she was feeling. Ekani loved Katarikari and he was beside himself because there was nothing he could do except hold her and caress her hair.

Finally she pulled back and looked at Ekani. She looked deep into his eyes. There was so much kindness and tenderness there. She sat on the edge of the bed and said, "Come, Ekani. Sit beside me." When he hesitated she pleaded, "Please."

He sat and she held his hand in her lap. "Ekani—do you remember when Mother traveled with Father to Rajasthan?"

"Yes, that was a few years ago."

"My father arranged for me to wed Prince Adheer when I turn seventeen." She buried her face in Ekani's chest and began crying again.

Ekani's whole world was just pulled out from under him. He was speechless. All he could do was hold Katarikari and rock back and forth gently.

The door opened and Ekani didn't care. He didn't care who was going to see him holding Katarikari and sitting on her bed. Canda walked in and closed the door. Neither Ekani nor Katarikari made any move to stand up or disengage. At this point neither one of them cared. Canda had heard rumors that the Princess had been promised to wed in an arranged marriage and when she saw the two of them, the Princess in tears, rush into her room and close the door, she thought perhaps her mother had told her daughter about the arrangement. This is why she had given the two some time by themselves before she intervened. She pulled over a chair and sat down facing them.

"I have known for a long time now that you two share a special love. But Ekani, you are a slave like me. You must have realized that you two have no future together. Princess, if you were to run off with Ekani, you must realize your father would hunt you both. He would never stop until he had found and killed you both. He would never allow you, Princess, to embarrass him."

"But I don't want to live without Ekani, Canda. I love him."

"I know you do, Princess, but you are nobility. Tell me why did your father promise you to wed?"

"Mother said uniting the two families would strengthen the Empire."

"Princess, with nobility comes much responsibility and whether you like it or not this seems to be your responsibility. I do not see that you have a choice.

"Women in India have never had equal say about their own lives and I don't know what can be done to improve it.

"I'm saying these things to you both because I have come to love you both as if you were my own children. You two have been so good for each other. I have often looked the other way when I knew you two were more than just friends. If there was anything I could do to help you, I would. But there isn't.

"You have a little more than three years before you are to be wed. All I can say is enjoy the time you have together, but you must be careful, always. I will help you when I can. But above all, you two must never engage in sex. Princess, you will be expected to be a virgin when you wed and if you aren't, the Prince will kill you and hunt down your lover."

Katarikari had stopped crying. She was leaning against Ekani and he had his arm around her. He was pretty subdued. His eyes were red and watery. This was the saddest day of his life, even more so than the day his father had left him at the palace when he was only six.

"Now you two go for a walk around the lake and learn to enjoy the time you have and forget what will come."

When Canda stood up and put the chair back, Ekani stood and said, "Thank you, Canda."

"Yes, thank you," the Princess also said.

* * * *

Once they were out of sight of the palace Ekani put his arm around Katarikari and they walked in silence around the lake. At the further end they sat down on a grassy bank and looked out across the water. They still had not said anything. There was not much that either one of them could say to comfort the other.

Ekani could feel his heart, his inner being, being stripped away. Katarikari had been his sole reason for staying at the palace and not running off. Now he would not even have her in three years.

Katarikari was thinking almost the same. She could not imagine life without him. They lay back on the grass watching the blue sky above. They laid hugging each other for hours. Neither one feeling much like talking. There was absolutely nothing that could be done.

* * * *

When they did return to the palace, Canda noticed a very downhearted mood. Neither one of them speaking. Katarikari went to her room and began crying again while Ekani stood outside her door. Neither one feeling much like eating. Canda saw Ekani standing near the Princess' door, looking straight ahead at the opposite marble wall, as if standing at attention as an honor guard. She was hurting also, but not to the same degree or the same reason. She had formed a special fondness for both and she wished there was something she could do. Her heart was aching also.

Katarikari lay on her bed fully clothed staring out the window, waiting for darkness to fill her bedroom. Maybe the darkness would erase the event of the day.

Ekani too, was lying on his sleeping mat fully dressed staring at the ceiling oblivious that darkness had filled his room. He lay there like that all night, not thinking about anything. He had blanked out the day.

Katarikari was thinking. Something Canda had said about her nobility responsibility. When she was born, her destiny had already been set into motion and the only person who could change it was her father. And she knew he would not. She knew in her heart she would never be able to forgive her father.

Then her Hindu teaching started talking to her. Where there exists no coincidences in life. This was then a lesson she would have to work through. *Maybe I can help all Maratha people and girls.*

Then she began to think about Ekani. *If there are no coincidences, then Ekani's destiny was to be sold into slavery and he and I fall in love. But to what end. How do either of us benefit from me being promised in an arranged marriage?*

Before she realized it the dawn's light was beginning to shine through her window. That in itself was confusing. She knew she had not been asleep. She had been thinking about Ekani and her own destinies and how much she loved him. Then suddenly it was daylight. The last thing she had been thinking about were her Hindu teachings—their destinies. Somehow through the night she had come to terms with her lot in life. *But where was I, and how did the night pass so quickly?*

Regardless, she was not happy about an arranged marriage and not being able to have Ekani's love, but she had accepted her fate and they still had three years in which they could continue seeing each other.

She got up, dressed and then opened Ekani's door and entered. He was still on his sleeping mat. "Hey sleepy head, time to get up." Playing, she sprinkled a little water on his face. This brought a smile and he was up and grinning.

"We have three years, Ekani. A lot can happen between now and then." This did make him feel better and he smiled again.

* * * *

Canda watched, when she could, Katarikari and Ekani and saw a change in them. At first she wasn't sure what it was. Then little by little she began to understand that they both had finally adapted to their own destiny and they both had grown inwardly over that long awful night. They had left the playful happy youngster in themselves behind. They were beginning the early years of adulthood at fourteen. No one else seemed to notice the change. Perhaps Canda had a closer relationship and understanding with them both.

Katarikari stopped visiting her mother and father and stopped talking with them. She looked upon Canda having more concern for her than her own mother. Canda was aware of this change and she secretly enjoyed the attention.

Ekani was more difficult to read. When he wasn't with the Princess or on some chore, he stayed to himself. But he did carry that same sense of knowing that Katarikari carried with her.

Shri Shivaji was too busy to notice the changes with his daughter. Only what his wife, Chira, had told him. He had an empire to oversee and couldn't be bothered with trivial women matters. He hardly saw his daughter before she was told about the arrangement.

But Katarikari's mother Chira was all too aware. Whenever her daughter saw her coming she would turn and walk away. If she was confronted unexpectedly by her mother, she refused to talk with her. When summoned to her mother's quarters she refused to go.

Canda was aware of the separation between the Princess and her mother and she stayed out of it. She didn't want to get involved.

Chapter 9

1665

The construction workers finished rebuilding the fort a year after Shri Shivaji declared Raigad as the Empire's Capital. The stone masons in particular had done a fantastic job. The floors were polished marble as were some of the interior walls. Many of the old timbers had been replaced. It was made larger. The 1703 steps of the main entrance were polished and the outside walls of the old fort were scrubbed clean and washed. The weeds and shrubs around the fort had been torn out by the roots and shade trees and flowers planted in their stead. Lake Ganga Sagar now sat in the middle of a huge park, with shade trees, flowers, pathways and benches to sit and enjoy the scenery.

Ankur Kumar, the architect, had surely built Shri Shivaji Maharaj a beautiful palace for his headquarters.

At first there were many people who would take a leisurely stroll through the park and around the lake and Ekani and Katarikari had to be very careful. They found a secluded place away from the lake near the base of one of the steep peaks behind the lake. Here they would lay on the grass and talk about their younger years at Satara and Katarikari wanted to know about his family.

"I'm not sure if there is much I can tell you Kari. I was six when my father sold me and now I'm fifteen; we're both fifteen." He told her what he could remember and that wasn't much. Life at the palace and tending to the Princess' every need consumed his whole life. There was no other life. And he didn't want it to change, as much as he knew it would.

When they were together like this, it wasn't as mistress and servant. They were equal and this seemed to please Katarikari that she was the equal of the man she loved.

"You know, Ekani, I am as much a slave as you are. I'm a slave only to serve my father's wishes. There are times—I have never said this before—but there have been times when I would envy you."

* * * *

Shri Shivaji Maharaj had sent word to all the Empire's Viceroys that their Generals should retire their older soldiers and replace them with younger men. The older soldiers, Shri Shivaji had decided, had seen their share of fighting and had served the Empire well and should be rewarded.

Some of Aurangzeb's force from the north of the Gujarat Peninsula tried a surprise attack on Fort Raigad. A Mughal ship had put in close to shore and after the men had left the ship, the ship pulled back into the Indian Ocean out of sight.

One squad flanked the fort and tried to scale the high cliffs behind the palace. Half of the men fell to their deaths; the cliffs were too steep.

The other squad tried a frontal attack and that meant going up the 1703 steps to the main entrance. The men who survived to return in their ship told Aurangzeb that Raigad was impenetrable. Shri Shivaji had a good laugh. He knew then that he had chosen well in Raigad as the Empire's Capital.

* * * *

One beautiful sunny day, not too much heat or humidity, Katarikari and Ekani climbed up on the cliff behind the palace as far as they could safely go. They stood on a rock promenade overlooking the lake and the palace beyond. They stood close together, their arms around each other. Ekani turned so he was facing Katarikari and kissed her with passion. She responded and kissed him. Then they stood there holding on to each other.

Katarikari said, "I love you, Ekani. But we cannot make any plans for the future. We must love in the moment and accept what comes. We cannot even let ourselves dream what it would be like to create a life together."

He knew she was right, but he didn't say anything. He kissed her again.

1667

Two more years had passed, and come spring Shri Shivaji Maharaj and family and caravan, accompanied by two hundred soldiers would start the trip for Rajasthan. Shivaji's oldest son Sambhaji had agreed to stay behind to protect Raigad. He was a great warrior like his father.

Katarikari and Ekani still refused to talk about the short time they had left. And in the last three years Katarikari had not spoken to her mother and father.

Preparations were being made and adequate shelters and transportation were being assembled below the mountain. And Shivaji left all preparations to one of his aides and he had an army of help.

Whenever Chira wanted to communicate with her daughter she had to go through Canda. Katarikari refused to see her mother.

Almost every day was spent packing and preparing for the month long trip. Besides a tremendous amount of food and water that had to be taken along for everyone, clothes—and there were the gifts Shri Shivaji was obligated to give to the Raman family.

Shivaji wanted to be in Rajasthan by the first of May, although the wedding wouldn't be for another two weeks. They all would need time to rest and get acquainted with the entire Raman family.

Katarikari and Ekani still found the time for their walks in the park, mostly due to Canda's help. She knew the two needed this time together. Still neither one would talk about how their life would be once she wed the prince.

The day finally had come. Ekani brought Katarikari her evening meal. "I can't eat, Ekani. I'm not hungry. You can have it." As Ekani was leaving Katarikari said, "Come back please when it is dark."

Ekani took the food to his room and he could only eat a little. He took the rest back to the kitchen. When the sun had set and it was dark outside the palace Ekani returned to Katarikari's room. "Come in, Ekani, and close the door."

When the door was closed Katarikari walked over to Ekani and put her arms around him and hugged him. "Hold me, Ekani." They stayed like that for a long time. Neither one talking. It was enough to simply hold each other.

Finally Katarikari said, "You know we leave tomorrow morning, Ekani."

"Yes I know."

"You cannot come with me, Ekani."

"Why not, Kari? I want to be with you wherever you go."

"I know, Ekani, and I wish to be with you too. But we cannot any longer. I love you so much Ekani. It wouldn't be long before Prince Raman learned this and he would have you killed or worse, and probably me also. You must leave here tonight, Ekani. Forever," she buried her face in his chest and began crying. He held her tight against him and caressed her hair. Tears were running down his cheeks also. Katarikari for him had been his whole reason for living.

"I love you Kari. I always will."

"Ekani, when we reincarnate in another life promise me you will look for me. I will look for you always, Ekani."

"Kari, we will find each other." He held her close feeling the warmth of her body.

"You must go now, Ekani, before you are discovered. I will always watch over you, Ekani."

Chapter 10

Ekani closed Katarikari's door gently. His face and eyes were red and wet with a tremendous sorrow. Canda was there in the corridor. "I'm sorry for you, Ekani. Good luck and be careful." He could only nod his head.

He left the palace and Katarikari behind. Not once looking back. He could remember his father telling him the same thing so many years ago. It now seemed like a lifetime.

He left Raigad and headed north. There was a bright moon so he could see enough to avoid obstacles. He came to a stream and a drink of water and rested for a while on the bank. He couldn't stop thinking about Katarikari. She had been his only reason for living. He thought.

All of a sudden all the penned up emotions of the last three years came pouring forth and he began to cry. Then in anger he began to run. He didn't care where he was going. He just ran. Trying to outrun all the emotions he had held inside of him. He ran and ran, without any idea where he was going, and caring much less.

He ran all night, not tiring, and he had no idea how much time had passed. All he could think about was how much he loved Katarikari and she him. And that loss would make him angry again and he would run faster. As he ran he was thinking how much he would like to hurt her father. It was because of him that all this was happening.

He was getting so tired he would often stumble and fall to the ground. He'd lay still for a brief moment until thoughts of Katarikari would wash through his mind like a flood. Then he'd pick himself up, mad again, and run until he would fall again. He kept this up most of the night, until just before daylight, when he stumbled and fell again because of exhaustion. Only this time he couldn't get back up. He passed out from exhaustion.

For four hours he slept. But it was anything but a restful sleep. Images of Katarikari kept flashing through his inner vision. He could hear her voice, feel her touching him, smell her perfume. These images tormented him for four hours.

When he awoke, his face was lying in dry dusty sand. For an instant he was confused. How did he get there? And where was he? Then it suddenly hit him. He was running away from Raigad and the memories of Katarikari. He stood up and his legs and feet were sore from running all night. He remembered Katarikari had said to go north. He checked the position of the sun and hoped he was heading north. The memories of Katarikari made him angry again, not because of her, but because their love for each other had been torn apart.

As he walked along a dusty path he kept looking around him. Everything seemed so strange. Then he understood he did not have much knowledge of India's countryside outside of the palace. He soon found a clear stream and stopped long enough for a drink. While he rested he soaked his sore feet in the cool water. But not for long. He had no idea if Shivaji would send out soldiers to find him or not, or would they be too busy with the caravan to Rajasthan. He remembered then that this morning Katarikari would be on her way to Rajasthan to wed.

And these thoughts mad him angry again and he continued on his way. He had no idea how far north to go or how long it would take him.

For two days he wandered through dusty and sandy countryside. Each morning he would check his position with the sun to make sure where north was. He was hungry but he wanted to put much distance between himself and Raigad. He had no idea how the Empire would punish a runaway slave.

On the third day out he came to a mountain range. The Eastern Ghat Mountain Range. He found a well used trail though a pass and decided to follow it. Darkness came before he was all the way through the pass and during the night there was constant noise of animals. Some were calling for a mate, a jackal had made a kill and was calling her young pups to feed and the pups started squabbling and fighting amongst themselves. An elephant trumpeted way off in the distance. Monkeys screamed at him from the tree tops. Not having any knowledge of the wilderness he was scared. If only he had a fire he would feel more comfortable. But he had no matches and he didn't know how to start a fire without them. And he was hungry.

He tried to sleep but he was too unnerved to close his eyes for long. There was too many animals all around him. It was an unsettling night and at the first hint of daylight the next morning he started his trek through the pass. It was odd. After all of the animal sounds during the night, he thought he would see them in the daylight. But the only sign of life was himself.

He was hungry and he knew if he didn't find some food soon he'd not be able to continue on his journey. When he came to the next stream he looked for fish. There were a few small ones that he tried to catch with his hands without any success. They were faster than he. There were two crayfish in the shade of a rock and he was able to catch both of them. He knew they'd be good cooked, but he had no way of starting a fire. He removed the head and ate the bodies raw. Except for the crunching shells they were pretty good. He looked for more but didn't find any.

He pulled up grass by the roots and washed them clean and ate the roots. Not bad when you are hungry. He picked and ate a few clover blossoms.

Feeling a little better he continued on his way, now always looking for food. At high noon the temperature was hot and Ekani had to sit in the shade of a tall tree. He leaned up against the trunk, trying to keep the memories of Katarikari from seeping through his conscious mind and overwhelming his emotional side of being.

Directly ahead he heard the chatter of monkeys. He sat still listening, then a Phayre's Langur monkey sitting on a limb directly overhead answered. Then a monkey dropped something that hit Ekani on the head. He look at the half eaten fig and picked it up and smelled of it. It smelled sweet. He ate a bite and it was delicious. He ate the rest of it and then searched the ground under the tree for more. There were two more half eaten pieces of figs. He decided to stay under the tree a while and see if the monkey would drop more fruit. He had never seen or known wild fig trees. Eaten like this they were delicious.

The monkey in the other tree was still screeching and Ekani found several figs on the ground. He looked at the tree and picked up a leaf trying to memorize how it looked so he might be able to find more figs.

He spent the rest of that day wandering around in the area and found four trees with fig dropping monkeys. It was odd why the monkeys would only eat half the fruit and throw it away. Lucky for him. He slept that night leaning up against one of those trees.

The moon was just coming up over the horizon and he wanted to stay awake and watch it but he soon was sound asleep. He was more exhausted than he had thought. With his stomach full of food he slept well until daylight the next morning when screaming monkeys awoke him. But it was an alarm screaming and then he saw it. A huge Indian tiger was only four hundred feet away directly in front of him. And what was worse there was a slight easterly breeze blowing his scent toward the tiger. Each year there were many cases of tigers killing and eating humans.

Ekani looked for a tree to climb, but all the branches were out of reach. He was too afraid to run. He knew he could never out run a tiger. The tiger kept coming closer, as if it was stalking something.

Then there was a clear voice; it was Katarikari. And her voice was as clear as if she had been standing next to him. "I will always watch over you, Ekani." He stood up and looked. He knew she was not there, but he had to look. Her voice was so clear. And he no longer was afraid.

He turned his attention back to the tiger and it was still coming closer. But when it was about two hundred feet away it stopped and looked at Ekani and then turned away and walked off.

The monkeys stopped screaming and the tiger was gone. He turned around and around even though he knew Katarikari had not been there. He wasn't certain now whether he had actually heard her voice or he was only remembering what she had said the night he left. He scratched his head and said, "Your voice was so clear, Kari, I know you were here."

There was nothing more to see there so he continued his trek, after checking the position of the sun. He knew that the middle of the country was jungle and he wanted to avoid it. So he started turning a little northwest. If he found later this wasn't enough he would correct his course then. He found a few more trees filled with monkeys eating the same kind of fruit. He ate a few and filled his hands to eat as he walked.

The monsoons would be arriving soon, if the rains followed the usual pattern. So he did not want to be in the low land or near major rivers or swamps.

With his stomach full again he had more energy since starting out from Raigad, and he quickened his pace. He soon came to a river and he had no idea what river it was. He had no knowledge of India outside his duties of the palace. Katarikari had taught him to read, write and some numbers, but she also knew nothing about the country.

The water was flowing southeasterly and he knew if he followed it downstream the water would get deeper. So he turned upstream and in a short distance he found shallow water that he could safely wade across.

Half way across he saw a silvery fish and when he tried to catch it he fell forward in the water. The fish swam off. He was wet, so in the shallows on the other side, he hunted for crayfish on his hands and knees. He found three together and managed to catch all three of them. He ate these in the water. Then he continued looking. He found a few more, but not enough to fill his stomach.

After wringing the water from his clothes he continued on. Two days later the monsoon rains started; so he thought. At night he'd sit under the canopy of trees and walk in the rain during the daylight.

Two days later the rain stopped. As he was about to start out that morning he saw movement in the distance and stopped until he was sure it was safe. Whatever it was was coming closer but angling off to the east. Finally he could just make out what it was. It was a marching column of soldiers. He swallowed hard and wondered if they were looking for him. Then he realized how ridiculous that was. Even Shivaji wouldn't waste time sending so many soldiers after him. Maybe one or two on horseback trying to run him to ground. In all honesty though he doubted if Shivaji had sent anyone after him. He would have been too busy with business at hand to bother with one runaway slave. But he still needed to be careful.

It was a long column and he waited even after they had passed out of sight. And even then he stayed in the cover of bushes and shadows. When he could see the road they were using, he decided to wait until dark before crossing in the open.

Hunger was nothing new for him now. Almost like living at home with his family when he was always hungry because there never was enough food. How long ago that life seemed to him now.

When darkness came he ran across the wide open meadow and road. There was nothing coming in either direction. The moon was on the other side of full, but there was still enough light for him to see. He traveled several miles beyond the road before stopping for the night.

As he leaned against a tree trying to go to sleep he tried to figure out how many days he had been on the run. As close as he could tell it was eight days. "How far have I gone in eight days?"

When he awoke the next morning he could remember dreaming about Katarikari. Then his heart started to shatter all over again, as the subtle truth started to take over. And this made him angry again and he stood up and continued his journey. But he couldn't let go of the images he saw in his dream and he became all the more angry and he began to run.

He ran and ran until he collapsed from exhaustion. He laid in the hot sun trying to catch his breath and he started crying and pounding the ground with his fists. His father Aamir had talked to him lovingly that day when he took him to the palace and explained he would have a better life as a servant than he could ever give him. He adjusted well to his new life and even liked it at the age of six. For eleven years he actually lived in royalty compared to the life he would have had at home. He even enjoyed his duties. His best friend was his mistress and then his love. She had taught him to read and write and his numbers because she cared about him at an early age. She had taught him so much and she healed him from the cobra bite and saved his life.

Now he had been torn away from that, the only life he could remember and away from the one person who made it all worthwhile.

The crying and pounding the ground finally stopped and he stood up and walked on. But still angry at his fate in life.

The days stretched on. Some days he was okay and there were others when, especially after memories of Katarikari or a dream of her just before awaking in the morning would be too much for him to bear, and he would become angry again and run. Trying to out run the memories and pain.

Some days food was very difficult to find and he'd have to survive on grassroots and clover and flower blossoms. He was losing weight and strength. He would tire soon each day. And now he had lost all concept of how much time had passed since leaving Raigad.

Also every day he saw animals, most were off at a distance and posed no threat. Some were curious and came closer until they winded him and then ran off. None of the animals had displayed any threatening behavior. Even one day a large bull elephant crossed his path. The elephant turned its head to look at the intruder and then walked on.

There was one day while he rested under a shade tree he had closed his eyes for a brief catnap and when he opened them there was a huge cobra snake near his feet. The snake had reared up so its head was more than a foot above the ground. The snake and Ekani stared at each other. At first he was terrified. Remembering the cobra that had bitten him. Sweat was breaking out on his face. He knew if he moved the cobra would strike. Then a strange thing began to happen. Ekani relaxed. The sweat dried up and he was no longer afraid. Katarikari's voice was back and as clear as if she was sitting beside him. "I will always look after you."

The snake lowered its head and left. He stood up and looked all around him. There was no one there, only him. But he knew as surely as he was standing there that he had heard Katarikari. Just as if she had been there with him.

This started the memories flooding his mind again and he started running. He was so intent in trying to run away from the memories, he wasn't aware that the land was changing. He ran across meadows of closely chomped grass, or that there were piles of droppings.

He was exhausted but he didn't care. He only wanted to run away from the memories. He was running up the slope of a small knoll. His heart was beating wildly and he was so dehydrated there was no more sweat. He collapsed before reaching the top. He was only conscious for a few seconds. Now he didn't care if he lived or died. He had surrendered to his fate, whatever was to be. He no longer cared. Then his world went black and he lay unconscious in the India sun.

* * * *

On the other side of the knoll was a shepherd's camp. Gopal Das had two dogs to help with the two flocks and they started barking and racing to the top of the knoll. Gopal Das ignored their barking at first, but when they didn't stop he stood up and climbed the knoll to investigate.

He saw nothing on top of the knoll but both dogs were facing toward the other side. When he saw a man's body lying there he stopped in shock. Not because of the still body. But because of the blue sphere of light that was surrounding the body. As he went closer the light suddenly disappeared.

Gopal knelt down beside the still body. He was still breathing, but just barely. Gopal was a man in his mid-fifties and he put his arms under Ekani's body and lifted, with no more effort than he would lifting a bucket of water.

He carried him down to his tent and laid him on his sleeping mat and opened the flaps in front and back of the tent so a breeze might blow through.

Ekani's clothes were dirty and in rags. Gopal stripped his clothes off and threw them outside and then checked Ekani's body for snake or scorpion bites. When he didn't see any he used a wet towel to wash off most of the dirt and then he put a cool compress loosely around his neck and another on his forehead. Then he sat back watching to see if this stranger would react to the cool compresses.

"I have no idea who you are, stranger, or what you are doing out here all alone. But I do know that that blue globe of light I saw around you, you are someone special. It had to be this light that alerted my dogs. I know this from my Hindustani teaching that someone is watching over you," Gopal said.

Gopal gently opened Ekani's lips a little and dropped

a few drops of water in his mouth. Ekani made no attempt to swallow. "When you are ready stranger, you will wake up." Gopal got up and fixed himself a bowl of stew and only a little for each dog. They were supposed to hunt for their own food.

Gopal kept replacing the cool compresses with new ones until he went to sleep. "Maybe in the morning you'll wake up, stranger," Gopal said and laid down another mat. His two dogs watched over the flocks during the night.

During the night the temperature had dropped and a cool breeze blew through the tent and in the morning Ekani opened his eyes. He looked around without turning his head. He had no idea where he was. Then he heard footsteps and turned to see a strange man a little darker than he was enter the tent and ask, "Your eyes are open. This is a good sign. Can you talk?"

Ekani's mouth and throat were parched from the hot dry air and he was having difficulty forming his words. Gopal recognized this and gave him a wooden dipper of water, "Drink slow. Sip it."

Ekani sipped at the water and it felt good trickling down his throat. Eventually he finished the dipper of water and asked for more, "Please."

"You have your voice back. Good. Can you tell me your name?" Gopal asked.

Ekani drank some more water and said, "Ekani—Ekani Mukul."

"I am called Gopal Das. Some people call me 'Old Das.' I like Das."

"Where am I, Das, and how did I get here?"

"I herd a flock of sheep and goats and you are in my tent. My dogs actually found you. You had collapsed almost on top of the knoll close to camp."

"The last thing I can remember is running for a long time."

"You must have collapsed in the heat from running. Enough talk for now. Are you hungry?" Das asked.

"Yes I am."

"I had to throw your clothes away. There were nothing more than dirty rags," Das laid out a change of his own clothes. "Here, these should fit you okay. While you dress I'll fix us something to eat," and he left the tent.

Das was back shortly with two steaming bowls of goat stew and goat cheese. "This smells delicious, Das. Thank you very much."

"Eat. We talk later."

They ate in silence and Ekani asked for more.

"Eat as much as you like, Ekani. There is plenty and plenty of cheese."

When they had finished Das made some tea and poured two cups. "I don't know how I'll ever be able to repay you, Das."

Das had decided to forego saying anything about the blue light until he had learned some more about this young man.

"Now, young Ekani, what are you doing out here in the wilderness alone, no food, no water, no weapon and only the rags you wore for clothes?" Das asked.

Ekani hesitated for a few moments wondering if he should be honest with Das. "I cannot lie to you, Das. I am a runaway slave."

"From where?"

"The Emperor's Palace in Raigad."

"Do you know what would happen if you are ever caught?"

"Yes, that's why I hesitated telling you," Ekani replied.

"Your secret is safe with me. Now where are you going?"

"I was told I should go north." He was determined not to bring Katarikari into this.

"How long have you been running?"

"What is the date, Das?"

"It is June 10th."

Ekani thought to himself. *Kari is wed.* "I left the palace the first of April. I guess I've been running for more than two months.

"You said June 10th, then where is the monsoon. This should be the rainy season, I understand."

"Well, we had a two day monsoon this year. The rest of the summer will be real dry. It happens sometimes. We'll probably get the heavy rains this fall after September," Das said.

"How long were you a slave?"

"My father sold me to Shivaji Maharaj when I was six. I am now seventeen."

"Your own father sold you, huh? That must have been terrible," Das said.

"Not really. I had a nice place to live and work. A room by myself, clean clothes and I didn't have to worry about anything as long as I did my duty."

"Then why are you running away?"

"I'd rather not say, Das. It is personal. I have done nothing wrong, except leave."

"I guess I can understand that. I tell you what, Ekani. I could use some help around here while you are recuperating. I can't pay you. But I'll feed you good."

"There is no need to pay me, Das, and yes I will help you."

"How do you feel now?"

"A little weak but other than that fine."

"Feel like going for a walk?"

"Yes."

"I want to show you my flocks. I have both sheep and goats. The goats are for food, meat, milk and I make cheese from the milk. There are more sheep and I shear the wool and put the wool in bags and haul it to market once a year. I just returned from town. I won't shear again until next spring. Soon I plan on taking a few sheep, some of the older ones, to town and sell.

"Right now we need to move the sheep to another meadow. It isn't far." Das whistled to his two dogs and pointed, and they bunched up the sheep, and kept any from straying, while Das and Ekani led one ewe. The others followed.

"Your dogs work well, Das."

"They do. They are especially trained for herding sheep."

"What about wild animals?"

"I do lose an occasional animal, but not often. The dogs are good protectors.

"Come I'll show you the goats now. The sheep will be alright here for a couple of days before we'll have to move them again.

"Goats like to eat bushes and tree bark as well as grass. They'll eat almost anything. There is so much feed around here I never have to worry about the goats or sheep straying too far."

There was a small stream running through the brush where the goats were feeding. "This is where I get my water also. Upstream away from the goats though. There are fifteen goats and thirty sheep. My flocks are not huge but sufficient for me to live out here."

"Do you have a family, Das?"

"My wife died two years ago. We were so happy living out here, just the two of us and the goats and sheep and the dogs."

"What happed to your wife?"

"She became ill and died two days later."

"I'm sorry. How do you cope without her?"

"With just me, the goats and sheep keep me busy. It did take a while to get accustomed to being alone."

Back at camp Das said, "Why don't you lie down and rest, I'm going to get some firewood and tender. If you feel up to it this afternoon we'll hunt for a few herbs to put in the stew pot."

Ekani laid down and he was asleep. But when Das came back he hollered, "Hey Ekani, I found a nice patch of mushrooms."

Ekani woke up and went outside. "I was asleep, Das. Did you say something?"

"You needed it, I guess. Yes, I was telling you I found a nice patch of mushrooms we can have with the stew."

It was a hot afternoon and since Ekani was still recovering from his ordeal they stayed in the shade of the tent and talked. "It is obvious to me Ekani you will need more than a day to recover enough for you to continue on with your journey. It'll be another couple of days," Das said.

"What is the nearest village, Das?"

"Assaye, about ten miles. Do you know where Mhasvad is?"

"No. How do you get your wool to Mhasvad? I don't see anything for a wagon or cart."

"Before I shear I go to Mhasvad and talk with a buyer of wool. To make sure the price is worth shearing the sheep. If we agree on a price then he comes here with a wagon."

While Ekani slept earlier Das had brought back enough wood for another day.

The sun was setting and the temperature had dropped. "Ekani, you start the fire and I'll put together something we can eat."

Ekani went out to the firepit and it was out. No hot coals at all. "The fire is out."

"Well, start a fire."

"How Das? I have never done this before," Ekani said, feeling a little stupid. Everyone knew how to start a fire. Everyone except Ekani who had been a personal servant.

Das went outside and looked at Ekani and said, "You really don't know, do you?"

"There was never any need of me knowing how, as a servant."

"Come with me, Ekani. First we must gather some dry tinder, dry grass or moss works okay, but I like to shave tinder from the dry underside of a dead tree. Come; I'll show you."

There was a dead tree not far away that Das had been using to shave tinder from. He took his knife and began scraping the wood, working up some fine shavings, then he passed the knife to Ekani. He soon had a couple of handfuls of tinder. "I'll hold onto this and you scrape some more for morning in case of rain tonight."

Ekani soon had another mess and they went back to camp. Das put his in the tent where it would stay dry. "Put yours in the pit Ekani. Now we have to get small dry twigs and sticks." They put those next to the tinder and Das brought out from the tent a piece of flint and his axe. He held the axe and hit the flint against the axe head and hot sparks flew. Ekani was as amazed as a small child would have been. Das showed him how to position the axe head to direct the sparks into the tender. "Okay, Ekani, you do it. That's right. Keep striking the axe head until you see some smoke."

Ekani kept striking the axe and much to his surprise there was a small column of smoke rising. "Okay pick up the tinder and blow gently on the hot ember until the tinder catches fire."

As Ekani blew air on the ember more and more smoke started to rise from the tinder pile and soon a bright flame shot up. "Okay put the tinder in the fire pit, Ekani, and put a few twigs and sticks on the tinder."

Ekani soon had a nice fire burning. "Wish I had had a fire during the nights I sat alone under a tree out there."

"It's simple once you know how it is done, Ekani."

Das had only a little stew left in the kettle so he put in the rest of the cured goat meat he had and then he added the fresh mushrooms, some onion grass and other herbs.

"It sure smells good."

"Tell me, Ekani, without being able to make a fire how did you survive? What did you eat?"

"Half eaten fruit the monkeys dropped from trees, raw crayfish and small fish, grass roots, clover and flower blossoms."

"I'm surprised you survived and didn't starve to death. You must have had a strong will to live."

"I did lose a lot of weight."

"There now, we put the kettle over the fire and we let it simmer until everything is cooked and tender. I only have a little rice left and before the stew is done, I'll put some rice in.

"There is a swamp nearby where I usually harvest some rice each fall. I only have to buy a little with some other staples.

While the stew was simmering Das made a pot of strong tea and added a few herbs.

"This is real good, Das. I would never have imagined food cooked out in the open like this with natural herbs and goat could be so good."

After they finished eating, they and the two dogs walked out to check on both flocks. They all had bedded down for the night. Das pointed towards the flocks and both dogs on cue circled the flocks and sat down near the outer perimeter. "They'll guard the goats and sheep tonight while we sleep," Das said.

They sat outside near the fire drinking—sipping the last of the tea. "I have an idea, Ekani. In good conscience I can't let you continue on your journey not knowing how to care for yourself. You didn't know how to start a fire. I'm not making fun of you, Ekani, but as a personal servant you never learned the basics of living or anything outside of the palace. You spend a year living here and helping me and I will teach you enough to take care of yourself. I can't afford to pay you. But I'll feed you, teach you and buy you some suitable clothes for this work and on your journey. I'll teach you enough so when you get to wherever you're going you'll be able to find work as a sheep and goat herder. Every man should have a skill." They both laughed.

"You know, Das, when I was a slave I never thought much about how much I didn't know of the practical side of life. As long as I did my job, everything that I needed was provided for me. This is quite an awakening."

* * * *

The next day they erected another tent from some canvas. Everything Das did Ekani watched and remembered. Das noticed this and smiled. "Ekani is a good pupil."

"Ekani, you have been here two weeks. Your weight and strength have returned and you handle the flocks well. I need you to drive ten sheep to Assaye. When you get paid you need yourself some clothes that fit. You are much taller than me and my trousers look like shorts on you. You'll also need a pair of sheep herder boots. You tell the shoe maker on the edge of town what you want them for and if he doesn't have a pair already made, he can make you a pair. And here is a list of a few supplies we'll be needing. You can leave early tomorrow morning and you should be able to reach Assaye before dark.

The next morning while they were finishing their tea, "Ekani, here are five more rupees in case the sale of the sheep won't pay for everything. Do not take less than two rupees per sheep."

Ekani had a rope on the lead sheep and the others were following behind it. Das stood by the fire pit watching until they had disappeared. Then he set about relocating the two flocks where there was more feed and some water. He had finished by noon and then he went in search of herbs and he set a few snares for rabbits and peacocks. Their meat was so delicious and the cape was actually worth what two sheep would sell for.

As he finished the last snare, he stood up thinking about Ekani and how delightful it was to have him helping. On his way back to camp he picked up some more firewood and tinder.

As Ekani led his little flock to Assaye, he suddenly realized he was happy again. For the first time in his life he had been given much responsibility for someone who had never before had to worry about it. It was a good feeling and he would not disappoint Das.

As the day wore on, the air was becoming much warmer. The sky was blue and the sun was directly overhead. It was hot, but he was so enjoying this new sense of responsibility that he was not too much aware of the heat. And the sheep didn't seem to be bothered by it also. When he would come to a stream he let the sheep drink and nibble some grass.

He had something now to keep his mind from thinking of Katarikari and the love they shared. And he was aware of this and each time images of Katarikari would start to come into his inner vision, he would start thinking of his task at hand. He did not want to disappoint Das.

He ate some goat cheese and washed it down with water and he was on his way again.

He reached Assaye two hours before dark. "Hello, are you Chava Ekram?"

"I am. Those are nice looking sheep. Are you selling?"

"Yes Sir, if the price is right," Ekani answered. "Five rupees each, Sir."

"No, that is too much. I'll give you two."

"No, I'll take five."

"They have no wool. They have already been sheared."

"That will save you the work. Look how fat and healthy they are. A butcher would get four times what I am asking. Or if you keep them until shearing time next year they'll be worth even more. Five rupees each, Sir," Ekani stood looking at Ekram with his hands on his hips.

Ekram looked each sheep over closely, looking for ticks or any sign of disease. "Three rupees."

"No, five or I sell them to the butcher tomorrow."

"You sure do drive a hard bargain. Five rupees each." He gave Ekani a handful of coins and started to leave.

"Wait just a minute, Ekram. You miscounted. There should be fifty rupees. You only gave me forty-five."

Ekram reached deeper in his pockets and handed twenty more rupees to Ekani.

"A pleasure doing business with you. Could I sleep in your barn tonight?"

"Help yourself."

* * * *

The next morning he found a place he could sit down and eat. Then he found the supply shop Das had told him about. The shoe maker was in the back. Ekani told him why he wanted boots and Gorg had a special made pair that were never picked up. It was soft goat leather soled with tough water buffalo hide. They were comfortable.

He purchased clothes for himself and the list of supplies Das wanted. Everything was tied in a bundle and a rope around the bundle so he could sling it over his shoulders. He really wanted to get back that day so he didn't waste any time talking with the shopkeeper.

On his way out of Assaye he met a patrol of soldiers just entering the little village. They paid him no attention.

His pack was heavy, but he wanted to make it back to camp before dark. He picked the pace up. Alone on the road he started thinking about Katarikari again and these thoughts were making him sad. He started running. But the pack on his back was too heavy for him to run far. He had to yield and walk at a fast pace. But angry.

He was so angry, he didn't take the time to rest or drink from the streams. He wasn't mad at Katarikari. How could he be. He was angry because they had been torn apart and upset his life forever.

As he was approaching a wet area, he saw a lone water buffalo, probably a bull. He was still too upset to take any caution. He just kept walking and the bull turned his head as it watched him pass. He was thinking how unfair life—his life was.

By the time he reached Das and his camp he had managed to calm his anger. "Hello, Ekani. I wasn't expecting you until tomorrow. You must be hungry and thirsty?"

"Yes, Das, I am." Ekani drank some water while Das dished up a bowl of stew. It was still warm. As he handed Ekani the bowl, Ekani gave him the small pouch with his money.

Das counted the rupees. He counted again. "This cannot

be. Did you buy boots and clothes?"

"Yes, everything is in the pack," Ekani said.

"But how can that be? I gave you twenty rupees and if you sold the sheep for two rupees each that's forty rupees yet you bought clothes, boots and my list of supplies and you still brought back fifty rupees."

"I got five rupees each for the sheep."

"Five each? I never get more than two. Are you sure?"

"You have the rupees, Das."

"But how did you get so much?"

"He asked how much I wanted and I told him five rupees each. He tried to meet me half way but I wouldn't bargain. I figured those sheep were worth more than two rupees apiece."

"Well, I'll let you do all the trading then. Thank you, Ekani."

"My pleasure."

As long as Ekani had something to occupy his mind he was able to thwart the memories of Katarikari and his sadness.

* * * *

The next day Das took Ekani with him checking his snares. "How many do you have set, Das?"

"Four."

They had one rabbit and one peacock. "This peacock, Ekani, is worth much more than a sheep. We'll skin it and rub wood ashes on the fleshy side of the skin to preserve it. The next time we go to Assaye we'll sell this."

"What is the rope you use for the snare?"

"It's a juniper root. When we have taken care of the peacock I'll show you how to find the roots. It's a lot of work."

"What do you do with the peacock carcass?" Ekani asked.

"We roast it over the fire and eat it. I like it much better than goat."

Das showed him how to skin the peacock and then how to rub wood ashes into the flesh. He opened up the bird and pulled out the innards and he saved the heart, liver and gizzard. "This is the gizzard Ekani. You slice it in half and then clean out the inside. Birds can't chew their food so they swallow it whole and it goes to the gizzard where it is ground up so the bird can swallow."

Das put a stick through the peacock for a spit over the fire. He put it close to the coals. "As soon as the meat is seared all around I'll lift it up higher so it'll cook slow. By searing it will help keep the juices in the meat and not dry it out."

Ekani roasted the heart, liver and gizzard, three hours later almost dark they ate their fill of delicious meat. "This is the best food I have ever eaten, Das."

"It is good, isn't it?"

The next day Das showed Ekani a juniper bush. "We can't just pull the bush out of the ground—the roots will break and we want the roots as long as we can get them. So we dig and find one the size we want. The roots in the center of the bush are too big and they go deep in the ground. We want the smaller ones that spread out close to the surface that'll produce more bushes."

They both started clearing the dirt away, a handful at a time. "Here's one, Ekani. See if you can find another one just like this. There usually are several with each bush."

Ekani watched as Das removed the dirt exposing the thin root. And he wasn't long before he had found another thin root and began removing the dirt around the root like he had seen Das do.

Das had done this many times and he wasn't long before he had uncovered ten feet of root and he pulled on it to break it off. Ekani's root was going off in another direction and he was only a bit longer before he had eight feet. "You might as well break it off now Ekani. It is getting to small to be of any use to us."

"You can braid these roots together and you have a strong rope, although it won't be very long. These roots are so strong I have caught and held a doe antelope. A buck would only knock the snare down with its antlers. Maybe later when this hot weather passes we'll try for a deer or antelope. The meat is as good as goat and I sell the hides in Assaye."

The rabbit and what was left of the peacock was put into a stew with herbs Das had found.

"We need to move both flocks again, Ekani. We'll move the sheep first. They need better grazing than the goats."

When they had both flocks moved Das taught Ekani the names of the trees, flowers, bushes and he named the animals and birds they saw. Das was thinking how anyone could go through life and not know his trees, flowers, birds and animals. And then he thought about from where Ekani had come. Yes he guessed he could understand. Not to find fault with Ekani, but it was like teaching a young boy the things in nature. And Ekani was just as interested and he remembered the names of everything.

Das couldn't imagine living in a world where you didn't know the names of trees or the animals. In a way he felt sorry for Ekani. But—he could read and write and he understood his numbers and he was able to get better prices for the sheep.

After eating the evening meal one day, while they were sitting around the soft glow of the fire, Das said, "Ekani, there is something I have been wanting to talk with you about."

"What is it, Das?" Ekani replied.

"When I found you on the other side of that knoll, neither me nor my dogs could see you. There was no wind so I doubt if either of them could smell you and you made no noise. But somehow both dogs knew there was someone in trouble on the other side. When I reached the top of the knoll I couldn't see you at first. But the dogs were pointing to the far side and there below the edge you were lying face down. Ekani, there was a beautiful blue globe of light around you. As if it was protecting you. I have learned through Hinduism that might be the manifestation of an inner being. A very special being. And this being has chosen you to protect. So I am believing that you, although you may not understand it yourself, are a special man."

Ekani knew who Das was speaking of and he dared not say a word about Princess Katarikari. For her protection. "I do not know what to say, Das. I have nothing special about me. I was born to a low class and sold into slavery. I do not know what to say."

"I'm thinking, Ekani, that you could walk unarmed into the jungles and this entity, this being would protect you."

Ekani had just learned something about himself this night and about Katarikari. He would not say anything about Katarikari's voice or that she had promised to always watch over him.

* * * *

The grazing for the goats and sheep was getting sparse. "Ekani, we need to move the two flocks to my winter area. Without the summer monsoons this year, the grazing is too sparse to stay any longer."

"How far do we have to travel?"

"Two days from here. Two days north in a small range of hills and a stream that flows through the valley."

"How do we move everything, Das?"

"We pack up everything we have. You and I carry it on our backs. The dogs will herd the flocks to follow behind us. Alone, of course, the move would take us longer because I'd have to make three trips. But I'm hoping you'll be able to carry the extra."

"I'm surprised you do not have a mule Das. A mule surely would make life easier for you."

"I have never had enough extra rupees to buy one, and buy all my supplies for the winter months."

"We have two peacock pelts. How many more would it take to buy a mule?"

"Probably two more at least."

The move to the new grazing location was made and Ekani had to make a second trip to haul everything up. He still thought Das should have a mule.

They set up camp and then walked the dogs around the area to familiarize them with the setting and for the dogs to leave their territorial boundary scent.

During the nights for two weeks predators would come close, but never crossing the boundary scent and the dogs would smell the predator and go off barking until the predator left. But never would the dogs go chasing after the predator. They simply chased them away from the flocks.

The rain started one day and Das said, "This might be the fall monsoon going to give us floods." But after three days the rain stopped and the flood pools dried up and the grass was growing so fast you could almost see it grow.

At the new location they snared three more peacocks and feasted for two weeks. They now had five pelts. The hot days of summer were gone. Although the average was only five degrees less, but the difference was noticeable and Ekani was glad he now had trousers to wear and not the traditional robe.

It was time for Ekani to make another trip to Assaye with the five peacock pelts and the doe antelope. "You take them to the same buyer. Do not take less than two rupees a piece for the peacocks or the antelope. You will have to travel back to the other camp to pick up the road to Assaye. It'll take you three days."

Das was enjoying Ekani's company. He was a good pupil and worker. He never had to show him more than once how to do something and he seemed to remember everything he saw and heard. He was also curious what it was about him, why the inner entity, being, protected him. He had never before seen a blue globe of light like that before. There was something special about Ekani. And something special about his inner protector. He was already missing his friendship and Ekani had only been gone two days.

Ekani went directly to see the buyer Chava Ekram. "No sheep this time?"

"No. I have five peacock pelts and one doe antelope." Ekani said.

"I'll give you two rupees apiece on everything."

"I'll take five each for the peacocks and four rupees for the antelope."

"Is your price firm?" Ekram asked.

"It is."

This time Ekram counted out the rupees into Ekani's hand. "Thank you, Chava Ekram. Do you know where I could buy a mule?"

"I have one I would sell. Eight rupees. And that's my firm price."

Ekani gave him the coins. "And I'll need a rope to lead him with."

Ekani led his mule down to the next shop where he bought Das' supplies.

Ekani led the mule out of Assaye, far enough so no one would see him as he climbed on the mule's back. He had never ridden a mule or horse before and he didn't want people watching if he should fall.

After he was over the shock, he decided it was so much easier to ride than walk the distance back. Once in a while he'd walk beside the mule to give it a break. What took three days now took almost two. Das was surprised to see Ekani ride into camp on a mule. "Just me, Das, this is so much better than walking."

"How many rupees did it cost you?"

"Eight rupees. Here is what is left and your supplies."

Das looked at the coins in his hand and counted eight. "I only expected two rupees left after you paid for the supplies. You gave me eight."

"I got five rupees each for the peacock and four for the

antelope hide. I think Ekram has been stealing you blind, Das."

"It would appear to be so."

* * * *

Like the spring monsoon the fall rains never really came. There was rain, once in a while, but not like it should be. Just enough to keep the grass green and not brown. For a herder, though, the weather was excellent. A few of the streams stopped flowing, but not the one they depended on for themselves and the goats and sheep.

Occasionally at night they could hear wolves howling off in the distance. "The wolves they come more south this year because there is not so much water. Probably the Tibetan wolf. Because of the monsoons, they usually stay to the north of here, in the foothills of the Himalayans. It is unusual to see them here. I have only seen it once before in my life and then too, there was no spring or fall monsoon."

"What about the goats and sheep Das?"

"We will have to watch over them. Maybe bring them in closer to camp each night."

"Then I will go now, Das, and walk around both flocks. The dogs are already out there, will you be okay here, Das?"

"I'll be okay. Thanks for asking."

Ekani left and Das was surprised when Ekani said he would go and then asking, *if I would be okay*. Das was beginning to wish Ekani would stay and work for him permanently. Of course then he would have to pay him. But he also knew there was something of great importance for Ekani at the end of his journey. No, he could not ask him to stay.

There was half a moon overhead and Ekani could see quite well. Most of the animals were bedded down and not the least disturbed. He had to make a wide swing to circle the sheep flock and at the back end he was on a slight knoll and he could see the profile of one of the dogs. Except he heard them barking near the goats. He stayed where he was and soon there were more, probably wolves with the first one. He was defenseless. The wolves had apparently scented him as they now were coming towards him and spreading out to encircle him. *No need to fear Ekani, I am watching over you.* He heard Katarikari's voice as clear as if she had been standing next to him. Then a blue globe of light appeared, surrounding him. The light looked almost as if it was emanating from himself. But he knew this was not so. Somehow he knew this was Katarikari.

All of his fears disappeared in that moment. He started walking towards the wolves. The blue light still surrounding him. The wolves stood still for a brief moment and then ran off. They never came back.

The two dogs came running up to Ekani from the direction of the goats. They could smell the wolves. "This was suppose to be your job." The dogs came up to him and licked his hands.

On his way back to camp he decided not to say anything to Das about Katarikari's voice or the blue light. There would be too many questions he was not prepared to answer.

"How are the goats and sheep, Ekani?"

"They're fine now. There was a pack of wolves but the dogs drove them off. I don't think they'll be back tonight, Das."

"Tomorrow night we bring them closer to camp for the night, "Das said.

With the goats and sheep so close to the camp there was little worry of predators for the rest of that fall and winter.

Not wanting to kill another goat for food they set more snares. "Sure would like to get us one of those boars. Their hide is the toughest leather I know and the meat is almost as good as peacock, only different. The snares we use wouldn't hold them. I've tried throwing a spear, but I couldn't get close enough."

"Das, what if we found a trail that was being used a lot with boar and we dug a pit?"

"I don't have a shovel. Then one of us would have to

jump down into the pit with the boar and cut its throat with a knife to kill it. Maybe we should forget the boar and get another antelope or deer."

"Of course a couple of peacocks would be good too," Ekani added and they both laughed.

They were able to snare a small deer and for Ekani it tasted much like the antelope had. Both very good. They harvested some wild rice, but there wasn't as much as past years because the monsoons never came. But what they found was good.

One thing about living in the tropics there were always herbs growing. Das' favorite herbs were onion grass and mushrooms. Although he could only positively identify a few. Those he learned by watching animals eat the mushrooms. Figuring an animal would know by smell if it was good or not.

As they were sitting around the fire sipping tea one night Ekani asked, "Das, what does Chava Ekram do with the peacocks?"

"He sells them to a dealer and they are eventually shipped to Europe to make hats for the noble ladies and to decorate their gowns."

From time to time while walking in the hills they would see a wide variety of animals. "It's strange Ekani, because of no monsoons this year there are many animals around; perhaps because of the water. But they do not come close to the goats, sheep or our camp."

Ekani knew the answer, but he didn't feel comfortable talking about her. After all she is a Princess and someday she'll be a Highness.

As fall changed to winter the temperatures were also changing. Ekani for all of his life had been acclimated to warm temps in the winter and hot in the summer. He wasn't that much further north than he had been at the palace, but he was aware of the lowering temperatures. During the day the temps were around 75-77 degrees. At night once in a while by sunrise the temps would drop as low as 50 degrees. Not cold but Ekani noticed.

Das made him a vest from the antelope hide. The leather was soft and Ekani was warmer.

Ekani was enjoying his life as a goat and sheep herder. And he liked the friendship of Gopal Das. If he hadn't taken him under his wing, so to speak, Ekani didn't know how long he would have survived out in the wilderness without any ability or knowledge to do so.

One day while Ekani was walking back from tending the goats and sheep four mounted soldiers rode into camp. He thought for sure they were after him. There was no sense in running. They had horses and he had already been seen.

"Will you join my friend and I with a cup of tea?" Das asked.

"First, are you the shepherd called Gopal Das?"

"I am."

They dismounted and accepted some tea and they sat down. "What is it I can do for you, since you have ridden all the way here to see me?"

"We are collecting taxes and the Viceroy has deemed that all shepherds should pay five rupees. Shri Shivaji Maharaj has just returned from weding his daughter to Prince Raman in the Rajasthan District." Das noticed how Ekani's facial expression changed at the mention of the Maharaj's daughter. "The war against the Afghan Muslims has been costly and the Viceroy has said the Empire needs this tax collection to rebuild the empire."

"Certainly. That is understandable." Das went into his tent and brought out the five rupees and gave them to the Lieutenant.

"Lieutenant, shouldn't you give Das a receipt for the taxes. Just in case someone else comes along to collect?"

The Lieutenant wrote out a receipt and gave it to Das and then the four mounted up and rode off.

"That was a good idea, Ekani, asking for a receipt. I

would not have thought of it. See, you have also taught this old man some things."

"Do they always come to collect taxes?"

"No, this is the first time. Either the Viceroy or the Maharaj needs the money."

As Das laid in his bed that night he was thinking about the change in expression he had seen on Ekani's face when the Lieutenant mentioned the Emperor's daughter's marriage. Ekani was a servant at the Maharaj's Palace. But what would a servant be doing with the daughter? Was that why he had run off? And most importantly, was the daughter, the Princess now watching over Ekani in her inner form of the globe of blue light? If so, then as a servant, Ekani had to be a special being. He knew enough not to ask him.

All except for the cooler temperatures that winter life as a shepherd went very well. Ekani, for the first time in his life understood what freedom and independence was all about. As a servant at the palace he had freedom to an extent. As long as he performed his duties. His decisions were always made for him. Out here with Das he had to learn to be responsible and he always had choices. As a servant his choices were usually made for him. But if he could once again be Katarikari's servant at the palace, without her husband, he would gladly return.

But that could never be, so his choices were his to be made now.

The antelope vest Das had made for Ekani was surprisingly warm. "This leather is so soft, Das. Maybe you should ask for more than four rupees next time."

* * * *

When spring came it was time to move to the summer camp. What the mule couldn't carry, the two carried the rest and they made the transition in one trip.

As soon as they were settled it was time to shear the

sheep. "I only have one set of shears. It would be a lot of help if you held the sheep while I sheared. After you have watched me I'll let you do a few."

With Ekani's help they sheared five sheep the first day. "I usually only shear one sheep a day." Ekani was doing good and he only nicked one sheep. "That is a lot of wool, Ekani. Now we have to bundle it and tie it off."

When they were finished they had five big bundles of wool. "How much is one bundle worth Das?"

"I usually average ten rupees a bundle."

"Maybe you should stand firm on twelve or fifteen rupees each. I think your buyers have been taking advantage of you."

Chapter 11

1668

They had moved to the summer grazing grounds and the sheep were all sheared. Earlier fifteen ewes had given birth to lambs that were doing very well and six goats had given birth to kids. One goat had twins. "You have large flocks now, Das. You'll be able to sell many and maybe buy a cart for the mule."

"You're getting ready to leave, are you not, Ekani?"

"Yes, Das. I must continue my journey to the north."

"Last summer I said you could stay and work with me for a year and I'd clothe, feed and teach you enough to survive on your own. But I have become accustomed to having you around. You have taught me things also, Ekani. If you stay I will give you half of the profit each year. You would have a good life here and you would not have to run anymore.

"Do you know where to the north you will go?"

"Delhi," Ekani answered.

"May I ask you this, Ekani? Why do you think you have to travel to the north? Do you know someone there? What's waiting for you in Delhi?"

"I know no one, Das, and there is nothing waiting for me. I go north because that is where I was told to go."

Das knew it had something to do with the Princess, the daughter of the Shri Shivaji Maharaj. And if he was correct

Ekani was playing with fire.

"I would like you to stay, Ekani, but I think I can understand your need to go. I wish you God speed, Ekani."

The next morning after eating, Ekani put his few possessions in a makeshift pack. "Ekani, I would like you to take these rupees. You may have need for them once you reach Delhi." And then Das gave him a mahogany walking staff. "I have been whittling this during the winter. You should walk with this, it could be a good weapon for you to keep jackals and other animals at bay."

Ekani handled it. "It fits my hand good. Thank you, Das. I will remember everything you have taught me."

"Goodbye my friend," Das said.

"Good-bye, Gopal Das, teacher, my friend."

Ekani left and started his long journey north. Das stood and watched until he was out of sight. He hadn't gone far when he realized just how much he had depended on Das' friendship to keep from thinking of Katarikari.

Now that he was alone and with no work to perform, his mind was once again flooded with images and thoughts of Katarikari. He felt so all alone now. And somehow his future, his destiny was lying to the north. He traveled all day, only stopping long enough to drink water. He wasn't even aware of the beautiful country he was walking through. He kept on a true north course and his mind away from Katarikari.

When he stopped for the night he didn't feel like eating. He did kindle a fire using the flint Das had given him and the back edge of his knife. Even though the night air was warm, he found comfort with the fire. He did make some tea and added some of Das' herbs.

He sat leaning back against a huge rock staring into the fire. The flames were hypnotic and soon his whole attention was drawn to the fire. He didn't hear the night sounds or feel the warm breeze on his face. The tin cup with the tea, he held in his hands in front of him. He was only conscious of two things. The fire he was staring into and the image of Katarikari.

Hours later the fire was only a few embers and the tea in his cup was cold. He drank the cold tea and set the cup down. He wasn't aware that he had been holding the tea cup so long that the tea had become cold and surprised to see the fire nothing more than embers. He wasn't aware so much time had passed. And he still wasn't sleepy, and still too warm to need a fire.

Instead of thinking of Katarikari he thought about his time with Gopal Das and herding goats and sheep.

In the morning he made another fire and then some tea and drank it while it was hot. He was lonely and sad. Until now he had not realized how beneficial working for Das had been for him. The work and companionship had kept him from dwelling on Katarikari, most of the time at least.

When the fire had burned out he shouldered his pack and moved on. The sun was hot, but he kept walking. Like the day before, he only stopped when he was thirsty and when he would come to a stream.

That night he ate some goat cheese with his tea. And later he fell asleep stretched out on the ground. The next morning he had more tea and cheese and then continued his journey.

This became a pattern every day. That is until he had eaten the last of the cheese. Two weeks had passed since leaving Das' camp and the sky was gray overcast. Thinking this might be the beginning of the spring monsoon he decided to spend some time here and he prepared a suitable shelter. He remembered Das telling him that when the rains come 'do not make your camp in a valley or gully.' So he looked on higher ground and by mid-morning he found an outcropping of ledge that would provide shelter, tucked under it.

Ekani built a wall leaning back against the ledge wall with woven palm fronds. He next brought in a good supply of firewood and then he set four snares in three well used game trails. He even had enough palm fronds left to make a comfortable sleeping mat.

Before the sun had set Ekani went in search of food. He found many herbs, thanks to Das teaching him to identify those that were edible. He owed a lot to Das.

He put some of the herbs in his tin cup with water and boiled it over the coals.

During the night the rain came. It came in thundering sheets. But Ekani was dry in his shelter. When lightening flashed, he could see for a great distance across the grassy savannah. He was tired and in spite of the heavy rain and thunder he slept surprisingly well. For now at least he had something to take his mind from thinking about Katarikari. As long as he had something to occupy his mind he was okay. It was when he was alone or nothing to work at that he began thinking of her.

The heavy rains continued all the next day and there were now rivulets in the shallow gullies and ravines. Birds stayed perched in the trees and all the animals were also taking shelter from the torrential rain as best they could. He knew it would be useless to go out in the rain to check the snares.

The next morning he had eaten the last of his herbs and he was hungry. There was only a steady rain now, not thundering down in sheets. Needing something to do more than food, he decided to brave the rain and check the snares. The rain had knocked the first three snares down. He reset and at the fourth snare he had a small monkey. The monkey had the snare around its neck and it was dead. Ekani was glad for that. He hated killing animals, even for food.

While the monkey cooked over the fire Ekani took his clothes off and hung them up to dry. Since the fire too was under the protection of the ledge smoke occasionally drifted back and filled the inside of the shelter.

As he sat watching the fire as the monkey meat cooked, he couldn't help but think how easy it was to start a fire using the flint and his knife. Fire was something he had never had cause to think about or how to start one working at the palace. He knew then that life at the palace had been a sheltered existence.

But one he would have been happy to endure if things had not changed.

After two more days the rain stopped, but it remained cloudy. Ekani decided to stay where he was for a while. When he checked his snares, he had a lamb antelope and a rabbit. He pulled his snares. He had enough food for a few days. The rest of the day he spent foraging for herbs and firewood. He had filled his back pack with herbs and figured he had enough wood to last him several days.

Needing something else to busy his time and mind, he cut more palm fronds to add to his bed.

When it started to rain again it wasn't the heavy down pour, but steady. Day and night for another five days. His food gone, he had no choice but to brave the rain and reset his snares and look for herbs. This time he found bountiful mushrooms, onion grass and other herbs that he did not know the names, only that Das had said they were good.

He found a large patch of shaggy mane mushrooms and these he relished more than the other herbs. The rain and two days of sunshine had brought them above ground. It was like walking through a food bazaar.

He roasted a few of the shaggy mane mushrooms, a few he ate raw and thankfully Das had given him a pot to boil water or simmer a stew. He made a herb stew that was quite delicious, but was even better when he added meat.

After two weeks at the shelter the sky cleared and Ekani was once again moving north. He carried his walking stick with him everywhere.

The streams were still swollen and there would be pools of water in low lying areas. There were animals everywhere taking advantage of the water, grass and new plant shoots. But none of them paid any attention to him as he passed through.

Two weeks after leaving there was another rainy spell when he had to build another shelter and stay put and wait for the rain to stop.

When the rain did stop, the sun baked the earth and much of the green grass began to wilt and the streams dried up. And he had never experienced days as hot as they were now. Instead of traveling during the hottest part of the day, he would lie still in the shade and travel at night until there was no light to see by. And then start out again as the morning sun began to rise. He knew he was not traveling as far each day. But there was nothing else he could do.

He was in the Vindhya Mountains now and the tall rocky peaks offered enough shade, so the ground was not as hot and parched. And he found water still flowing in the gullies and streams. Only a little and that soon vanished in the savannah.

He worked his way slowly across and through the range of mountains and while standing on a rocky precipice he could look out over a parched grassland. He knew he would die if he tried to cross in this heat, so he built another shelter back away from the grassland in the shade of the high peaks.

The temperatures stayed too hot to travel right up to the beginning of the fall monsoons. He had found fish in two deep pools in the stream that flowed through the valley where he had made his shelter. Try as he might, he just could not catch one using only his hands. So he made a spear from a bamboo stalk and after two days and many attempts he was finally able to spear a rather large fish; with no practical knowledge of the wilderness, he had no idea what kind of fish it was. He put it on a spit and roasted it over the fire. It was delicious whatever it was.

The fall monsoon was not the heavy thundering rain of the spring, but the streams filled up and he could see pools of water on the grassland. Not knowing what he would encounter crossing the savannah he decided to wait until after the monsoon and the water had receded. He had security there in the mountain valley and there was plenty of food.

He missed the camaraderie of his friend Das. He had certainly learned a lot from him. *If it hadn't been for Das I would not have lasted out here this long. It was divine guidance that led me to him.*

He stopped there and thought a minute. Then he said aloud. "Katarikari—she was the divine guidance that showed me the way to Das' camp." And then he added, "Just like she is doing now. She told me to go north. But not where in the north I should go."

And that's all it took to make him sad and tears started to run. Being away from Katarikari was like splitting him in two. One half could not live without the other.

He spent another sleepless night watching the flames of the fire shoot up into the air. Come daylight he decided he had to leave, even if the rains started again. He needed to be on the move to put the sadness and emptiness from his thoughts.

As he was sitting outside his shelter waiting for the first rays of sunlight to appear, a peacock walked within six feet of him. But if he killed the beautiful bird he would have to skin and clean the pelt and cook the meat before it had a chance to spoil in the heat and he would not be able to leave. He decided he wanted to leave, more than he wanted a peacock.

The peacock stopped and turned its head to look at Ekani. Ekani started smiling and he said, "This is your lucky day, peacock." Then he stood up and shouldered his pack and picked up his walking stick and started out across the grassy savannah.

While it was relatively cool he started off at a fast pace. He had no idea how far the savannah reached. And much to his surprise he found waving rolling knolls. The savannah was not as flat as it had appeared. And there were still shallow streams. And an abundance of herbs. He'd stop often for a drink of stream water and pick a few herbs that he ate while walking.

The savannah stretched on for two days travel. There were many grazing animals, but he didn't see any predators. Herds of water buffalo, deer and many elephants. He even saw a few cobra snakes, that seemed to sense his urgency and gave him a wide berth. As did the elephants and water buffalo.

He began to realize that if not for the monsoon rains and he deciding to wait until they had passed, he would never have survived the crossing without water and in the heat. And he was beginning to understand that survival was about making the right choices.

The weather was nice and the heat was not as bad. By year's end Ekani had reached Gwalior, almost five hundred miles from Assaye. He had no idea of the distance, only his clothes and boots were about worn out. But he had developed a tough rugged body since leaving Raigad.

He found a shop where he bought new clothes and another shop where he found a comfortable pair of boots. He still had a few rupees left that Das had given him.

Not feeling comfortable around people or safe, he left the little village, preferring the wilderness and finding his food along the journey.

He was now considerably further north than previously at Das' camp and the temperature change was that noticeable. For the first time since leaving Das, he pulled on his antelope vest. It was warmer and he liked the feel of the soft leather.

The nights were cool enough now so he needed a fire to keep warm. Three days beyond Gwalior, he decided to build a shelter and rest a day before continuing on. If the weather kept getting colder the further north he traveled, he wasn't sure how far north he wanted to go until warmer weather.

Even three days north of Gwalior the temperature at night rarely dropped below fifty degrees, but that was cold for him. He was acclimated to warmer weather. So this shelter would only be temporary while he scouted out a good area with water, herbs and small animals.

This part of India he found was pretty flat. Another savannah. But there were many animal trails through the grass and bushes. Now he needed to find water and a supply of wood. He made a circle around his camp and then a wider circle and about a mile away he found just what he wanted. A stream and a stand of trees and bushes which would block the wind.

The next day he moved his few belongings to this new site and began building a new shelter. Before meeting Das, he would not have known how to do any of this; living off the land.

There was a tall ledge precipice and he made his shelter like the others, woven fronds and boughs. This time he closed in both sides and left an opening for an entrance. It was already dark when he had finished, and there was only enough wood for a small fire. Enough to make some tea and some herb broth. Tomorrow he'd look for meat.

He was tired after working all day making his shelter and he sat warming himself beside the fire until there were only embers left.

With the fire burned out he was getting cool, so he went inside and laid down on the ground. Tomorrow he'd have to make a sleeping mat.

There was an abundance of small wildlife living on the grassland. Before he had all of his snares set, he had caught two peacocks. He pulled his snares skinned the birds and set both of them roasting over the fire. While they cooked, he rubbed wood ash into the flesh of the two pelts and then set them to dry.

What he really wanted to catch in one of his snares was an antelope, so he could turn the hide into a blanket.

Three days later with the peacock meat almost gone he set snares in game trails in the bush where the antelope would go for refuge.

Game was plentiful and he had one nice antelope in one of his snares. It was a large doe and he was surprised the juniper root snare had held her. He set some meat to roasting while he scrapped all the sinew from the hide and rubbed ashes into it. He knew he'd never be able to eat all the meat before it spoiled, but he needed the hide to use as a blanket.

He slept much warmer with the soft hide over him.

That winter Ekani spent much of his time exploring

around him. He saw and discovered a variety of animals. But none paid him any attention.

Each evening he'd sit by the fire with the antelope hide draped around his shoulders and thinking about his future. He had found it so easy living off the land. Maybe he could get a few goats and sheep like Das.

And then he would think about Katarikari telling him to go north. 'How far north? Am I suppose to find something? Or was being in the north, far enough away from Shri Shivaji Maharaj and Rajasthan and Katarikari? Is there something that I am suppose to do?'

Questions ran through his mind all night and he awoke the next morning still sitting by the fire. There were a few embers left and he put enough wood on to warm up some tea, then he let the fire burn out. Sitting there drinking tea, he had just about decided that all he was doing was surviving, with no real purpose in his life. Did he really want to spend the rest of his life only surviving? It would be a very lonely life. "It is lonely already," he said aloud.

He knew he had to stop thinking like that or the sadness would engulf him and make him miserable. So he got up and went exploring again. For something to do and to keep his mind occupied.

He would check his snares first. If there was anything caught, the scent of death might attract a predator. He had two more peacocks. He took these back to his shelter and removed the skins and treated them and put the meat inside where it was still cool. Then he went for his walk.

Only a few minutes into the savannah he heard something wrestling in the grass. He stopped to listen and the noise stopped. He waited and there it was again. Using his walking stick he parted the grass beside him and there, a head raised a foot above the ground was a king cobra snake. It was huge. Ekani's first reaction was panic and then he heard Katarikari's voice as clear as if she was beside him. 'I will always watch over you.' And the cobra made a detour around him.

But this started him thinking about Katarikari and that was all he could think about for the rest of the day. He sat down on a rock in the savannah. But he saw nothing that was around him. He had withdrawn into the recess of his mind. Where he could escape the physical world and its problems. He was watching images of he and Katarikari playing in the park in Satara when they were children. Images of him lying in the Princess' bed recovering from the cobra bite. And Katarikari sitting by his side and then when she had healed him.

He didn't see the black cloud covering the sun. Or the ant crawling on his leg. And he wasn't aware of the huge tiger fifty feet in front of him that was slowly coming closer. The tiger sniffed the air, Ekani was another source of food for him. The only thing Ekani was aware of was the life he had had as Katarikari's servant and the love they shared.

The tiger was now only ten feet away when something like an electric shock across the shoulders brought Ekani back to the present. The tiger made a deep throttled sound and licking its jaws. Ekani at first was frozen with fear. Then he didn't care if the tiger killed him or not. Then he began hoping the tiger would put him out of his misery.

"Ekani!" her voice was so loud and clear, it seemed as if she had shouted at him. "Do not fear Ekani, I will watch over you." Very slowly the tiger turned and left. And Ekani stood up and like a zombie he walked back to his camp. Built a fire, made some tea and then sat back starring into the flames. He was beside himself now. Katarikari was that close to him. How he wished he could reach out and take her in his arms.

He drank his tea and sat there for two days and nights. The fire had long since burned out. He wasn't aware of the cold or that he was thirsty and hungry. He honestly didn't know if he had the will to go on.

Ekani's physical form was there sitting by his shelter, but as soul, he and Katarikari were in the finer, more beautiful inner world, where they did not have to hide their love for each other. It was a time of pure happiness, to be with the one person he had loved for most of his physical life.

* * * *

On the third day Ekani slowly opened his eyes and he recognized his camp. The happiness he and Katarikari had shared in the inner world was now fading, like a dream until there was no memory at all of a happier time.

He drank some water and packed his things. The two peacocks had spoiled. He'd leave those for the scavengers. The skins he packed, and then shouldered his pack and picked up his walking stick and walked off.

The morning air was cool and crisp. But he was too numb with sadness to feel anything or even care. He walked on with no particular destination. Just one foot in front of the other, and looking straight ahead.

He walked all day like that and into the night until it was too dark to go on. Then he laid down where he was. Sometimes he would sit up and cross his legs and stare into the darkness. Sometimes he would make a fire and warm some tea and then sit and watch as it burned out.

Day after day was the same. The only nourishment was the herb tea or he would find an edible herb while walking and eat it. Never going out of his way to find food. He never was aware of the animals that sometimes followed him or lay just beyond the illumination of his fire at night. And not once had any of the stalkers attempted to attack.

He had no idea how long it had been since he left his shelter, nor had he any idea how far he had traveled. He was aware though that the days were getting warmer.

There were some mornings where Ekani would remain in a sitting position staring at absolutely nothing. His mind a complete blank. During these mornings he would remain like this to mid-morning. Then he'd stand up and walk, without stopping until the sun had set.

One morning as he sat staring at the last embers of his fire, he could hear noise coming from beyond the knoll about one hundred yards in front of him. This noise, disturbance piqued his curiosity and brought him out of the stupor demeanor of the last several days.

From on top of the knoll the noise was louder. In the distance and across the Yamuna River was a huge Red Fort, and it was called The Red Fort because of the red sandstone that it had been built with.

Ekani was awe-struck. He had never expected to find anything like this, this far north. Even from this distance the palace was beautiful. He wasn't sure if it was the morning sun, or the distance, but the palace looked red.

This sudden discovery made him for now forget about his sadness.

In 1648 after fifteen years of construction, Shah Jahan, the Emperor of the fifth Empire of the Mughal Empire built The Red Fort as his personal palace in what he declared the capital of the fifth Empire, Shahjohahabad. "This has to be Delhi," Ekani said out loud.

Ekani crossed the narrow bridge over the Yamuna River and through the south gate of the city. It wasn't difficult to find a shop that would buy his peacocks. He had four skins and the buyer was impressed how well Ekani had cared for them. He gave Ekani thirty-five rupees and asked, "Where is your turban my friend? You do not want to be seen on the streets without one. There still are many in the city who still prefer to follow Islam rather than Hinduism."

Quick thinking Ekani replied, "A monkey came down out of the trees and stole it."

"Here are a few that I sell."

Ekani chose a white one and wrapped it around his head, and he paid the dealer.

The weather was too warm now for a jacket so he would wait until he would need one. He visited other shops to satisfy his own curiosity. He found a shop selling cookware and he purchased a fry pan and a larger kettle for stews. He knew if he stayed in the city long he would spend most of the few rupees he had.

As he was exiting the north gate he passed a livery with five mules in a corral. "Would you sell me one mule?"

"I sell mules, yes."

"How much for one mule?"

"Twelve rupees please."

"I'll give you ten rupees with a rope halter."

"Twelve rupees with halter."

Ekani counted out eleven and said, "This is all I will give you."

The livery guy shrugged his shoulders and took the money, and as soon as Ekani had his heavier pack tied on the mule he left the city. And he still had twenty-six rupees.

"Apparently if I am suppose to find something in the north, Delhi wasn't the place. Or maybe I didn't recognize it," he said to his mule.

The Yamuna River was heading in the general direction of north; maybe a little east of north, but he decided to follow it up stream. It was getting late so he decided to stop for the night. There was good grazing close by for the mule and he found enough herbs and mushrooms for a stew.

He found the river water much colder than anything he had experienced so far and wondered why. As darkness came upon the land, he noticed that the air was much cooler close to the river and he had to wrap the antelope hide around his shoulders and he added more wood to the fire.

By traveling close to the river he was still seeing a wide variety of birds and animals and all along the river, when ever he came to a small tributary of cold water, he looked for a deep pool with fish. He was wanting fresh fish to eat.

He and his mule followed the sandy bottom stream for a

long way before he found what he wanted. After making camp and staking the mule to graze, he fashioned a bamboo spear and went fishing. It took a few tries before he speared the first fish and then a second. Two was all he could eat, so he stopped with these two and put a stick through them to cook over the fire.

The fish were a good change from red meet and birds. He was hungrier than he thought. He ate both fish and they each were big.

* * * *

Traveling beside the river was becoming difficult. If the land was too rugged, then there were thickets of alders and bushes, too thick to travel through. So he turned east and the traveling was much better.

Two days after turning east he came to another smaller river and he decided to follow that for a while. The water was not as swift or deep and he could see fish in pools close to shore.

He followed this river and it soon turned north and the summer heat was upon him. But it was not as hot as he had experienced during the last two summers.

A month after leaving Delhi he awoke before sunrise and decided to get an early start before the sun was too high. There was just enough light for him to lead his mule safely. When he reached the top of a high rocky flateau he stopped to catch his breath. Looking to the north there was a layer of clouds close to the ground and behind that on the far distant horizon he could see white capped mountains. The first time he had ever seen snow. As he stood there looking at the snow covered peaks he wondered to himself 'how far north have I come?'

A week later he walked into the town of Saharanpur. He had managed to catch three more peacocks and an antelope. He decided to sell the hide along with the three peacocks.

"I'll give you five rupees for the antelope hide and four each for the peacock."

"For two years I have been selling them for five rupees each," Ekani said.

"I can't do five, because it cost too much to ship them to Bombay for shipping to Europe from here. Four or leave it."

"Okay, four each."

He went in search next for a jacket or coat. After seeing the snowcapped mountains in the summer, he decided he would need one. At a shop in the center of town he found an antelope jacket. It was just what he needed.

It was late in the afternoon when he had all of this business done and instead of staying the night in town, he would feel safer and more comfortable in the wilderness.

He only went far enough to get beyond the noise of the town and so he would not be seen traveling on the road. He still wasn't sure if he was suppose to be this far north, to escape the Shri's soldiers, or if there was something he was suppose to do or recognize. Katarikari had not been precise. He did know though that he wanted to be further away from Saharanpur.

The spring monsoon would be arriving anytime now and he wanted to be prepared. So the next morning he left without eating in search of a likely place to build a tight shelter against the weather and rain. He didn't think he should be this close to any river so he left the low land in search of a flateau.

He was all day finding what he wanted and he began to make a shelter, leaning poles up against a ledge wall. Another day passed before he had finished with plenty of dry wood piled inside the shelter also. The next day he went in search of herbs and he set three snares.

The rains began during the night and come morning he had no choice but to brave the rain and check his snares. He had two rabbits and something that looked like a chicken, only gray. He would roast the bird and make a stew with the rabbits.

The rain continued for two weeks before stopping for three days and then rained for another two weeks. He was so glad he had moved away from the river. He relocated his fire to one of the side openings, so the smoke would not fill the interior and he could sit where he would be dry and watch the flames and the warmth would keep him warm.

One night as he sat in the dark in the protection of his shelter and bathing in the warmth of the flames, he began to wonder what it was that had told or convinced him to move away from the river? Was it knowledge he had learned from living two years in the wild? Had it been Das? Or was it the inner voice that was always protecting him. If he had not moved to the flateau —that whole area below him was now under water.

He had even made a crude shelter for his mule to keep it protected from most of the rain.

When the rain stopped he worked for two days making improvements to his shelter and also the mule's, so it could have cool shade during the hot summer months. He found plenty of small animals and a variety of birds for food and still there were plenty of edible herbs. He had decided to stay for a while. He continued caring for the peacock pelts and antelope hides whenever he caught one in one of the snares. These would give him a few rupees.

One clear nice morning, he staked his mule where it could feed and where there was some tree shade and he decided to make an arc to the east of his camp and circle back to the river up stream and then back to camp. He needed to know what was around him.

The country side this far north did not seem to be as parched as the country he had traveled through. Once he had left the tropical woodlands behind the ground had been dry and often dusty and often the green savannahs had turned brown with the lack of rain. But here there was a subtle difference.

As he explored, he kept looking for a high knoll from which he would be able to see the snowcapped peaks again. This snow in the summer, when it was so warm, could cover the mountains was amazing to him. And how strange it seemed.

As he was swinging north making his arc there was

a strong north wind and that brought the cold down from the mountains. This made him shiver and goose bumps formed on his arm from the sudden cold. This had never happened before and he looked at both arms. Puzzled he began to rub both arms and soon the goose bumps were gone. *This*, he thought, *had been strange.*

As suddenly as the cold wind had blown down from the mountains, a wind from the south was blowing even stronger, bringing with it the hot air of the sub-continent. Trees were being blown over so the tops could almost touch the ground. When this blast of hot air hit the cold north wind, the air mass started swirling and Ekani watched in amazement as a cyclone formed. The funnel grew bigger and bigger and the roar of the whirling wind was almost deafening. Trees were being uprooted and thrown about. Huge rocks hurled through the air.

Ekani was being buffeted with the strong wind and as he started to run a—it was not the wind that had knocked him to the ground in a depression, but it felt more like someone had pushed him. And then he heard Katarikari saying, "No harm will come to you, Ekani. Stay here until the wind stops."

He laid on his stomach and used his hands to cover his face. When it was over he rolled over and then sat up. He stood up and looked around him. There was so much damage—he had never seen damage like this before, nor did he know anything about cyclones.

If it had not been for Kari; I would have been killed, and he looked again at the hole in the ground where he had been pushed and then told to stay.

As he made his way back to the river, he kept seeing images of Katarikari in his mind and it wasn't long before he was no longer conscious of his surroundings or anything except reliving the love he and Katarikari had shared.

When he was back at the river, it had receded a lot during the day. He knew where he was now and he sat down on a grass bank under a tree in the shade.

Saddened again by the images and thoughts of Katarikari, he sat and stared forlornly at the flowing water. But seeing not the river nor anything else. His mind was blank and he was sad, remembering the happy years with Katarikari. Nor was he aware of the lone man approaching him from downstream. The stranger walked up beside Ekani and stopped. Ekani still wasn't aware he was not alone.

In a kind voice the stranger wearing sandals and a brown robe standing six feet tall said, "Why do you sit with your face in your hands? What can be so wrong to make you this sad?"

Ekani wasn't startled by the sudden voice speaking to him nor of the stranger's presence.

"I was thinking of happier years and these memories sadden me," Ekani replied.

"Then your sadness can only be but one thing, since you are alone in the wilderness watching the water flow in the river. Which is a grand symbol of life. Your sadness must be the lost love for a woman."

"Yes."

"How far have you journeyed trying to escape this sadness?"

"I left two and a half years ago. I have traveled maybe a thousand miles."

"Oh my, this sadness of yours must be a great burden. But you said you left, not this woman that you love. Are you running away from something?"

Ekani was silent for a long while, thinking whether he should answer this stranger or not. Then the thought came to him and an electric shock went across his shoulders. *Could this stranger be the reason I have come this far north?*

"I have traveled here from Raigad. My father sold me into slavery when I was six years old."

"The Maharaj recently traveled to Rajasthan. His daughter wed Prince Adheer Raman. Oh my! You were in love with the Princess Katarikari. Not surprising you have traveled such a great distance.

"Are you in any legal trouble?"

"No, and I have never known if the soldiers were sent to find me or not. I have not wasted much time in villages."

"I believe the camp and mule I found downstream must belong to you," Chapal said.

"Yes, and maybe we should go there before it is completely dark. I can offer you rabbit stew with herbs and herb tea."

"That sounds inviting and I am hungry," he said. "What is your name? I am called Chapal."

"Ekani," and he stood up and led the way back to his camp. It was only ten minutes away.

Ekani started a fire and then brought his mule in closer to the shelter. Nothing more was said about Ekani and Katarikari until after they had eaten.

"How old are you, Ekani?"

"What is the date?"

"This is 1669 September."

"Then I was nineteen in May."

"For someone so young you possess a great understanding of the ways of the wilderness."

"I had a little help. I was almost dead and a sheep herder found me. I stayed with him for nine months helping with the goats and sheep and he taught me everything I know about the wilderness."

"What was this shepherd's name?

"Gopal Das, but he preferred just Das."

"I know Das. He is a Way Shower and he has helped many on their way to enlightenment.

"Why did you travel so far north?"

"When Katarikari told me I would have to leave for my own safety and for hers, she told me to go north. Not how far. I just kept going north, trying to leave my sadness behind."

"Why are you so sad, Ekani? A broken heart can heal.

Did you not know or understand that some day the Princess would have to leave. She is nobility. The two of you could not have expected a future together."

"I would have been content to be her servant for the rest of my life." He told Chapal then about their special relationship and how it began. The daily walks the two would take in the park. The night Katarikari saved his life after the cobra bite.

"So, Ekani, what exactly is your problem?"

"Katarikari and I were so in love—life isn't fair. Why did we have to be torn apart? Sometimes I get so angry, because life treated me this way," Ekani said.

"Ekani, have you once thought how Katarikari must feel? She lost the same as you. Only she now is wed to someone she does not love. Because she is nobility. It was expected of her. Did you ever think this was her destiny? Just as you are here now. Everyone has their own destiny. Sometimes it takes on hard rough paths, but there is a reason for this also. Nothing happens, Ekani, by coincidence. There is a purpose, a lesson for each event."

"I never stopped to think how Katarikari might be hurting also. All I could think about was my own grief. My own bad luck."

"The sooner you can accept the fact that you each are exactly where you are supposed to be, the happier you'll become."

There was a bright moon out tonight and even after the fire burned down to embers they sat outside and talked. It was after midnight when they lay down to sleep.

* * * *

The next morning while they were eating and sipping tea Chapal asked, "What are your plans, Ekani?"

"I was thinking about staying here and living off the land. Maybe get a few goats and sheep like Das."

"I have a hut three days travel from here. You could come with me and I can help you to understand life and your own destiny. You will be free to leave any time you wish."

"You said earlier that Das was a Way Shower, is that what you are?"

"In a manner of speaking. I am what is called a Sadhu, Holy Man. It is not a position or a title, but a level of consciousness one obtains after many trials and tribulations and finally leaves behind the need for materialism and desires.

"Now if you are interested I suggest you pack your mule so we can be on our way."

For two and a half years Ekani, whenever he traveled, was always alone. Now he had company. And this helped to keep him from sliding back into thinking of Katarikari and feeling sad.

Chapal reminded him a lot of Das. They had no physical similarities, but it was more like how they portrayed themselves, their knowledge and their willingness to help him.

As they journeyed north, once in a while Ekani would feel a cool breeze on his face, Chapal did not seem to notice. Ekani was wondering if Chapal's hut was in amongst the snow covered mountains. They carried on an almost steady conversation. Ekani wanted to know all about this north country and if it ever snowed where Chapal lived. "Yes, once in a while a strong north wind will bring a storm down into the foothills. But this is very rare."

The second day out they stopped mid-afternoon, so Ekani could set snares and hopefully catch something for their evening meal. While he was busy with snares Chapal made a quick shelter. There were gray storm clouds forming overhead.

When the snares were set, Ekani gathered herbs. While they waited for the snares to work, Ekani made some strong tea from teaberry leaves and juniper bark. As they sipped tea they talked constantly. Ekani knew as long as he could keep the conversation going with Chapal, he would not be thinking about Katarikari.

When they checked the snares they had a guinea hen in each set." I don't know what these birds are but they are very good eating."

"They are guinea hens. If you can follow one back to their nest, sometimes you can find several eggs."

As the hens were roasting over the fire, "Ekani, you say you have been two and a half years traveling from the palace at Raigad. You have always traveled alone. With all of the wild animals in India and you without any weapon, I'm surprised you have made it this far without being attacked by predators or trampled by water buffalo or elephants or bitten by another cobra."

"This may be difficult for you to understand, Chapal. I don't understand it completely myself. The night that I left Raigad, Katarikari and I were together. Crying in each others arms. She told me to go north and then she said, 'I will always watch over you, Ekani.' I have been confronted by a pack of wolves, jackals, a water buffalo, a bull elephant, a tiger sneaked up to strike and the day you found me, Chapal, I was in the middle of a cyclone. I have never been injured. And with each encounter I hear, as clearly as I hear you sitting there, Katarikari's voice telling me, she will always watch over me.

"When Das found me unconscious he said there was a globe of blue light surrounding me and he said it was this light that alerted his two dogs that something was wrong. I too have seen this blue light. Protecting me it seems. I don't know any more than that, Chapal. And each time I hear her voice I start reliving the love we had and I become sad and sometimes angry that life can be so cruel."

"First of all, Ekani, life wasn't being cruel when you and the Princess were torn apart. But we will get into that yet later. There is much I must help you to understand first.

"Apparently Princess Katarikari is a very special Atman. The inner self or soul. I think you will agree with this. I am just discovering it. When she told you she would always watch over you, she was literal. It is also apparent that she also has a great love for you, Ekani. She is working from a high level of consciousness. And with this level of consciousness comes great knowledge and abilities—and responsibilities. Not every Atman can operate or function in this physical or human side of life. But she can. When the blue globe of light has appeared around you, it is Katarikari in her astral form protecting you. She has allowed you to see this energy because you also, Ekani, apparently have this consciousness. But your understanding probably hasn't been developed yet. If you can follow me. You have the ability. You simply have to realize it.

"When Das saw the light, well, he also is working from a high level of consciousness. She appeared then, so he would help you.

"When you hear her voice, you are actually hearing her, but with your inner ear, that of Atman. When the Princess said she would always watch over you, this is exactly what she is doing. Her inner self, Ekani, her Atman is always with you. You cannot see her human form because of the difference between the structure of the human body and the inner self.

"Does this help you?" Chapal asked.

"I think I understand. Katarikari in her Atman body or inner self is always with me. Watching over me.

"I only wish I could see her and hold her in my arms," Ekani said.

"That will probably never happen my friend. Not in this lifetime. Perhaps when the two of you reincarnate into another life you will find each again. My advice to you, Ekani, you will only keep on hurting yourself if you daydream or think too much about the Princess, with the hope of seeing her again."

Ekani didn't like hearing those words. All he had left of Katarikari were the memories of their years together. But he also understood what Chapal had said.

They were both silent for a long time. Chapal knew Ekani had much to think over. Ekani was trying to come to an understanding of his life.

"I was six years old when my father took me to the palace in Satara. At first I was frightened because I couldn't understand why he had sold me into slavery. Why me and not either of my two brothers or my sister.

"My father told me I would be a servant to the Maharaj's daughter and she was of the same age as I. That I would always have a clean place to live and sleep, clean clothes and a full belly always. I knew I'd be seeing grand things that I otherwise could not even imagine. I asked my father if being a slave for the rest of my life was my destiny. I don't remember his exact words, but that's what it amounts to. He told me never to look back. That I should always live in the moment." Ekani was quiet then, thinking about what he had said before continuing.

"Your father was correct, Ekani. He sounds like a good man," Chapal said.

"When we arrived at the palace I was not afraid and I soon accepted my position as servant, and I was not upset that a servant I would always be. Because I enjoyed what I did. I had a good life. But now I have to ask you, Chapal, was being a servant my destiny or is this my destiny here in Northern India? Which is it, Chapal?"

"Life, enlightenment and destiny all depend on choices, Ekani. If we continually make the wrong choices then when we reincarnate we'll have to go through the same lessons again until we get it right. Your destiny, Ekani, was laid out for you when you were six and your father left you at the palace in Satara. Your father only did what he had to do, so you could follow your destiny.

"You have obviously made the right choices in your life, Ekani, or you would not be here now. Has your destiny changed? I wouldn't think so. Katarikari was only part of it. You and Katarikari truly found divine love and this you can witness as she watches over you Ekani. It would be a terrible mistake for you to try and find her during this life. Knowing the ways of the nobility, you and she both would be killed and she understood this when she said you must leave. When you two reincarnate into another life, it would be my guess that you two will find each other. Think on this, Ekani, and try not to dwell on what was. Live in the moment like your father said."

* * * *

Chapal was right about the rain; it came down heavy after they lay down to sleep. There were a few leaks but they survived. By morning the clouds had blown out and blue sky returned.

They camped out one more night and by noon the next day they arrived at Chapal's hut in the foothills, a day travel northeast from Shimla.

"What is it that you do, Chapal? I know you said you are a Sadhu. But you live alone in the foothills away from any village."

"Well I suppose you could say in a way I too am a 'Way Shower'. I not only help those looking for enlightenment and answers to life, but I help other 'Way Showers'. Now you seem to be good at catching food with your snares. So while you are making sets I'll gather some herbs. On your way back to the hut, would you pick up some firewood?"

For two days they relaxed at the hut stocking up with firewood and snaring small animals for food. Chapal suggested one morning before daylight that they hike to the top of a high ridge. Through the years Chapal had worn a path in the ground that was easy to follow in the dawning twilight.

It was still dark when they reached the top and they sat down to rest. Ekani had no idea what was the point of climbing the ridge before sunlight, but he waited.

Way off in the eastern horizon they watched as the first golden rays broke the night sky. It was a pretty sight to watch the sun rise. Ekani had never witnessed this before.

The sun was visible now; a golden ball sitting on the horizon. After the sun had risen a little Chapal said, "This is what I wanted you to see Ekani, look towards the north."

Ekani turned to look and was amazed with the spectacular beauty of the highest mountains in the world. Their snowcapped peaks now were covered with gold, as the morning sun cast its awakening rays upon the snow covered mountain. "This is really beautiful, Chapal. What mountain range is that?"

"The grand Himalayan Mountains. The tallest mountains in the known world. I come up here often to watch the sun rise."

"They are beautiful," Ekani said.

A layer of clouds was beginning to form below the tops of the mountains giving the golden snowcaps a mysterious apparition.

"Come, by the time we return to the hut, it'll be time for hot tea and maybe some cheese that I have fermenting in a shallow hollow behind the hut."

The cheese was strong, but very good with hot tea.

"While you were a servant at the palace did you ever study Hinduism?"

"Not actually study, but Katarikari and I would sometimes talk about it and how it is woven around our lives."

"People who participate in Hinduism are naturally called Hindus. This word is actually an Arabic term which means the people who live on the other side of the Indus River. This would be the Maratha Empire—our people, Ekani."

"Chapal, what is all the fighting and wars about between the Mughal Empire and the Marathas?"

"The Afghan Mughals would like to control all of India to the Bangladesh Peninsula and force Islam onto all people of India. Our Maratha Army is trying to stop the Afghans and preserve our way of life (Sanatana Dhorma). Trying to push the Mughals out of India and not conquering the Empire.

"Our Eternal Way of Life, Ekani, is very important to all Hindu people. This is our religion."

"Who started Hinduism, Chapal?"

"That is difficult to answer, Ekani. There is not a known founder. It is a way of life that has evolved into doing everything in our life, the Right Way. These traditions have been passed down from generation to generation as far back in history that has ever been written.

"We discussed earlier about making the right choices in ones life, well there is a right way and a wrong way to do things in our life, a right and wrong way to live. If you practice always doing the wrong, you will be a victim of karma that has to be worked off, debts that must be paid in full before one can achieve Moksha. Which is release from the wheel of reincarnation. Liberation.

"The 'Eternal Way' is sometimes said to be 'Eternal Law' such as: restraint from lust and anger, more towards honesty, mercy, purity, charity, patience, refraining from injuring living things. These are only a few, but I think you can understand the meanings.

"In Hinduism we don't have a strict regime of beliefs. We conduct our life and affairs on principles."

"What you said a moment ago about the Eternal Laws— at the palace I had to live by those same laws or be punished."

"There you go Ekani, you have discovered for yourself part of your destiny. There is no such thing as a coincidence. Everything has a purpose. And more often than not, to teach us a lesson," Chapal said.

* * * *

Ekani thought often about what Chapal had told him about Hinduism and its principles and especially his own destiny. The days were kept busy, but at night when he was laying on his sleeping mat listening to the only sound, the wind blowing over the top of the ridge. Sometimes just a gentle breeze and sometimes a strong wind.

He was becoming happy as he was slowly discovering self-realization and all the time wondering where his destiny was taking him now.

He had not heard Katarikari's voice since the day of the cyclone. That night as he laid on his sleeping mat, in his inner self he began talking with Katarikari and thanked her for always looking after him. From his first day as her servant and now. And he told her he was sorry for not understanding the heartache that she too was feeling.

He went to sleep that night as he and Katarikari talked while in the inner world.

When he awoke the next morning he was feeling good. Happy. And the images of he and Katarikari during the night were fading like dreams do. He tried to hold on to the images he could remember about their night together, but eventually his mind shut out all the images of the night before.

But his inner self, soul, could remember and was able to convey this happiness to Ekani's conscious mind. And this was why he awoke with an aura of happiness around him.

Chapal was aware of this change in Ekani and he knew Ekani had been able to move on, beyond a great obstacle in his path.

Not Katarikari, but his own attachment to her. Chapal knew Katarikari was a very special being and some day he knew Ekani would be also and he also knew Katarikari would always be there to guide him.

Chapter 12

1672

Three years had passed since Ekani had met Chapal and became his student. He had changed much from what he was when they first met, as much as ice and water. He walked and carried himself with realization, confidence and an enlightened inner self which was evident with his happiness.

Ekani no longer dwelled on his sadness or the loss of the woman he loved. He would always love Katarikari and the great difference in him now was that he knew and realized that Katarikari would always be part of him and she was always watching over him.

For two years, except during the cooler months of winter, they roamed among the foothills of the Himalayan Mountains helping Way Showers and those in pursuit of self-realization and illumination. They traveled from Srinagar Kashmir to Bangladesh.

Returning from Srinagar, two days south of the city, they were accosted by a band of six thieves. They saw the mule laden with supplies and they had mistaken them as mule freighters packing valuable supplies. The six gruff looking bandits all had scimitars and waving them about threateningly.

Chapal and Ekani stopped. The bandits were still approaching cautiously. A blue globe of light appeared in front of them and Katarikari said, "Do not be afraid. I am watching over you."

Ekani looked at Chapal and smiled and said, "We are in no danger, Chapal."

The six bandits stopped, wondering why these two men were smiling and not afraid. This was peculiar, and the leader changed his mind and the bandits stepped away from the road and let them pass.

"I saw the blue light, Ekani, but you heard Katarikari didn't you?"

"Yes, Chapal, I did."

"What did she tell you?"

"She said we did not have to fear, she was watching over us."

"I wish I could have heard her. But then again it is you, my friend, whom she is protecting."

The rest of the trip back to their hut was uneventful. They arrived at their hut as the cold winter wind started to blow off the mountains.

"The wind and cold this year, Ekani, is not normal. You may yet see your snowstorm."

Through the years they had built a crude shelter for the mule and had added another room onto the hut for Ekani and a small food storage room, dug out into the hill where their food could be kept cool.

* * * *

Warmer weather arrived and they both were glad for that. Ekani had experienced his first snowstorm with the new year. When they woke up one morning there were four inches of snow on the ground and still snowing. As the sun climbed high in the sky the storm blew out and the snow melted.

One evening while sitting outside sipping tea and watching the sunset, Chapal said, "It is time, Ekani, that you were on your own. A Way Shower for a few years and then when you know you are ready, a Sadhu."

"Where should I go, Chapal?"

"Do you remember when we passed through Pauri a year ago and how much you liked the country? And do you remember how many people were looking for answers?"

"Yes I do."

"This will be a good location for you. You can purchase goats and sheep in Pauri and set up camp in the hills like Das."

Ekani had learned a lot from Chapal and he was eager to be on his own once again.

"I'll leave tomorrow morning."

* * * *

The mule packed with his few possessions and walking stick in hand, Ekani said, "I first said this to Gobal Das and now I say it to you, Chapal. I would not have made it, if not for you. I was drowning in my own sorrow, and you held my head up and made me face what I could not. Thank you, Chapal."

"I'll check on you once in a while. I know you'll be safe and well taken care of, my friend."

Ekani left the hut behind and his head held high and smiling. He was glad to be starting on another leg of his destiny and the prospect of starting anew and becoming his own man and being a goat and sheep herder excited him.

He only stopped twice during the day to let the mule rest and drink water. He would eat herbs and tea until he would have to stay put a couple of days because of the weather. He was hiking through beautiful valleys and hill tops. Flowers were blooming and the grass was green like a carpet.

As he sat next to the fire that first night out he was beginning to plan ahead for his existence. He still had a few rupees, but he would need more to purchase a few goats and sheep and other necessities he would have to have to set up camp.

Two days later dark clouds rolled in and he decided now would be a good time to make a temporary shelter. When that was done he gathered firewood and then he set two snares. The third snare had broke long ago.

Then he set to work digging out juniper roots. He had two he was uncovering side-by-each and it was taking him a long time. When he had finished he coiled the roots up and headed back to camp. He had a guinea hen in each snare. He reset both snares hoping for an antelope. Das had said antelope with the shorter summer hair was more valuable than the coarser winter hair.

He actually had to stay three days before the weather broke. He had caught a peacock and a rabbit. The peacock was a large male and he took particular care skinning and rubbing ashes into the flesh side.

He slow roasted the peacock and made a stew with the rabbit. The next day he was getting restless and he decided to move on even in the light drizzle. By noon the sky was clear and the air hot.

There was a slow leak overhead in his shelter, but he was so happy he hardly noticed it. He was really feeling an extraordinary exhilaration. He was feeling good about himself and the change with his understanding. Here he was sitting by himself watching the fire and instead of brooding about his sadness, he was happy. As difficult as it was for him to accept, he and Katarikari were exactly where they were supposed to be, fulfilling their own destiny. And now whenever he thought about Katarikari he could smile. Because he also understood that she was always close by in her inner self and in another life when they reincarnate, they will once again find each other. He didn't believe this. He understood it to be so.

* * * *

The weather was fine for traveling and a month after

leaving Chapal, he arrived in Pauri. It was situated on the west side of rugged hills. This wasn't what he was looking for so he went east away from the high country. There was an old wooden bridge in Pauri that crossed the Ganges River.

Three days later he found what he wanted. Grassy meadows on side hills facing south. Nearer to Rishikesh than Pauri. Exploring the area for grazing goats and sheep, he found thick grassy meadows. In one meadow yellow flowers were growing so thick that it looked like a yellow blanket covering the meadow. While looking for a place to build his shelter he saw numerous animals. Deer, antelope, rabbits, peacocks, guinea hens and some kind of spotted cat.

He set two snares where he had seen the peacock and guinea hens and then he started building a shelter, while also tending his snares. Two days later he had an adequate shelter near a spring.

By late summer he had his camp as he wanted and it was time to travel to Hardwar. He now had ten peacock, four antelope hides, one cat hide and two deer hides. Everything secured on the mule, he left for Hardwar. He still had ten rupees.

He found a dealer in hides at the edge of the village. "Let's see what you have. You're new around here." Statement not a question. "You take nice care of these. Five rupees each for the peacock, six for the antelope, twenty for the fishing cat and five for the deer."

"That's a hundred and four rupees total," Ekani said. "I'll take one hundred ten."

Hakim resisted, but eventually he agreed. "One hundred ten rupees," and he counted them out as he gave them to Ekani.

"Where can I buy some sheep and goats, Hakim?"

"At the other end of the village. Stay on this road you'll come to it."

Before going to the other end of the village, Ekani purchased other supplies he would be needing and packed them on the mule.

"Do you sell sheep?" he asked the farmer.

"I do."

"And goats?"

"I do."

"How many rupees for each?"

"Sheep ten rupees each. Goats eight."

"The sheep are already sheared so there is no wool. I'll give you eight for the goats and sheep. One billy and one doe goat. Five ewes and one ram."

After Ekani paid him he still had forty rupees left. He bought canvas, some tools and rope. "How about a good dog?"

"Five rupees."

Ekani tied a rope around one of the sheep and began to lead his entourage through the village and back to camp.

The dog was a big help.

* * * *

Ekani had his own camp set up the way he wanted it and the dog instinctively knew how to herd sheep and goats and how to respond to his commands.

Many times that fall while out exploring his new surroundings, he would come upon someone or a young couple who were looking for answers. And much like Das and Chapal had done with him, he would sit by the light of his fire in the evening and discuss with them the concept of Hinduism. And after each time, he would feel gratifying pleasure of being able to help someone.

The years passed and with each passing year Ekani grew into a more subtle being. Neither his outer actions, inner thinking or planning were rash or random. Everything he did and said, now had a purpose. He immensely enjoyed being a Way Shower and word was spreading throughout northern India about the shepherd between Hardwar and Pauri. People were coming from as far away as Delhi to listen to him, looking for help along their individual path and journey to enlightenment and understanding.

He no longer had to snare animals for food or their hides and feathers. People looking for help and guidance would bring him gifts of food. He still kept a few goats and sheep to help pay for the things he needed to maintain his camp.

He often thought about Gobal Das and their first meeting and how he had literally saved his life. He had descended emotionally as far as anyone could go, and Das had brought him back to the living.

And again when he was at an emotional low, Chapal had taught him understanding and realization.

Sometimes on a warm evening he would sit outside to watch the sunset and Katarikari would appear as a blue globe of light and he was comforted by her presence and love.

Above all else Ekani finally realized that his destiny was to be exactly what he had become. A Way Shower, to help others find their own understanding and their real inner self, like his father had said on that trip to the palace in Satara, 'There are no coincidences in life, son. Everything has a purpose.' He now understood that his entire life had been preparing him for his duties now as a Way Shower. Even the love he and Katarikari had found with each other. Without her Ekani knew he would never have made it this far.

That evening he wrote a letter to his mother and father telling them all about his life and that he was now a Way Shower. But he did not mention Katarikari or why he had run away. And he thanked them for their part of his destiny and wished them well. He sealed the letter and the next day he made a special trip to Hardwar where a courier would take it to Delhi and eventually to Satara and then to the small farming community two days travel south, near Karad.

* * * *

In 1680, word spread throughout the sub-continent of India that the Great Chhatrapati Shri Shivaji Maharaj had died and his oldest son Sambhaji was the new Shri Maharaj. As much contempt as Ekani had had for Shivaji for two and a half years after leaving Katarikari, he now was thanking him for his part in his unfolding destiny.

He finally became so involved and too busy to herd sheep and goats and he took them to Hardwar and sold them. He still had his dog and the two of them roamed freely in the foothills of northern India, with staff in hand.

There were streaks of gray in his hair and an aura of well being and knowing that surrounded him and all that came into contact with him responded to this well being.

Ekani was only spending time at his hut during the monsoons or on an occasional stop over while passing near his hut. There was never any sadness in his voice or on his face. After all these years away from Katarikari he still had the same divine love for her. The difference being, now he had realization and understanding.

1685

Five more years had passed and one evening in the spring, before the monsoon, Chapal arrived. As they sat and talked Chapal said, "You have come a long way, Ekani. Many people have found their way to me that had spent time with you first. They all say the same thing. That if not for you they would not have known what they would have done. You have done so well, Ekani, it is time that you become a Sadhu and take my place." Chapal removed a golden colored robe from his pack and gave it to Ekani. "It is time, Ekani, to put this on. You have earned it.

"My time is over, Ekani, and I have but one wish of you. Tomorrow morning I want you to take my body, and leave it by the stream in this valley. My body will be a gift to all the other sentient beings to eat and take nourishment. I have taken enough from them to sustain this body. Now I want to give something back."

There were no tears, no sadness. Ekani only nodded his head that he would.

The next morning Chapal had left his body as he said he would. There was no more life in it. Ekani picked the cold body up and put it over his shoulder and then carried it down to the stream and laid it on the ground.

Chapter 13

When Ekani left the palace in Raigad in 1667, Canda had offered her services to the Princess and her assistant at the palace became the new chief of staff in the palace. A week had passed on the journey to Rajasthan before the Maharaj and his wife knew anything about their daughter's servant running away. They didn't object to Canda taking his place. She had always served the family well.

Prince Adheer Raman had become viceroy after his father's death and now Katarikari was My Lady Katarikari. One afternoon while Katarikari was sitting in the shade under a huge tree, Canda walked over and addressed her, "My Lady Katarikari, may I have a word with you?"

"Of course, Canda, what is it?"

"When I was at the market place yesterday I heard people talking. And some of the servants here, My Lady, are talking about the same thing."

"What is it, Canda?"

"There is a *Sadhu* (holy man) who walks the foothills to the north of here with a dog and staff. He wears a golden colored robe. People are saying how he has helped them and how kind he is to everyone, My Lady. That he is a special Hindu Sadhu. That he has a special ability of knowing."

"And who is this holy man, Canda?"

"My Lady—My Lady, it is Ekani," and Canda started

157

crying. There was so much joy and happiness flowing through her, that they finally now knew what had become of him.

Tears were running down Katarikari's cheeks and she asked, "Are you sure, Canda?"

"Yes, My Lady. People are calling him by his name."

Katarikari stood up and stepped closer to Canda and for the first time in her life she hugged her like she would have her mother. Canda hugged her back.

"Oh Canda, I have always loved him so much. I'm so glad you have told me this."

"I have always loved him too, My Lady. But as a mother. Now, no Maharaj, Prince or Viceroy would ever attempt to harm a Hindu Holy Man. He is finally safe, My Lady."

1715

The years passed without Ekani paying much attention to their passing. He wandered among the foothills for decades helping people find what they needed in life. He had helped many to become Way Showers and a few he had bestowed them to *Sadhu* (holy man).

His dog had died of old age and he found another. He walked among the wild animals in India without any fear and the wild animals could sense the goodness in him and they too were not afraid.

A new century came without much ado. It was only the start of another year. For forty two years Ekani walked among the foothills of the Himalayan Mountains, teaching the principles of Hinduism and helping some find their self-realization.

He knew his time was near, so one day he stopped and turned around and headed back to his hut. He met a couple on the way and gave them his dog.

It was late in the afternoon on a warm spring day when he arrived back at his hut. Instead of stopping there he walked down to the cool stream. Had a drink of water and sat under a huge shade tree and leaned back against it. Remembering this is where he had left Chapal's body. Now he would give his to the animals to eat and take nourishment. This would be his gift to them, like Chapal had done.

He sat there not really thinking much about anything. But he was happy and smiling. The sun was below the tree tops and it was twilight. He was feeling happy and excited and a warm golden ray encompassed his body. Then a beautiful blue globe of light appeared in front of him. He knew Katarikari was there.

Then suddenly the blue light changed and now Katarikari stood in front of him smiling. She looked just as she had when they had said good-bye so many years earlier. She extended her hand to Ekani and said, "Are you ready, Ekani, my love? Take my hand and step out of that body of clay. I stepped from mine a month ago," she said.

Ekani took her hand in his and suddenly the last forty-two years vanished. All there was was this moment. Nothing else mattered. He and Katarikari were once again together. "Come, Ekani, we'll have a long time together before we have to reincarnate again. This is our time now, my love."

Chapter 14

Ekani and Katarikari spent many years together in the inner worlds of Brahma, the ruler of the three worlds of Hinduism. Their life of sadness apart, while in the physical, now was forgotten. All that was important or mattered was they were now together. Always, wrapped with divine love and happiness. Here Katarikari was not a princess and Ekani not a slave. They were equal.

But this happiness had to wait for a while as Ekani and Katarikari each reincarnated again into another physical body on the Earth Plane. Katarikari had lessons she needed for her development towards Moksha, the liberation of material needs and illumination of spirit. Ekani had his own lessons which would not include Katarikari in this life.

"We will be okay, Ekani. Even though we will not be together in this new life, when we go to sleep at night we will always have each other for a few hours each night. Just remember, Ekani, I will always be watching over you." Ekani hugged her and smiled. There was no sadness.

* * * *

On January 3, 1740, in Norwich, Connecticut, Ekani reincarnated into the body of Benedict Arnold and all past memories of another life, Katarikari and the inner worlds were erased, forgotten. He had more lessons to learn before achieving Moksha and those lessons could only be learned now as Benedict Arnold, named after his father Benedict who died in 1761. Through his grandmother, Arnold was a descendant of John Lothropp.

Arnold and his sister Hannah were the only Arnold siblings who survived the yellow fever. Benedict's father was a successful businessman. After the deaths of a son and daughter, Absalom and Elizabeth, Mr. Arnold started drinking and became an alcoholic, losing most of his fortune and mercantile business.

Benedict had wanted to attend Yale College, but there were no family fortune now to send him. Benedict became an apprentice in the apothecary and mercantile business.

But after seven years, Benedict became restless and tired of working for his mother's family; at the age of sixteen he decided to enlist in the Connecticut Militia and fought against the French at Albany and Lake George. The French were defeated and the militia took possession of Fort William Henry, in New York.

Benedict soon realized there was no money to be made in the militia, so he with the help of the Lothropps, started his own bookshop and pharmacy business in New Haven, Connecticut.

In 1764 Benedict went into business with Adam Babcock and they purchased three ships. They traded extensively in Quebec, Canada and the West Indies. On one trip, while in Honduras, Benedict had gotten into an argument with a British sea captain who had insulted him, damning his character. The British captain was wounded on the first volley of shots and before Benedict could reload for another shot the Captain apologized. This began Benedict's hatred for the British.

Britain had established the sugar and stamp act and in 1765 Benedict joined the chorus of opposition and his hatred for the British was renewed.

Benedict always had a restless side of him and he found it difficult to stay in one place for long. He was aware of this restlessness, but neither did he understand it. Arnold married Margaret Mansfield February 12, 1767; their first son was also named Benedict.

He was in the West Indies at the time of the Boston Massacre on March 5, 1770, and this furthered his hatred. So when war broke out in 1775 Arnold was a Captain in Connecticut's Militia, but soon was offered a Colonel's rank in May of 1775. Along with Ethan Allen and his Green Mountain Boys, they captured from the British Fort Ticonderoga.

Colonel Arnold boldly fought the British anywhere he could find them. He was always in the forefront of the fighting and his men had a lot of respect for him, for his fighting and he was being called a military genius, which caused much jealously with other Continental officers.

At the second Continental Congress in 1775 after the victory at Ticonderoga, Arnold and Ethan Allen both spoke up and said that Quebec City in Canada should be taken to prevent the British from using the city port as a staging point for attacking New England and New York and down the Hudson River Valley. And much to the disappointment of both Arnold and Allen the invasion task was given to General Phillip Schuyler of New York.

General Washington personally requested Arnold to take a northern overland route to Quebec. Traveling light and fast up rivers and through forests. While Schuyler wanted General Richard Montgomery to go by boats from Lake Champlain to the St. Lawrence. Montgomery would be able to carry food and provisions for Arnold's expedition when they met on the St. Lawrence.

When Arnold said he would canoe up the Kennebec River to the Dead River, and north of Flagstaff across the Chain of Ponds, then to Lac Megantic and Chaudiere River, General Schuyler countermanded this and said, "You will take bateaux. It'll take fewer boats for your men and you'll be able to carry more provisions."

Arnold rebelled against the bateaux, but Schuyler ordered

him to take the bateaux and not canoes.

Washington introduced Arnold to Reuben Colburn, a boat builder from Gardinerston, Maine.

Arnold planned an expedition of 1100 men and Colburn said he would have the bateaux ready.

Arnold had to have them ready by the middle of September, but the expedition's departure from Newburyport was delayed because of strong winds.

This timetable for so many bateaux to be built on time, Colburn had to employ many more men. Green lumber had to be used in many of the boats as there wasn't enough dried lumber for them all.

Arnold still would rather go with lightweight canoes, but both Washington and Schuyler convinced him otherwise. Washington handed Arnold a crude map of the Kennebec and Dead Rivers he had obtained from Colburn. "This map, Benedict, doesn't show any obstacles all the way to Chaudiere River. There may be some shallows the men will have to drag the boats over, but I don't see much difficulty and I'm sure the bateauxs will be more stable on the lakes than canoes. Especially if you run into foul weather," Washington said.

Arnold had one huge difficulty at the onset. The Continental Congress had not provided any funds to supply the expedition. Frustrated, Arnold used his own funds to supply the expedition of 1100 men. He kept all of his receipts in hopes of being reimbursed at a later date.

The temperatures were already cool at night and Arnold was concerned about his men. But Schuyler advised him that the trek to the St. Lawrence River should be a quick one and he would probably arrive there before Montgomery.

While the bateaux were being built, Colburn's friend whom had obtained the maps of the Kennebec and Dead River was snickering. He was a loyalist and he knew the maps were inaccurate. Enough so that Arnold would be delayed sufficiently until winter had set in around Quebec.

Colonel Arnold employed the assistance of five scouts from the Penobscot Indian Tribe who seemed to have some familiarity with the route Arnold had chosen. They would scout ahead of his men and see what obstacles lay ahead, kill moose and caribou for food and find suitable places to camp.

Arnold was tired of the constant delays and blamed both Montgomery and Schuyler and the Continental Congress. He had planned to take Quebec City before cold weather, but that seemed unlikely now.

The expedition arrived at Colburn's place in Gardinerston on September 22, 1775. When he inspected the bateaux, he wasn't happy. They were too heavy and he could see any number of problems they would have with them. But time was of the essence and Arnold had no choice. He would have to use these. "Oh, I wished I'd been allowed to take canoes rather than these cumbersome bullocks."

Before Arnold left Colburn asked, "Colonel Arnold, may I have a word with you?"

"Yes what is it, Colburn?"

"The scouts I sent out, sir, have brought back word of a large concentration of Mohawk Indians encamped near the headwaters of Chaudiere River."

"Did they see these Mohawks or is it only rumors, Colburn?"

"Word was given to them from Natanis, a Norridgewock Indian. There are rumors though that he is spying for the British and the Quebec Governor General Guy Carleton.

"Hum, your scouts did not see any Mohawks, Colburn?"

"No. This is what they said was told to them by Natanis."

"I have never known any Mohawks to be in that part of Canada." Arnold decided to discount the information.

With not a minute to waste, Arnold and the expedition finally set out from Fort Western (Augusta) on September 25th.

There were already problems and men were grumbling. The river was too shallow in places to float the heavy cumbersome bateaux and men would have to wade the river and pull the bateaux upstream. The temperatures were dropping and the men slept in wet clothes at night.

They reached the Norridgewock settlement on October 2nd and already behind Arnold's schedule.

"Hey Colonel, do you need help carrying all the boats over the portage?"

"It would help us out."

Men from the settlement came out to help and they brought what oxen they could to help. "My, these bateaux sure are heavy!" The same man said, "You could travel much faster in canoes, young fella. What ya going to do when you come to what the Indians call The Carrying Place? Ain't never been there myself, but I've heard tell it's a hard hike. Let alone dragging one of these bateaux behind you.

"Haven't your own scouts, Colonel, told ya about The Carrying Place?"

"All I have been told is that it is an easy carry," Arnold replied.

"Well, I hope you do. If you meet up with a lone Indian on your trek, name is Natanis. Hire him and get rid of your other guides. Natanis knows every inch of The Carry, besides the Dead River Country all the way to the St. Lawrence."

"Thank you Rusty, and thank everybody that's helped us with this portage."

With each passing day and portage, Arnold knew he should have insisted on taking canoes. But he was determined to take Quebec City.

With deep enough water for the bateaux and no portages, they actually were making good time. The scouts had shot two moose and a caribou and this fed 1100 men for three days only. There wasn't the plentiful game available for food that Washington was assured would be there. The scouts caught and shot beaver, squirrels and partridges. Anything that would keep the men from starving.

They finally reached The Carrying Place trail and Arnold ordered a day of rest before starting the gruesome chore of dragging the heavy bateaux overland to Flagstaff Lake.

Arnold asked his Indian scouts, "Are you sure this is the best way to go? That we cannot continue up the Dead River?"

"Yes Sir. From here to lake too much rock, rough water and Grand Falls. Indians always find Carry Place much easier."

The Carrying Place portage was twelve miles to Flagstaff Lake. The height of the land before reaching the lake was 1,000 feet in elevation. No one was looking forward to the Carry. Some even left during the night. Walking back home.

At daylight the next morning Natanis and his brother Sabatis walked into Arnold's camp and offered to guide them across Carrying Place to the Dead River and then onto Chaudiere River. "We know this trail better than Penobscot Brothers."

The portage across and up the Carrying Place was brutal, even with Natanis and Sabatis' help, scouting ahead for the easiest route and killing game to feed the men. In spite of its difficulty they reached the shore of Flagstaff by the end of the second day. Natanis and Sabatis had left a cache of food and went on ahead to scout, by canoe.

After filling their bellies and a night of rest the expedition moved on up the lake. They were all glad to be traveling by boat and not having to drag or carry it.

Natanis found beaver dams across the Dead River and after killing a few for food he tore the dams out enough so the bulky bateaux could glide through.

But once they were above the effects of the lake, the river became too shallow for the bateaux and the men had to drag them along.

"Arnold, why you bring boats so big, so heavy? Canoe not bateaux?"

"I'm following orders, Natanis. I wanted the canoe but I was ordered to use the bateaux. The man who built these bateaux, Colburn, also gave me a map and said the water was good all the way to Megantic."

"How many time Colburn go by bateaux to Megantic?"

Arnold was suppose to wait at the lower end of The Chain of Ponds for Lt. Col. Greene, but because he was already behind schedule, Arnold wanted to press on. But many of his subordinates wanted to go back.

The officers voted and Lt. Col. Enos was the tie breaking vote and he sided with Arnold, until he returned to his men and they all wanted to turn back. Enos changed his vote and he and 450 men left Arnold and the expedition and returned.

The Chain of Ponds were about twelve miles long and the expedition reached the head of the lake before dark. Sabatis had another cache of food. All of their provisions were now water soaked and ruined, so Arnold depended on Natanis and Sabatis' ability to hunt to provide food for his remaining men.

Colburn's crude map did not show the swamp around the south end of Lac Megantic and it was a rough trip through the swamp and alders. The little river would later be called Arnold Riviere.

Once across Lac Megantic they proceeded down the Chaudiere River at Sartigan, the southern most French village on the Chaudiere. The locals were sympathetic to the Colonies quest for independence and helped Arnold, but would not join the revolution.

Arnold's expedition reached the St. Lawrence River at Pointe Levi on November 9th. His men were tired and almost starving. Of the 1100 men that started on the expedition, Arnold now had 600, poorly equipped men.

Arnold knew he was poorly equipped to attack such a fortified city. But if only he could defeat the British here, the war would have to come to a quick end. Lt. Col. Allen Maclean had nearly 1100 well equipped men, against Arnold's tired and starving 600 men. Lt. Col. Maclean also had two Royal Naval ships, *HMS Hunter* and *HMS Lizard* protecting the river and city.

In desperation, Arnold sent a courier under a white flag

to Maclean with terms for their surrender. It was a ruse. But Arnold had to try. When it failed, Arnold decided to withdraw to Pointe aux Trembles and wait for Montgomery. Montgomery had managed to capture Montreal.

On December 31st Arnold and Montgomery's combined forces crossed the St. Lawrence. They were helped by the Abenaki people and the French. Supplying canoes and boats to take the troops across. But Maclean was ready for them. Montgomery was killed, Arnold was wounded in the left leg, and supposedly Natanis and his brother Sabatis were also wounded.

Arnold had to retreat before he lost everything. While his remaining men retreated to Fort Ticonderoga New York, Arnold personally commanded the rear guard, even though he had been wounded in the left leg. He was an inspiration to his entire army, or what was left of it. But he delayed the advancing British long enough to prevent them from reaching the Hudson River, New York.

While Arnold was recovering from his leg wound, he thought often of his family and his wife Margaret. They were married in 1764; she died June 19, 1775. Arnold's sister Hannah was caring for his three sons. He also learned he had been promoted to Brigadier General. Washington gave him high praise for his efforts and delaying the British from advancing on Ticonderoga and his actions at Saint-Jean.

The men in Arnold's army told other soldiers about Arnold's valor and how he was at the front of the fighting with his men and not at the rear where it was safe, like a lot of generals and commanding officers. Washington was impressed, and this made other commanders jealous of Arnold and the respect Washington had for him. Washington held General Benedict Arnold in high esteem.

Arnold had a restless persona and he could not remain idle for long. He was searching for something, but he didn't even realize that his search was misinterpreted as restlessness.

For a while Washington requested Arnold to the defense

of Rhode Island. The British had captured Newport.

The British knowing Arnold was defending Rhode Island, they did not want another encounter with him.

During a trip to Philadelphia to see Washington, he was alerted that a British force was advancing on Danbury, Connecticut. He helped David Wooster and General Gold Stilliman to organize troops to stop the British. During the battle Arnold was again wounded in the left leg. After the battle he was patched up and continued on to Philadelphia where he met with Washington.

Before Arnold had completely recovered from his second wound in the same leg, he returned to the Hudson. General Gates was now in command of the American Army. During the first battle at Saratoga, Gates and Arnold had strong disagreements and Gates, outranking Arnold, took him out of the front line fighting.

Arnold ignored Gates dismissal and led attacks against the British. The British surrendered and Arnold was wounded a third time in the same leg. The field doctors wanted to amputate his leg and Arnold wouldn't allow it. He told the doctor what would happen to him if he removed his leg. His leg was crudely set and now was two inches shorter and he had to walk with a cane. He was several months recovering.

In June of 1778 the British withdrew from Philadelphia and Washington appointed Arnold military commander of the city.

With each passing day he was getting more and more restless. He wanted to be in the field fighting the British and not confined in a city and to a desk. He began looking around, searching, and he found ways to keep his mind busy and engaged in a few profitable business alliances. While all the time making plans how to attack the British where it would hurt them the most.

While in Philadelphia he met Peggy Shippen, a loyalist sympathizer. Peggy knew, quite well, British Major John Andre during the time England occupied the city.

To solidify the plan he was working on in his head, on April 8, 1779, he married Peggy Shippen. Arnold had also befriended Joseph Stansbury, a reputable merchant in Philadelphia and loyalist. Arnold would use him to carry messages back and forth.

Washington traveled to Philadelphia to talk with Arnold after he had received some derogative information about his close association with loyalist and possibly the enemy.

When Washington arrived Arnold knew his plan was working, since Washington had traveled to Philadelphia to talk with him after hearing rumors about his loyalties.

"General, let's you and I go for a walk, where we can be alone and not interrupted," Arnold said.

As they were walking along a park path, Arnold began thinking how extraordinarily familiar this walking in a park seemed. He had never experienced this familiarity before.

They found a park bench away from other strollers. "Sit down, General, please."

"What is this all about, Ben?"

"Sir, it is obvious that because of my leg I am not fit for any field command. And this is where I should be. But it is as it is. I have opened a door to the British through my wife Peggy and her loyalist family and their British friends."

"Yes, I am well aware of this, Ben, and there are many in the Continental Army that say you have gone over to the enemy," Washington replied.

"Sir, I have not changed my allegiance. I am still as committed to defeating the British as ever. But I can see that my plans are working. Our own people believe I am going or gone over to the enemy and I have the British believing that they can swing me."

"You're telling me, Ben, that you have done this on purpose?"

"Yes Sir."

"But why?"

"Sir, give me command at West Point. If you do I believe

I can draw the British into a trap and take enough pressure off the other fronts to allow you to sweep the British out of this country.

"When I have important information about the British I can send a reliable courier to bring you the information."

"This would work to our benefit. Ben, you'll be walking a very thin line. What about your family and what will you do when this revolution is over and the British are defeated. There are some men in Congress and a few of my officers already asking for court marshal proceedings against you."

"If our own people already feel like this, General, then it will be easy for me to gain the trust of Major Andre and General Clinton. Once I have their trust, the rest will be easy."

"If I give you command of West Point, people are going to be asking a lot of questions. I'll have to discuss this with some of my officers, Ben."

"No Sir, you can't. I'm sure you are aware there are loyalists and British spies in every command in your army. For my safety and my family's, and for this plan to succeed, you cannot share any of this with anyone, Sir."

"You're correct, of course. When this is all over I don't know if I'll ever be able to clear your name and reputation, Ben. But I want you to know I'll always hold you in the highest regard."

"I need to do this, Sir. I'm wasting away here in Philadelphia. I need to be in the field fighting. We can't let the British return to govern us, Sir."

"I will think on this, Ben, and I'll give you my decision before I leave Philadelphia."

* * * *

On August 3, 1780 Arnold took command of West Point. Major Andre fully trusted Arnold, but Clinton wasn't easily convinced. So Arnold, as any good spy would, walked the fine edge of a razor blade, gave Clinton information about some insignificant army movements. He slowly gained Clinton's trust.

At the same time Arnold was sending, via a special trusted friend and courier, valuable information about the British.

Arnold knew the British wanted West Point. Arnold passed information that he would set circumstances to work to have Major Andre travel overland back to New York. The *HMS Vulture* had intended to take Andre by ship to New York, but through channels Arnold fed information about Andre's movements and Colonel James Livingston at the outpost at Verplanck Point fired on the *HMS Vulture* causing sufficient damage, so the ship retreated back to New York. Andre had no choice now but to travel overland, while carrying maps and information Arnold had given him.

Andre was captured in Tarrytown. The maps and information were found. The letters and maps were delivered to Washington and he secretly smiled when he understood the British attempt to seize West Point had failed. But Major General Benedict Arnold was now called a traitor, a turncoat, once the information of Andre's capture reached the public.

Arnold hated the idea that he would be considered a traitor by his countrymen forever. But he did what he considered he had to do to defeat the British.

When the British were defeated in 1781, Arnold had no choice but to move his family to England. In January 1801 Arnold's health was declining due largely in part to the wounds he had received in battle. Then on June 14, 1801, on his death bed he said, "Let me die in this old uniform in which I fought my battles. May God forgive me for ever having put on another." [1]

As Arnold's body lay still as he was breathing his last breaths, he saw a beautiful blue globe of light at the foot of his bed. And he knew Katarikari was watching over him and waiting for Ekani to emerge from the clay body of Benedict Arnold.

Now in his soul body, free of the physical limitations,

---

1   Wikipedia

Ekani and Katarikari hugged. "Do you understand, Ekani, that this life as Benedict Arnold was a lesson?"

"Yes." And then Ekani surprised her when he said, "It was a lesson where I had to learn that one sometimes has to give for the benefit of many."

Katarikari smiled and kissed him and said, "Come, we will have much time together now in the inner worlds."

Chapter 15

1860

Sixteen old Alexander William Roberts was walking around the farm fields bordering the Monongahela River after chores one morning. His father William Alexander and two older brothers were working at the steel mill across the river in Pittsburgh. His grandfather who he was named after—Alexander William—died a few months earlier. Alexander preferred to be called Will.

He sat down on the edge of the field looking across the river at the mill. He hated the idea of going to work every day in that damned mill for the rest of his working life, as his grandfather had done and as his father and two brothers were now doing.

The Roberts had a small family farm and now most of the work fell on his shoulders. He didn't mind farming, but nothing was his own. He was working for the whole family and not making a life of his own.

He had to quit school that year because he couldn't keep up with the studies and work the farm every day. He had hoped to go to college and become a civil engineer. Those dreams were gone now.

Each morning he milked ten cows, fed the chickens and gathered eggs and fed the hogs. There was a large garden to weed also. The heavy cream was separated from the milk and his mother Lorna made cheese and butter. Most of the milk products were sold and the money went into the family coffer. Will hardly ever had any money he could call his own. Will had two younger sisters who helped their mother around the house. Most of what the family needed for food was grown or produced on the farm.

The first crop of hay was done and in the barn. He had to hire help this year, because when the weather was good his father and two brothers were at the mill. It was a good crop of hay and Will was hoping for a good second crop also.

The only recreation he had was a community barn dance every Saturday night in the town square. Will had a girlfriend, Katie Albert, and they both enjoyed dancing, but Saturday nights were the only times when they could see each other. Will's day started at sunrise and ended when the last cow was milked. Because of the farm work he was a rugged sixteen year old.

Rumors of war were everywhere. It seemed that's all people were talking about now. Even at the Saturday night dances. Everyone at the mill was talking about what would happen when Lincoln would win the presidential vote in the fall. Many people were packing up and moving west and even into Canada.

Pennsylvania was a free state, but there were still a few who would prefer to have slavery. Will's oldest brother Carl was already talking about quitting the mill and enlisting in the Pennsylvania Volunteers. Daniel said he'd wait to be drafted.

Once the second crop of hay was cut and in, Will would have some spare time each day that he would usually spend hiking in the woods or around the farm. He had a restless itch and now since his dream of becoming a civil engineer had come to an end, he was listening to others talking about going west. To the big open country. There were still places that had never seen man. White man at least.

One afternoon in late September Will had time to take a horse and wagon into town for supplies. Before leaving he bought a newspaper. On the front page in bold lettering was 'Seven Slave States Threaten to Secede from the Union if Abraham Lincoln wins the fall election.'

There was no doubt in Will's mind that Lincoln would win the presidency, but would the seven states keep the threat and leave. What would that mean to the whole nation?

Will wasn't old enough yet to vote, but if he were, he wouldn't hesitate to vote for Lincoln, inspite of the South's threat. Abandoning slavery was one thing and probably the right thing to do, but splitting the nation was wrong. Any way you wanted to look at it.

Will's father didn't want to hear about any of his sons going to war. Will just wanted to go west. But if Carl enlisted and Daniel probably would be drafted if war came and if Will went west, that would leave his father to run the farm all alone and he would have to quit the mill. *Could he eke out a living on the farm?*

Will's mother Lorna just wanted her family to stay on the farm. And maybe milk more cows, acquire more hogs and chickens, so they could sell the meat and eggs. She did not want her sons to fight in the war, even if it was for a good cause.

With a little spare time on his hands now, with each passing day he was becoming more and more restless. He began walking more and more, always searching for something. But he had no idea that he was searching or for what. He began to feel that there was something he was supposed to do. But there again, he didn't know what or why.

Sometimes he would sit on a stump in the woods and watch the small animals around him. They didn't seem to have any fear of him. He would often bring butternuts or acorns with him to feed the squirrels. He discovered that deer would eat the nuts also. They wouldn't come close to him, but when he tossed a nut or acorn in their direction they would find it and eat it.

Other times he would just sit and listen to the sounds, until it was time to return home and start the late milking.

Through the years Will had developed a natural ability to doctor the farm animals. Many times where his father would have put the animal down, Will would tend to it and heal the problem.

One day when his father and the two brothers returned home from working at the mill Carl had a bad cut on his upper left arm. Someone had bandaged it with a dirty piece of cloth.

"That's an awful dirty cloth Carl. You'll be lucky if you don't get an infection." Will took the old cloth off and said, "Go wash up then I'll clean it and stitch it together."

While Carl was washing up Will prepared a needle and thread. Then he laid a towel on the kitchen table, "Lay face down on the towel Carl. Pa, get me your bottle of whiskey."

"What for?"

"So I can sterilize the wound; the alcohol will kill the germs and infection."

"You sure you know what you're doing son? I'd hate to waste a bottle of whiskey."

"I'm sure, Pa."

When Will poured a little whiskey in the open cut, it was about three inches long, Carl let the screams out of him. "Damn Will? That hurts more'n the cut. You sure you know what you're doing?" Carl squealed.

"Oh brother, you ain't felt nothing yet. Wait until I go to sewing you up."

When Will figured he had all the dirt out of the wound he dried it with a clean towel.

When he started to sew the wound together Carl flinched when the needle pierced the skin. "Pa, Dan, you'll have to hold him down so I can stitch him proper."

Every time the needle pierced the skin Carl let the squeals from him and Pa and Dan had all they could do to hold Carl down. When Will had finished, the wound had closed nicely and the bleeding had stopped.

His mother Lorna said, "Nice job son. How do you know

to do this medicine stuff? I don't remember anyone ever teaching you."

"I don't know, Ma. I just do."

He wrapped a clean bandage around it and said, "Now keep this clean Carl. If you don't and infection sets in I'll have to open the wound and we do this all over again." Carl got up from the table and pulled his shirt on. Sweat had beaded up on his forehead.

"Thanks brother. Maybe you should think about becoming a doctor, instead of farming," Carl said jokingly.

* * * *

Shortly after bandaging his brother Carl, Will was busy butchering two hogs and smoking the bacon and ham. When that chore was taken care of he went hunting for deer. It really wasn't much of a hunt. As there were so many deer on the farm, they were actually a nuisance. He shot three nice bucks and after stripping the meat away from the bone, Lorna canned it. It took her three days to finish, with all of her other household chores.

Later when the weather would turn cold he'd kill a few of the chickens that were not laying enough to make their keep worth it.

Voting day arrived and Will and his two brothers were not twenty-one yet so only the father could vote. And naturally he voted for Abraham Lincoln.

It took several days before all of the votes were counted and the returns telegraphed to Washington. Two weeks later it was announced that Lincoln had won the presidency by a landslide.

Great Britain declared it would remain neutral. But the elite secretly wanted to support the south in hopes of splitting the nation. The popular opinion in England, though, was neutrality.

The confederate states were disappointed. The Confederacy had been supplying both England and France with king cotton and had assumed naturally both countries would support their secession.

Before Lincoln's inaugural address to the nation, seven slave states informed Lincoln they had formed a confederacy and were making plans to secede.

This secession irritated thousands of northern working men and they rushed to volunteer into local militaries and the Union Army. This is when Carl made his decision to quit work at the mill and leave his family and farm and join the Union Army.

The whole country was in an uproar. Dan soon received a notice that he was being required to join a state militia unit. So the only bread winner in the family now was Will's father Alex. The money from the sale of milk, cheese, butter, eggs and an occasional beef, that money supported the farm and household. But Will never had any money of his own.

Things really came to a head when on April 12, 1861 the confederates fired upon Fort Sumter in South Carolina. It was an important Union Fort. Lincoln immediately ordered that all states provide troops for the Union Army.

With Carl and Dan both gone now, what help they did provide on the weekends was now gone. Plus the money they were earning at the steel mill. Will noticed their absence more during the haying season or when garden crops needed to be harvested. But not so much food was required to feed two less men and Will and his mother sold more dairy products, ham and bacon in town. But that money never went into Will's pocket.

During the summer of 1861 the south was still sending some cotton to England in exchange for munitions, and the British were successful with slipping their cargo ships through the Union blockades.

John Laird and Sons, a British ship building company, was building two warships for the south over the protest of the United States. England would rejoice if they could successfully split the United States.

Will and the whole family read the daily newspaper every

day. Looking for words of ending the war. The Union Army wasn't by far winning all the battles. The south was winning about as many as the north.

Will no longer had any spare time to go off by himself hiking or just sitting on the riverbank watching the water flow by. His father was just as busy. Sometimes he'd have to help Will until late at night after working all day in the mill.

In the fall of 1861 U.S. Naval Captain Charles Wilkes had seized and boarded a British ship, The Trent, and took custody of two confederate diplomats. James M. Mason was on his way to England and John Slidell was on route to France. Both diplomats were seeking help to defeat the Union Army. Britain was appalled by the boarding, but even though the United States was fighting a war with the south, Britain did not want to declare war against the United States. They had failed to defeat her in two earlier attempts.

That fall Will and his father only shot one deer each, for meat for the family. With only two deer this year to can Lorna didn't have as much work to do. There was also less laundry and mending to do. Her two daughters Becky and Rachel were old enough now to help out around the house when they were not in school.

Carl and Dan would write home when they could. Lorna prayed every night for their safe return home. The boys had actually seen a lot of fighting. And in some instances the southern army had driven them back.

Christmas that year, as with many families throughout the country, was a solemn holiday, especially for the families who had lost loved ones.

1862 started off frigging cold and water was freezing that never had before. The steel mill was advertising for more workers. The U.S. Army and Navy were using much of the steel produced in the Pittsburgh mill. Will's father was asked to work longer days, but he said he couldn't.

Will would be turning eighteen soon and he was seriously

thinking about joining one of the volunteer regiments. He was careful not to say anything to his family about what he was thinking. And he wasn't sure why he thought he had to join a regiment and get involved. It was more like he knew he had to, without any possible reason. The Roberts' Christmas festival was filled with worry and apprehension.

The north was defeating the south in a few battles and likewise the south was winning a few. The war was yet too indecisive to declare one side or the other as coming out on top.

During the winter of 1862 Alex, Will's father, was beginning to work a few longer days, since Will was able to handle the farm without any extra help.

During the cold winter months Will had heard rumors of a new volunteer regiment being formed in the fall and possibly being commanded by Col. Richard P. Roberts.

"Pa, a Colonel Roberts is forming a new volunteer regiment. Would he be a relative?"

"I don't think so, son. There are as many Roberts in Pennsylvania as there are Smiths in the rest of the country."

With the spring planting in and the vegetable garden planted, Alex was still working twelve hour days at the steel mill and every other Sunday. Will had two more milking cows, he sold the old bull for beef, there were six new piglets and he had to kill several hens that weren't laying. The farm was prospering, but Will was tired. He was now doing everything by himself, and he still had no money in his pockets. He had made up his mind to join this new regiment when it would form up. He read the newspaper every day looking for word of a new volunteer regiment forming and commanded by Col. Roberts.

Alex knew there was something going on in his son's mind. He had become very quiet and subdued since the first of the year. He thought maybe a good woman would help to cheer his son up.

By late August of that summer of 1862, the haying done and stored in the barns and sheds, firewood worked up enough for a year, an old bull butchered and taken to market, one evening Will stood in the doorway to the livingroom and said, "Colonel Roberts is forming another volunteer regiment. The 140th, and I have decided to join up."

His father exploded and his mother cried. "I won't hear of it Will! You can't leave. Who will look after the farm? You get that idea out of your head now."

"I'm going, Pa. I turned eighteen in May. I'm of legal age now and I make my own decisions."

"But why, Will? I thought you liked it on the farm. You have always done such a good job," his father said.

"You can't go son," Lorna wailed. "I can't lose all my boys in this awful war."

"What about the farm, Will? You can't just abandon this. You have done so well with farming. I can't run the farm and work in the steel mill."

"Pa, you'll have to make a choice. You quit the mill and farm or you sell off the stock and spend the rest of your life in the mill. Ever since you made me quit school I have worked this farm, much of the time alone and the money has always gone to you, Pa. I don't have a penny to put in my pockets. I wanted to go to college and become a civil engineer. I wanted to build things. To be part of this country. But you did away with those dreams, Pa, when you made me quit school.

"I want to do something for my country, Pa, and I want to get off the farm and discover the world and who I am. I get so restless sometimes I can't stand it. It's like I'm searching for something without knowing what I'm searching for. Maybe in the Army I'll find it. And the way I feel now when the war is over, I'm going west. I don't hate the farm, Pa, and maybe when the war is over I'll want to come back. I just don't know." Then in a more solemn note, "There's something mighty big, Pa, that wants me to find it. This is just something that I have to do. I hope you can understand."

"How soon will you go, son?" his father asked.

"The article in the newspaper said if anyone wanted to join they had until September 8th to be in Washington. That's only a day coach ride from here. Today is Friday, I'll leave Monday morning.

"Everything is all done for the winter, Pa. Until spring planting. Even the firewood. Maybe you could hire someone to milk and take care of the animals until spring. That would give you some time in the mill."

"I'll work it out, son," Alex said.

* * * *

Monday morning came; it seemed early. Will hugged both his mother and father. Alex walked with him to the bridge where he had to cross over to the mill and Will turned right to the stage stop. "Take care, son," Alex said.

Will boarded the stage an hour later and stepped off in Washington just as the sun was setting. There was a soldier in uniform to direct all the new recruits to Camp Curtin.

At Camp Curtin the new recruits received two weeks training and then they boarded a train for Parkton, Maryland guarding the North Central Railway. Captain Horace Green set up a twenty-four security at the station hub and along the main spur and the Dauphin and Susquehanna connecting line and the Lykens Valley line. The railway was so important to the Union Army. Besides transporting troops, the rail also carried war supplies, food, clothing, coal, iron products and passengers. The confederates would like nothing more than to seize the railway or do enough damage so it would not be so vital to the Union Army.

Will and another new recruit, Howard Drake, had a security detail two miles north on the line at a bridge crossing. Their second night out they saw two men trying to set dynamite charges. When Will hollered to them to stop and stand up, they were fired at. Will and Howie shot back killing both confederate saboteurs. That same night two other groups of two were also shot at two other bridge crossings.

This awakened Will. He decided being a Union soldier and protecting the railway was serious business. Here, like the farm, Will was working seven days a week. And he still didn't have a penny in his pocket. But he was feeling good about protecting America.

The 140th volunteers now had almost three months experience and training to be Union soldiers. On December 12th 1862 the 140th regiment had been issued and still using the old and heavy Vincennes muskets. They were so heavy they made for a good battering club at close quarters. On the 18th they were issued the new Springfield rifle muskets, lighter and more accurate.

The 140th still had not been involved in any battles, only a few skirmishes. But that was all about to change, as on April 28, 1863 the 140th marched around Gen. Lee's left flank and on to Chancellorsville. They arrived at their designated position on May 1st and waited for orders. Every soldier there knew this was going to be a major battle and Will hoped he was up to it. He and Howie Drake had become buddies and they now shared a common position behind a rock wall. Howie asked, "Will, are you scared?"

"I don't know, to be honest with you Howie, I just feel sort of numb all over. Like this is a bad dream or something."

"I wish it were just a dream." Howie was quiet then.

From somewhere deep in the recesses of his mind, Will knew he had experienced worse than what this battle would be. And for some reason that he couldn't explain, he knew he had survived that experience and he would this battle also. But try as hard as he could, he could not remember where he had been or what he had experienced that was now coming to his attention. But he knew he would be okay.

That was a long night. Howie was too scared to sleep, other than short catnaps, and Will spent most of the night trying to recall the memories or feelings of another time, another place.

In the morning, May 2nd, the 140th was ordered to join the 1st Division picket line, commanded by Col. Miles. On May 3rd, Battery E, 5th Maine Light Artillery was threatened to be overrun by the confederate troops, so Will, along with a squad of the 140th, were able to remove the artillery back to their own lines before the south could seize them.

When the fighting had finally stopped both Will and Howie had come through it without a scratch. The 140th regiment returned to their base at Falmouth.

"You know Will I was too busy to be scared during the fighting. I know a lot of our own boys were killed and I feel sorry for their families."

"I think it is a good thing, Howie, to be a little scared when going into a battle. It'll keep you from doing something stupid or foolhardy. I don't like killing much, but the south started this damn war and I think we have to do everything we can to hold the union together."

When the 140th wasn't fighting or securing the railway, they were training. There was a rumor going around the regiment that they would soon be getting a new repeating rifle, called the Henry. Will had never heard of a repeating rifle and decided it would give the Union Army a sizable advantage. A few of the new Henry rifles were issued to the 140th, for the more senior and experienced soldiers. Will and Howie did not qualify there. But they each had a chance to look it over and try it out on the range.

"Oh man alive, Will! What we couldn't do if every Union soldier had one of these."

"Yeah, good thing they are being produced in New Haven, Connecticut and not in the south," Will said.

Capt. Green gave the order, "If during the battle anyone comes upon a fallen Union soldier who has a Henry, be sure and take it. We wouldn't want the south to have any of these. To be of any use to you and if you have the time, make sure you grab the ammunition too."

By July the 140th had been snapped into a sharp disciplined fighting regiment. They were no longer bumbling new recruits, but not yet seasoned veterans either.

"Will, what will you do when this war is over?" Howie asked.

"I'm going west, out where there is big blue sky and the air isn't filled with fumes of a steel mill. How about you, Howie?"

"I want to farm."

"I should introduce you to my father. If he stays working in the mill he'll need a good man on the farm."

"What's the matter with you, Will? Don't you like farming?"

"Farming is good. You never go hungry. I want to be on my own." Then on a more serious note, "All of my life, Howie, I have always felt that deep down inside me, I'm looking for something."

"Looking for what, Will?"

"That's just it, I don't know. Only that this searching causes a restlessness in me. I don't even know if I'll recognize it if I ever find it. I hope I will."

"I hear rumors that Lee may be pushing into Pennsylvania soon. The south needs the steel manufacturing capabilities and the farms would be an added bonus," Will said.

"I wonder how soon and how many men we'll be facing when it happens?" Howie said.

* * * *

The 140th regiment had a reprieve from fighting for a while, but as rumors of Lee's advent into Pennsylvania became fact the regiment boarded the train and disembarked south of Gettysburg.

"This is going to be a big battle, Howie."

"Yeah, 'fraid so."

The actual battle had started the day before on July 1st. The 140th assisted Gen. Daniel Sickles' III Corps. The 140th had two days of the dirtiest and highest mortality rate of any battle. Before the end would come on the third day, all who fought there would be seasoned fighters.

Both Howie and Will found fallen comrades who had been issued the new Henry rifle, and a satchel of ammunition. During one charge on the morning of the third day both Will and Howie suddenly found themselves alone facing a squad of confederates. A cannon roared and shrapnel hit both Will and Howie in the head dazing them both long enough to be captured and taken back behind the enemy's line.

The battle continued, but more and more confederate soldiers began retreating until it was obvious that the Union Army had defeated the rebels at Gettysburg. Many men in the 140th regiment died in that battle. Will and Howie were taken to a prison camp in Virginia.

After Lee's army returned to Virginia and all the prisoners accounted for, it soon became apparent that a new prison camp was needed to house so many union prisoners. A new camp was hastily constructed in Sumter County Georgia, known as Andersonville. It was situated close to the Southwestern Railway.

The prison camp in Virginia soon became overcrowded and a few thousand prisoners were systematically transferred further to the south and finally on February 27, 1864 arriving at Andersonville. It was a sixteen acre stockade enclosure with a small stream flowing through the middle, which was designed to be portable water for the thousands of prisoners.

At first it didn't seem to be too awful. But soon Will and every prisoner there would soon experience the atrocities of the south. The only escape the prisoners had from the weather were tattered and weather beaten tents.

The men's spirits were low. "Will, we'll be lucky to survive this cesspool." Their first meal, one a day, was a watery soup with only a few vegetables added, no meat or protein. There were already men sick with disease, dysentery and malnutrition. Their biggest problem, other than no food, was the water supply. There was a stream that ran through the stockade but because of the overcrowding of thousands of men, the stream soon became filthy, and the prisoners were using it as a sewer.

With that many men all crammed in together in a relatively small area there didn't seem to be any one in charge. A few men had banded together and called themselves 'Raiders'. They would steal food and valuables from other prisoners, and sometimes killing a fellow prisoner for his clothes.

Will and Howie helped to organize another group of prisoners called the 'Regulators' who captured the men doing the raiding. The Raiders' punishment was usually a ball and chain, but there were a few who were hung.

Prisoners were dying daily at an alarming rate. One night Will awoke in the middle of the night from what he though was a dream. A woman's voice was saying, "You can do it. I will help you help these men." He lay awake for the rest of that night wondering who the woman was that had spoken to him and saying he could do what? *Help these men. With her help?* And who was she?

Come daylight, though, he understood. And he went to see the Prison Commandant Captain Henry Wirz. There was a so-called *deadline*. There was a solid log stockade about 15 feet high surrounding the compound and a light wire fence built around the stockade. The deadline was 20 feet between the wire fence and the log stockade. Any prisoners found in this area were shot.

Will walked over to one of the guard towers and asked the guard for permission to speak to Captain Wirz. The guard made Will stand there at attention while he went and informed the Commandant that a prisoner wished to speak with him. He stood there for three hours at attention before the guard returned.

"The Commandant will see you. Do not move until another guard comes to escort you to the deadline," the guard hollered down to Will.

When the escort came, Will's knees were hurting so much from standing at attention for so long he wasn't sure if he'd be able to walk the distance. As he began to move his joints were loosening and he was actually feeling better.

His escort waited with him for the commandant. The commandant came walking smartly out into the deadline in a clean uniform. "Name and rank?" He demanded.

"Private Alexander William Roberts."

"Where are you from, Roberts?"

"Pennsylvania, Pittsburgh area."

"I don't have much time, so make it quick."

"Sir, I can help a lot of the sick prisoners. But I will need clean bandages and something for an antiseptic and shovels to clean out the stream so we can have clean water."

"The medical supplies are out of the question. We barely have enough for our fighting troops. I will give you one shovel and before sunset each day it must be turned over to one of the guards. Then you can request it each morning. Now back inside the compound. Guard, find this soldier one shovel."

It was a square point shovel, but it would be better than nothing. Will had the Regulator Group gather and explained, "We're getting sick for two reasons. One, no food which we have no control over, two the filthy water in the stream. We need to clean out all the waste and garbage so clean water will flow. Then we must stay out of the water. We also need to dig a latrine in one corner of the compound and everyone must use it. We are living in our own filth. The commandant gave us one shovel to use and it has to be turned in to a guard each day before sunset."

No one had much strength or energy and the prisoners were a week cleaning up the stream and another two weeks digging a deep enough latrine hole.

"Even though the stream is running clear now we must boil the water before we drink it," Will tried to explain.

The latrine was dug, the stream was cleaned and Will thought everyone was boiling the water before they drank it. Will now had clean water to wash open wounds, but clean bandages were hard to come by. Men were still dying, but Will knew not as fast as if he hadn't convinced the Regulators to clean up the stream.

He hadn't gotten sick yet, but he was a skeleton of the man he once was. He asked a guard for permission to speak to the Commandant again and again he was made to stand at attention, until he knew if Captain Wirz didn't soon give him permission he would soon collapse.

Then finally he was escorted to the deadline. This time Wirz was there waiting for him. "Yes, Private, what is it this time?"

"We have cleaned the sanitation up and the stream is now running with clean water. But too-too many men are dying from disease and scurvy from malnutrition. Captain, we need some food."

"Out of the question, Private! My guards' rations have been cut as well. All thanks to you Yankees!" Wirz was so angry now he was screaming.

"I don't understand, Sir," Will replied.

"What! What do you mean you don't understand?"

"I'm sorry, Sir, I have no idea what you are talking about."

"I'll tell you! Your Major General Sherman marched on Atlanta in November and December. That bastard burnt the city. And before that his troops stole food, grain, horses, mules, anything they could use and then burnt the farms and grain bins and storage barns. After Atlanta he continued onto Savannah doing the same thing. Our troops, Private, and the peoples of Georgia have very little to eat themselves, let alone feeding 30,000 prisoners.

"The North's glorious General Sherman destroyed the state of Georgia. Every industrial plant was destroyed. What livestock wasn't taken was slaughtered. And you stand there wanting me to give the prisoners food I don't have?"

"Then Captain, why not release us? We are out of the war and there isn't one of us who could fight now, the shape we are in. We were brought here and the Confederate Army has the responsibility to our survival. What General Sherman did was an act of attrition in war. To cut off supplies to the enemy. That's war, Captain. What the Confederate Army is doing here is nothing short of murder."

Captain Wirz was so furious now he withdrew his service revolver and pistol whipped Will on the side of his head. Will collapsed unconscious and Wirz walked off and left Will there lying in the deadline.

The guard on the tower thought Wirz had killed him. Will lay in the dirt not moving. Then the guard saw something that frightened him and he was the only one in the entire compound who saw a blue globe of light surround Will. The guard had no idea what was happening, and he watched in fascination, because he was too frightened to move.

After a few minutes Will stood up and walked back into the compound. Even he was not aware of what had just happened. But where Wirz had pistol whipped him, his head no longer was hurting.

From that moment, the guard who had witnessed the blue light stayed away from Will, and he told no one what he had seen. And for some strange reason what he had seen made him believe Will must be someone very special. That hit on the side of the head should have killed the private. But the guard saw him stand and walk off like nothing had happened.

Will kept trying to keep the men from dying. Always stressing to boil the water before they drank, and to keep their bodies as clean as possible. But even still 200 to 300 men were dying daily.

With the Union Army now in Georgia, Will had expected some relief. But it never came. Then he wondered if what Wirz had said about General Sherman marching through Georgia was true.

Will had heard rumors that General Sherman was on his way north to join up with General Grant to oppose Lee.

Sherman's army fought and won battles as he marched through South and North Carolina.

Will told Howie what he had heard. Howie was deathly ill and Will knew he would not last the night. The next morning Howie lay cold and stiff in the only bed he had. Will buried him in the camp mass grave that day.

But there was news that Grant, without Sherman's army, had marched to Richmond, Virginia to oppose Lee. Will and all the Union prisoners knew that if Grant defeated Lee the South would have to surrender.

On April 19, 1865 after a grueling and exhausting battle the south was bested by Grant's Army. The South had no choice now but to surrender.

But the news of the defeated South took several days to reach Andersonville Prison. The South's line of communication was in ruins and there was no longer an army. On May 7, 1865 Union troops arrived and liberated the prison and took Wirz and his second in command James W. Duncan into custody and they were taken to Washington D.C. where they would remain in jail until their trial in November of that year.

Over 12,000 Union soldiers had died or were killed in that prison during its fourteen months of operation. Many of the men were angry and rightfully so and wanted Wirz shot before leaving Andersonville.

There were times when Will had wanted to kill Wirz himself. But now as he watched as the Union officials took him and Duncan into custody, he was actually feeling some empathy towards the man. Not so much that he would be held accountable for these men he murdered or the 12,000 who died of starvation, but that his consciousness was so low that allowed him to conduct the operations at the prison as he had without feeling any remorse.

* * * *

Will was one of the more healthy ones who survived and after a month recuperating at Fort Meade in Maryland, he was allowed to return home. He had a lot of back pay and he had made a deal with Colonel Smith. Will had found his true calling while at the prison caring for, as best he could, the sick prisoners. He wanted to go to college and study medicine and become a doctor. Colonel Smith said the U.S. Army would send him to college all expenses paid, if he agreed to go west and be an army doctor for five years with a Captain's commission. Will accepted readily.

On his trip home he was remembering the dream he had had and now he knew that none of this had been a coincidence. Everything had played out just as it was supposed to. Then he started thinking, somewhere, sometime, he had been aware of this same conclusion about no such a thing as a coincidence. But for the life of him he couldn't remember when or where. But the concept was not new to him. Of that he was sure.

He had sent his folks a telegram while he was recuperating and another the morning he boarded the train for home.

Carl and Dan both had survived the war, but Dan had lost part of his left arm. And after it had healed he refused to go home, he said, "I can still do clerical work or in supplies." He had an excellent attitude. Carl had been wounded but it wasn't severe. They both were at the train station waiting for their brother.

It was an emotional reunion. All three had survived the war. Dan was missing part of an arm, Carl, as Will, had been affected emotionally which neither one wanted to talk about.

Lorna and Alex were the most excited and thankful that all three sons had survived. Carl and Dan were planning to carry on the farm and his mother and father were clearly supportive about Will studying medicine.

"The farm looks good, Pa."

"I had a good man."

Will's two sisters Becky and Rachel were teenagers now and they had really changed. His mother looked ragged and tired, as did his father. Too many long days of worrying and working.

Will only had two weeks at home before he had to leave for the university in Philadelphia.

* * * *

Five years later in May of 1870 Will Roberts was now Captain Doctor Roberts. He had thirty days before he had to be on a train for the Montana Territory. He wanted to be as far away from the south as he could.

Becky and Rachel were both married now and the men had built two new houses on the Roberts' farm. Will knew now his family was well taken care of and he knew he would be also.

"Will, after you have served your five years in Montana as an army doctor, do you suppose you'll come home then?" his mother asked.

"When my five years are done, Ma, I'll come home. But I don't know for how long. There's something calling me west, Ma. A voice that I hear in my dreams. It is this same voice that kept me alive in every battle and again at Andersonville. I can't explain it any more than that, Ma. I'll write often and before you know it the five years will be up and I'll be back.

* * * *

Life was sure being good for Will Roberts now. He was a doctor with a Captain's Commission in the U.S. Army. He sat next to the window every daylight hour. He didn't want to miss anything.

The train went up to Duluth, Wisconsin. Lake Superior looked as big as the ocean. From Duluth the train went to North Dakota and then west to Fort Ellis a little east of Bozeman, Montana. Will had never seen such wilderness.

The doctor Will was replacing, Doctor Jim Harris, retired and left the following day of Will's arrival.

The Indian wars were at their height of fighting and now most of Dr. Robert's practice was removing bullets and patching up wounds. But he enjoyed his work and his patients began to trust a younger doctor.

He was beginning to feel sorry for the plight of the natives and on his time off he would travel into the wilderness among the different villages of the Blackfeet and offer his assistance. They too soon began to trust him.

1876

Good to his word after he had worked his agreed five years, he took a leave of absence and returned to the family farm across the river from Pittsburgh.

When he had left Fort Ellis he wasn't sure if he would return or not. But now a month after arriving home he knew he would return. He understood it, as he had to. He was still searching for something and he knew he'd never find it on the farm or in Pennsylvania. After two months of home life he said good-bye again and boarded the train for Montana.

* * * *

Will Roberts never returned home to the family farm again. He had found a life in Montana as a doctor suitable for his lifestyle. He never married. Never really had a woman of his own. But if asked if he ever became lonely because he didn't have a woman's companionship, he would always reply that he had a loving woman in his dreams. As he grew older the dreams of this same woman were more frequent. But he could never remember upon waking who she was or what her name was.

Then one day in May this woman in the inner world asked him, "Do you know my name?"

"Yes, of course I do. You are Katarikari."

Ekani never returned to the body of Will Roberts again. He was free of the flesh and clay prison. Now he was once again with his beloved Katarikari.

"This life wasn't a lesson, was it, Kari?"

"No. What do you think it was all about?"

"I think I came into the body of Will Roberts to help people. To help those imprisoned in Andersonville and the Indians. I do think I learned a great deal from helping people."

Ekani would take all the lessons he had learned from his many lifetimes and grow from them into a more sentient and conscious being. And as he looked at Katarikari, he was now seeing her with a much deeper and clearer understanding and love.

Chapter 16

1959

Just before daylight on September 9, 1959, Kyler Pardy was having what he thought at the time, a dream. But it surely didn't seem much like any dream. It all seemed so real and colorful. Kyler and a girl about his own age were running and playing in a beautiful park. The grass was so soft on bare feet and there were many flowers growing. Kyler and this girl were having so much fun playing. There was no one else around. Then towards the end of this inner experience (dream) Kyler and the girl transformed into young adults. They were hugging and saying good-bye. It was time to leave. Then the girl was saying something special just for Kyler.

But at that moment someone was rapping on his bedroom door saying it was time to get up. Kyler laid on his back for a few more minutes still living the moment with the girl he had been with on the inner. Only now he didn't know who she was, or what she had been saying to him when someone rapped on his bedroom door. But the rest of the experience he could remember and relive over and over. In fact every day for the rest of his life he would see images of this experience and the girl. He would never forget. And he would always wonder what she had been saying to him.

Kyler's bedroom was a closed in porch with windows

on three sides. As he laid in bed staring out the window by his bed looking up through the branches of the huge tree that grew close to the porch, he was wondering why he couldn't remember who the girl was or what she had last said to him, when he could clearly remember everything else about the experience.

There was another rap on the door, "Come, Kyler, breakfast is ready," his father Kyle said.

Kyler finally got up and dressed. The rest of the family was already eating. He was quiet, still thinking about the woman in his dreams. As he ate, he was thinking to himself that that experience was no dream. He didn't know what it was, but it was no dream. It was as real as the breakfast table in front of him.

He ate in silence and no one in the family seemed to notice he was exceptionally quiet. Even during school that day he was quiet and again no one seemed to notice. All that day all he could think about was that experience with the girl.

Four days later the whole family went for a picnic at Sarampus Falls on the Dead River near Chain of Ponds. While Kyle was getting the charcoal briquettes going to cook hot dogs and hamburgers, Kyler's mother Katie said, "Benedict Arnold came up this river on his way to Quebec City during the Revolutionary War. Story has it that some of his men camped out here."

"When we finish lunch we'll ride up to the Chain of Ponds. I was told where we could find Natanis' grave. He was the Indian who guided Arnold from the Kennebec River to Quebec."

The mention of Benedict Arnold hit a familiar chord with Kyler and he didn't know why. His two brothers and sister were fishing in the river without much success. Kyler was listening to his folks talk about Arnold and his trip to Quebec.

His mother said, "I have never believed Arnold was a traitor. After everything he did to stop the British."

Listening to his folks, Kyler knew Benedict Arnold was no traitor. He didn't understand how he did—he just knew he did. In school while studying Maine history they had only touched upon the Arnold Expedition.

No one else had stopped for a picnic nor had there been a lot of traffic on the road. This was a corner of the state that didn't see much traffic.

After lunch they picked up everything and followed the twisting road along the shore of Chain of Ponds. At times the shoreline of the water was right next to the road. "I think this is the spot Murray was talking about."

They all walked around the small point and up and down the shoreline and didn't find anything. They spent the afternoon there at Chain of Ponds looking for the gravesite of the Indian guide Natanis, but never found it.

On the way home Arnold's story kept echoing old memories in Kyler's mind. Echoing but nothing definitive. But he knew Arnold had not been a traitor.

At school the next day Kyler's teacher overheard him telling friends about looking for the gravesite of Natanis. Before ending his talk, young Kyler also said, "And I don't believe Benedict Arnold was a traitor." When his teacher asked him why he thought like that, he said, "I just know."

Even when Kyler was in the 8th grade and the class was studying Maine history, Arnold's expedition covered one chapter. But there was nothing to support Kyler's opinion of Arnold. And then again there wasn't enough to declare him a traitor either. He just knew.

All during his youth when Kyler wasn't working on chores or raking and mowing other people's lawns or haying for other farmers, he could usually be found in the woods hiking and exploring. Kyler had hiked and explored a square mile around his home. Always searching for something. He was very comfortable alone in the woods. But he always had this feeling he was looking for something without knowing what it was.

Even when he was in the woods, where he often felt more comfortable, he could not sit in one place for long. He always needed to see what was on the other side of the knoll. Even though he had been there before. Something new or different.

When he was old enough to hunt by himself, he would find a likely spot and sit. Only for a few minutes though and he'd be up looking for something different.

The summer between his junior and senior high school class his father allowed him to buy a car with money he had in the savings bank. This opened a whole new world for Kyler. That summer he was working 50-60 hours a week on a huge dairy farm and now his mother Katie wouldn't have to drive him to work each day. There were many times during the peak of the haying season Kyler wouldn't get home from work until long after sunset.

Kyler dated some but he never had what you'd call a steady girlfriend. That summer when he wasn't working late, he and two other friends would spend several hours fishing for eel, with the idea of having a fish fry at the end of summer. Mariann, a local pretty girl, would show up sometimes and sit by the fire with the three boys and talk the night away.

Sometimes Mariann would use one of the fish poles and fish awhile. One night when Kyler's two friends didn't show, Mariann did.

They started a small fire next to the water to attract the eels. They sat side by each on a log talking and watching the fish pole. Kyler felt very comfortable with Mariann and he soon had his arm around her and she snuggled close. Before the night was over they both had stopped fishing for eels and were wrapped in each other's arms making love.

Kyler was happy whenever he was around Mariann. She was always smiling and happy even though she might not have too much to be happy about. They would see each other off and on for years. Though Kyler never thought of her as a steady girlfriend.

When the three boys had the fish fry at the end of that summer, Mariann was there also.

* * * *

During this time in Kyler's life the United States became heavily involved in the Vietnam War. Many older boys from town had already done their time in the rice paddies and jungles of Vietnam. The national draft board devised a cleaver system to make the draft of young men fair for all. A lottery system. Kyler's number was not enough he figured to skate clear of the war.

In industrial arts class his junior year the shop teacher Sewall Pettengill got permission for his students to purchase old WWII German 8mm mouser rifles that would have to be disassembled, cleaned, reblued and new wooden stocks made. When Kyler had his finished it looked like a new rifle.

In the spring of his senior year Kyler went for a long walk across the family farm and next to the neighboring farms. He found a quiet place to sit and think about his future. If he waited to be drafted, he would probably end up in an infantry unit. If he enlisted maybe he'd have somewhat of a choice.

The next week he drove to an Army recruiting office in Lewiston.

"What are you interested in doing, Kyler?" the recruiter asked.

"The Army Corp of Engineers. I'd like to be a civil engineer."

"Do you have any training? Any college? Any civil engineering studies?"

"No. I won't graduate from high school until June. I can't afford college. I didn't know but maybe I could get my training in the Army."

"I can help you there, Kyler. If you decide to enlist then after basic training you'll be assigned to the Army Corp of Engineers. From there you'll be reassigned to one of their units.

"Do you think this is something you'd like?"

"Yes, I think I would. When would I train for engineering?"

"Glad you reminded me, I almost forgot. The enlistment will be for three years, then if you re-enlist you would be

201

enrolled in one of our engineering classes. We don't have mid-term breaks or summer vacations so a three year course with a Master's degree will take you two years. At that time you'd be asked to re-enlist again in part for the Army training you."

"Do you still think this might interest you?"

"Yes. Where would I go for basic training?"

"Fort Dix, New Jersey. When would you want to go?"

"I'd like to wait until September if that would be possible."

"Certainly. If you are sure, we can fill out the enlistment forms now and I'll give you a date to report."

A half hour later paper forms all filled in, "Be at this address on September 9th", and the recruiter handed Kyler another paper with the address, time and date. On the drive home the date September 9th started him thinking again about that inner experience he had nine years ago with that beautiful woman.

* * * *

After graduation Kyler went to work in one of the several mills in town and he wasn't long deciding that mill work wasn't what he wanted in life. He didn't mind the hard back breaking work or his weekly paycheck, but he found it boring.

September came and Kyler's father drove him to the address in Lewiston. "Good luck, son. You'll be okay."

"Thanks, Dad."

Before leaving Maine for Fort Dix the bus was full. They arrived at Fort Dix ten hours later.

It was late when the bus stopped inside the camp. After the new recruits had their bedding and beds made it was midnight. The next morning reveille was at 0600 hours. No one had been issued uniforms or gear and they marched into mess wearing civilian clothes. They had thirty minutes to eat and then they had to report to their barracks. Drill Sergeant Luke Davis was now in charge of them.

Kyler did well with basic training. Some of the new men acted like they knew more than their drill instructor and they had a more difficult time. Kyler was used to doing what he was told and he always tried to do his best, no matter what he was doing. With all the exercise and three meals each day, he filled out where it mattered and put on lean tough tissue in other places. No one knew where they were going once basic was over.

President Nixon wanted to step up the war in hopes of bringing it to an end. But Congress was the obstacle. Like Korea, Vietnam was being called a police action and not a war. But Nixon insisted on stepping up booming in Cambodia. The supply line into North Vietnam.

Many of the new recruits would be going straight to South Vietnam after basic and leave time. Those going into specialized fields would be going directly to their particular training without the usual thirty day leave before going to combat. They would get a few days leave though.

Kyler telephoned his folks, "I'm through with the basic training and tomorrow morning I'm going to Fort Hamilton in Brooklyn, New York to The United States Army Engineering School. I'll be at Fort Hamilton for thirty days then two weeks leave, during which I plan to come home, and then Vietnam."

His mother Katie didn't want to hear that. Her husband had fought in WWII and she worried about him every day until he was discharged after the war. His father was more understanding.

The next day after arriving home in the evening, he drove down to see Mariann. They both seemed to have the same idea and they rode up Gilky Hill to a friend's camp. Mariann felt good in his arms, but he knew better than to get too involved. He explained that he would be leaving for Vietnam in a few days, and he didn't know how long he'd be gone. So they enjoyed the moment.

Kyler couldn't just sit around in the house, so he often

would do what he had been doing all his life. He went for a walk in the woods. He was still searching for something, only he was not aware of it. He simply thought his restlessness was because he was bored.

His whole family went for a picnic at Sarampus Falls. The entire family enjoyed the wilderness here and the Chain of Ponds. They took a hike into Bug Eye Pond, not far from Sarampus Falls. It was cool and they didn't stay long. With the foliage gone they could see through the trees on the other shore and they could see two huge bull moose fighting.

A breeze started to stir, breaking up the thin film of ice along the shoreline. It sounded like soft wind chimes. Kyler was really enjoying the day, and he knew his father was also.

His leave was coming to an end and his folks drove him to the Portland airport. His mother was trying not to cry as she hugged her son and said, "Good-bye, son. You be careful over there."

His father hugged him without saying anything.

Kyler was in uniform and people he met on the way to his plane were exceptionally polite.

* * * *

At Fort Hamilton in Brooklyn, New York, the headquarters for the North Atlantic Division, the regiment that would be going to Vietnam gathered in the conference room. Colonel David Elbridge entered the room, "Gentlemen you were to have a month of training before going to Vietnam, but things have changed and this regiment is needed there as soon as possible. You'll be replacing a regiment that is rotating stateside.

"Our intelligence service has picked up chatter of a massive build up along the Cambodian border in the southwest of South Vietnam. We have been clearing a defensive line along the border from the Mekong River to the sea. To date only half of the border has been cleared and two bases built. We need to clear the rest and build two more bases and a landing strip.

"We now have only two days to train you on heavy equipment. Our job will be clearing the border and areas for the bases and landing strip. Another unit will be responsible for the buildings. All of the equipment is already in place. We have two days to train you on equipment and then another two days to get you to the border. You'll be flown to Saigon first, then flown by a smaller plane to Binh Thuy. From there helicoptered to Chau Doc.

"The information is Cambodia has joined forces with North Vietnam and when they push towards Saigon from the south the V-C are planning to push on to Da Nang at the same time trying to split our forces.

"We have maybe two months to finish and complete our operations."

"I'm handing out a list of each name and what piece of equipment you'll be trained on. As soon as you have seen the list a bus is waiting to take you to your training area.

"Master Sergeant Avril Monahan. Thank you gentlemen, I won't see you again until you arrive at Chau Doc. I'm leaving now."

Kyler check his list, "Wow, a D-7 bulldozer!" He had operated a small dozer on the dairy farm, but never imagined of being on something this big.

There were thirty men in the unit and thirty pieces of equipment. Each man had a ride-along trainer with him. "Every unit, Kyler, will have a set of headphones just like this one. The radio is built into the dash. On and off switch and this knob changes channels. We use channel 5; same as in Chau Doc. The Cambodians sometimes send out a patrol. If you see or hear any rifle fire, put it on the radio. Then turn your machine facing the firing and lift your blade. That'll give you a lot of protection. No one has been killed yet. Three wounded and not seriously. We'll always have patrols out looking for their patrols. If there is a fire fight, you'll be expected to help out. You'll be carrying an AR-15 just like this one with plenty of ammo. And in this compartment under your left armrest will be a dozen hand grenades and a small first aid kit. Each piece of equipment will be outfitted just like this. You'll wear a flakjacket and helmet always when you're in the field. There's more, but you'll pick that up in Chau Doc. Now I'll show you how to start it, then I'll shut it down and let you start it."

Kyler watched him start the pony engine and open the diesel throttle a little. When the pony engine was running smooth Corporal Dan engaged the diesel clutch and black exhaust bellowed from the stack. "Any questions?"

"No." Cpl. Dan shut it down by closing the throttle completely. Shorting off the fuel.

Kyler took the seat and he started the big machine first try. At the end of that day, "This machine has to be greased each day. We usually do it in the morning. Then check the oil levels."

By the end of the second day Kyler could operate the D-7 pretty well; all except for grading level. But for clearing a strip, level grading wouldn't be necessary, "That'll come with experience," Corporal Dan said.

The next day they boarded a C-135 Troop Transport. It wasn't even light out yet. They stopped in San Diego for fuel and again at Pearl Harbor.

"I never realized, Jeff, how damn big this world is," Kyler said.

They stopped next at Clark Air Force Base in the Philippines for fuel. From there everyone was quiet. Soon after leaving the Philippines air space, they were now in the war zone and they were being escorted by four F-16s.

Soon the Captain announced, "Gentlemen if you look out the starboard side you'll see the Saigon River and Fung Tao."

"Looks like a forest fire has burned everything on both sides of the river," Kyler said.

"That was no fire men, thick foliage used to grow right

down to the water and the V-C would dig out caves in the banks and wait for ships loaded with supplies and fire hand held rockets. We patrol the river with patrol boats and mounted 50 caliber guns and we still couldn't stop it. So we sprayed everything with Agent Orange. A defoliant," Corporal Dan said.

The C-135 was approaching the Saigon Air Base, "Men our next plane is already waiting for us. We need to get to Binh Thuy as soon as possible. We eat and rest after we land. At 0400 we'll be helicoptered to Chau Doc. Less chance of being shot down if we fly out before it's light," Cpl. Dan said.

It was beginning to sink in now. They were in the war.

From Saigon to Binh Thuy was mostly dense tree cover with open rice cultivation towards the sea. With a few small shanty villages. Binh Thuy was an Army Base with Army personnel only.

"Enjoy your supper men. There is no refrigeration at Chau Doc. Much of your meals will either be dry powder mixtures or k-ration. You'll have k-ration out at the border.

"In the morning you'll have ham, bacon, eggs and oatmeal, and coffee. Make sure your field packs are ready before you go to sleep tonight. If not you'll not have time in the morning. Reveille is at 0400. You must be aboard the helicopters by 0445. If you miss your flight you'll be thrown in the brig. Literally."

Kyler, Jeff and most everyone else slept in their fatigues. And probably many like Kyler laid awake for much of the night thinking about the morrow and the next. For some strange reason which he couldn't explain, Kyler was not feeling apprehensive about Chau Doc or being shot at by a sniper.

The next morning at breakfast Jeff noticed how calm Kyler seemed to be. "Hey Kyler, the rest of us are a bundle of nerves. You sit there as calm as can be. What's your secret?"

"No secret Jeff. Whatever will be will be. I don't believe in coincidences. If some thing is supposed to happen, then it will. If not, it won't."

Kyler enjoyed the flight out. It was still too dark to see much below them. Or for the V-C to see them. Just as the sun was beginning to rise above the horizon they were landing at the temporary base camp at Chau Doc.

"Okay men you'll notice we don't push up a raised bank of debris on the opposite side. This would give the V-C a nice hiding place to take pot shots at us. We try to push the burnable stuff into piles in the middle. Once we have the border strip finished we'll come back and burn it.

"Okay find your equipment number and go to work," Sgt. Monahan said.

Kyler greased his D-7 and checked the fluid levels. Then he started the big machine. As he sat while the machine warmed up, he checked his radio and put on the head phones. Checked the rifle, ammunition, and the hand grenades and the first aid kit.

It was exhilarating operating the D-7 with so much power. There was nothing he couldn't knock down or push. The soil was soft and the tree roots were not deep. But he had to constantly watch for the V-C.

The heat from the big engine blew back on him and he was beginning to sweat and he was thirsty. Tomorrow he'd have to remember to bring water.

That first day the team had cleared a mile long strip. While the equipment was working during the day, another smaller team had moved their temporary camp behind them. That night for supper the cook had used the last of the dried beef and vegetables for a stew. Everyone was hungry and had second bowls. "For the next four days, men, we'll have to subsist on k-rations. You guys cleared a mile today. That's good work for the first day."

Everyone was tired and complaining about an aching back. There was no one lying awake that night.

The next day they cleared a mile and a half. And Kyler remembered to bring along a canteen of water as did they all.

On the fourth day in the middle of the afternoon, Kyler

this time was on the border side pushing the slash towards the center pile when a bullet ricocheted off one of the vertical cab supports. The bullet disintegrated and a small piece grazed Kyler's cheek. He instinctively radioed the shot, and turned his D-7 towards the border using the blade as a shield.

As he was swinging the D-7 he saw six V-C. They were still shooting at him and other machines. He heard a voice in his head that said, "Go after them. I am watching over you." He looked around to see who was talking. There was no one there but him. Another bullet ricocheted off his D-7.

He pulled out two grenades from the armrest cubby and put those inside his shirt. He shifted to a higher gear and at full tilt started for the V-C patrol. They ran back a little, figuring Kyler would stop at the edge of the forest. Their mistake. The D-7 plowed through the trees knocking them over forward towards the six V-C as they ran. The tree tops coming down around them.

Kyler lobbed a hand grenade as far as he could in front of the big machine. When it exploded shrapnel and rocks and dirt came flying back at him. But he was pretty well protected in the cab.

"Has anyone been hit?" Sgt. Monahan called on the radio.

Everybody except Kyler replied no. "Where is Private Pardy? Is he down? Has he been hit?" The excitement and concern clearly in the tone of his voice.

Jeff replied, "I'm not sure if Kyler has been hit or not."

"Where is he?" Monahan wanted to know.

"The last I saw of him Sarg, he was chasing the V-C through the woods."

"On foot!" he hollered.

"No Sarg. He's chasing them with the D-7."

"He's what!"

"He is chasing after the V-C with the D-7," Jeff said again.

"Hell! You guys that are closest jump down and go after him. Be careful. Watch your perimeter."

When the grenades exploded the six V-C fell to the ground for cover. And Kyler and his D-7 plowed into a grove of six tall palm trees that were pushed forward and the tops came down on top of the six V-C soldiers pinning them to the ground. Kyler stopped and looked around for the six men and when he couldn't see them he grabbed his AR-15 and the one grenade in his shirt and jumped down off the machine.

He couldn't see them anywhere. He proceeded slowly forward, scanning both sides. He couldn't believe they had disappeared so quick. Then over the noise of the D-7 he could hear someone moaning. He walked up to the sound and saw the six soldiers pinned under the tree tops. He removed their rifles and searched them for explosives.

Jeff, and Sammy were the first to reach the idling machine. Jeff checked the cab and Kyler wasn't there. Neither was his rifle. "That son of a bitch took off on foot after them by himself."

Monahan arrived next. "Where is he?"

"He and his rifle are gone. He must be chasing after them."

"Jesus Christ! Come on let's see if we can catch up with him. Watch your sides, I'll watch forward."

They inched their way behind the big blade and Monahan looked over the top and saw the downed palm tree and Pardy sitting on the top of one of them. "I see Pardy."

"What's he doing Sarg?" Jeff asked.

"He's just sitting on a tree top looking at the ground. With his rifle pointing at the ground."

"Let's move up men. Be careful." They moved out. All three could see Kyler now, sitting on one of the downed trees.

When Sarg was standing beside Kyler, he looked down and saw the six V-C soldiers pinned under the tops. Monahan began laughing and said, "Well I'll be to go to hell!"

Kyler turned to look at Monahan and Sarg saw blood on his cheek. "Are you okay, Pardy? You have blood running down your cheek."

"Just a piece of shrapnel. Not serious, Sarg, I'm going to need help getting these guys out from under the tops. I searched them, Sarg, and they're clean."

The three of them working together removed each V-C while Kyler kept his rifle trained on them. "If this don't beat all," Jeff said while laughing. "Chased down by a D-7 and pinned to the ground by a tree top." All three began laughing again.

"Bring their rifles and we'll take 'em back to camp and call in a copter to take them to Binh Thuy. They'll be interrogated there by the South Vietnamese.

"You three get back to work and I'll take these guys to camp," Monahan said.

Kyler went back after his D-7 and worked it back to the strip. His cheek was beginning to burn a little but he'd have to live with it. For the rest of that day he kept wondering about the voice he heard in his head. At least he thought it was in his head. It was so clear and precise. It sounded like someone had been sitting beside him.

Col. Elbridge and Capt. Raynalds flew out from Binh Thuy when they received word Sgt. Monahan's men had captured six V-C soldiers. The Col. was staying and the Lt. would be taking the prisoners back to Binh Thuy.

It was after dark when they arrived at the Chau Doc camp. "Hello Sergeant," Col. Elbridge said.

"Good evening Colonel—Captain."

"Where are the prisoners, Sergeant?" Capt. Raynalds asked.

"They're locked up in the utility shed, Sir," Monahan replied.

"I'll take charge of them now and we must be leaving," Capt. Raynalds said.

After the copter and prisoners had left Elbridge poured himself a cup of coffee and sat down. "Tell me how you managed to capture six V-Cs, Sarg."

"I didn't, Sir. Private Pardy did by himself."

"Wasn't he operating a piece of equipment? At least he was supposed to be. Why don't you explain, Sarg," Elbridge said.

When Sgt. Monahan had finished, Elbridge broke out laughing. "Chased them down with a D-7. Damn! These people are superstitious and when word gets back to Cambodia, that D-7 episode will put the fear of God in 'em," he laughed again.

"I want to meet this Pardy, Sergeant, but in the morning. What about that wound on his cheek? Is he okay?"

"Oh yeah, just a superficial shrapnel graze, from when a bullet hit a cab vertical support beam. I cleaned the wound with an antiseptic and put a couple of band aids on it. He'll be fine."

"After I talk with him in the morning, I'd like you to take me where he chased them. Can you imagine how afraid those six soldiers must have been. Chased by a huge D-7 and a maniac? Unbelievable, Sarg. You have yourself a good man. But don't let him get careless."

"I'll be here for a few days until Captain Mellows comes in with the next supply flight.

"Now, Sarg. I need a cot."

* * * *

The next morning after a breakfast of powdered eggs, "Private Pardy," Col. Elbridge said, "would you remain behind. The rest of you may go.

"Sit down Private. That was quite an accomplishment yesterday. We should be able to obtain some valuable information from them. You surprise me, Private. You haven't even gotten your feet wet yet over here and you performed well, like an experienced soldier. But tell me one thing, Pardy, whatever made you decide to chase them down with your D-7?" Elbridge and Monahan began to laugh.

Kyler didn't want to say anything about the voice he heard. They'd probably send him to a psychiatric ward. "It seemed like the thing to do. I thought it might scare the hell out of them. Besides, Sir, they tried to kill me," and he rubbed his cheek.

"How is your wound, Pardy?"

"I guess it's okay. Burns like a bad sunburn."

"I'll see that you get a purple heart for that."

"Thank you, Sir."

"That's all, Pardy. You're dismissed. But be careful out there. We can't afford to lose good men like you."

"Yes Sir," and Kyler left and walked out to his machine and greased it and went to work.

"How are the rest of the men working out, Monahan?"

"They are all doing a good job. I think we'll have this strip finished before schedule," Monahan answered.

"When I get back to headquarters, I'll write up Pardy for a bronze star. I think he has earned it."

"So do I, Colonel."

"Damned! Chased them down with a D-7!" They both laughed again. "This technique of fighting the enemy will have to be studied at West Point."

The crew were clearing almost two miles a day now. Helicopters started routinely patrolling the length of the cleared strip looking for enemy combatants and any supply trains crossing. Colonel Elbridge knew instead of the supplies being moved by vehicles, they would be carried in by people. There were no roads close to the Cambodian border and the terrain and soft soil would make vehicle traffic difficult. No the supply train would be hundreds of men carrying the supplies across. So the helicopter patrols were also looking for a stock pile of supplies and any concentration of men.

Four days after Col. Elbridge's arrival, Capt. Raynalds was helicoptered in with food, supplies and other necessities.

"Have a good flight, Colonel," Sgt. Monahan said.

"Sergeant, this unit seems to be functioning better than the previous unit," Raynalds said.

"Yes Captain, they surely are. I estimate another three weeks tops and we'll have this project completed."

The food stores were certainly appreciated but they only lasted a week and they were back to powdered food and k-rations. The sleeping quarters, office/mess hall were both in two quonset huts on skids and they were dragged daily to keep up with the crew.

"Captain Raynalds, if all goes well, I expect to have this completed in another week," Monahan said.

"Thanks. Sounds good, Sergeant. Thank you for the up-date."

Three days before completion Capt. Raynalds was walking along the clearing watching the bulldozer work when he was shot by a sniper. Kyler heard the shot and saw the Capt. go down. "The Captain has been shot and he is down. About two hundred feet from me. I heard the shot and it sounded like it came from directly in front of me. Some of you men go get the sniper. I'll go see to the Captain," Kyler announced over the radio. Kyler grabbed his rifle and first aid kit and ran over to the Capt.

Kyler rolled him onto his back and saw an entrance wound in his right shoulder. He packed off the wound to stop the bleeding and radioed to Sgt. Monahan. "Sergeant, the Captain was hit on his right side just below the shoulder. He's alive and I've packed off the wound. I'll need some help to carry him to camp."

Just then gunfire had erupted where Kyler had heard the shot. He naturally assumed his buddies had targeted the sniper.

Monahan helped Kyler carry the Capt. back to camp. They laid him on a mess table and removed his flakjacket and shirt. "Hit just above the flakjacket. The bullet didn't go all the way through, and that ain't good. Our radios won't reach Binh Thuy from here and it'll be at least another two days before the resupply flight arrives."

"Sarg," Kyler said real serious, "that bullet will have to come out. He can't wait two days or he'll surely die of infection."

Private Kyler Pardy again heard that same voice and this time it was telling him, "You can do it. I'll be watching over you."

He turned around and around looking for the person who had said this to him. There was no one there but he and Sarg, and the Capt. "Roll him on his left side, Sarg, so I can feel the skin."

They rolled him up carefully and Kyler felt of his back. "It's right here Sarg. Maybe an inch deep. I can feel where the muscle issue has a bump. I can do it Sarg., remove the bullet and dress the wound."

"Are you sure, Pardy? If not, you could kill him."

"I'm sure, Sarg, and if I don't he won't survive until the helicopter returns.

"Okay, we need to clean this tabletop with antiseptic from the first aid kit. I'll hold the Captain up while you clean the table, Sarg." When the table was clean, "Okay we need to turn him on his stomach."

"Now what?" Monahan asked.

"I'll get what I need for instruments. You cut away his shirt and wash his back and then clean it with antiseptic."

Kyler found what he would need and boiled some water to sterilize them. When Jeff opened the door Kyler said, "Jeff, you can't come in; we're sterilizing everything. We have to remove the bullet from the Captain." Jeff closed the door without answering.

Monahan turned on the overhead light. "Thanks," Kyler said.

"Are you sure you can do this?"

Just then Kyler saw a blue globe of light surrounding the Captain's body. He had no idea what he was seeing but he knew whatever it was, it was going to help him. "Do you see that, Sarg?"

"See what, Pardy? I don't see anything."

Kyler smiled and he knew whatever this blue light was was there to help him. *Sarg couldn't see it.*

"Oh nothing, Sarg. I'm ready."

Kyler used the scalpel and made a two inch incision over the top of the bulge. He made it a little deeper and then using a pair of tweezers he probed for the bullet. "I can feel the bullet."

He worked around the bullet until he had the tweezers holding it and then he pulled it out. He wiped the blood off from around the incision and flushed the wound with antiseptic and then he stitched the incision up. "That was the easy part, Sarg. Now we have to roll him on his back and look at the entry wound.

"It's only a small wound," Kyler said, "but there may be damage inside, but I don't think the bullet hit any bone and there wasn't enough blood for a severed vein or artery. I'll wash it out with some more antiseptic and then stitch it closed."

After he had stitched the entry wound he said, "There, that's all we can do for him."

"So now what, Pardy?"

"We put him in his bed and check on him often. Make sure the wound doesn't become infected."

When they had Raynalds in his own bed Monahan went outside to talk with the others. "There was only the one, Sarg. We found this map in his pocket, but none of us can read Vietnamese."

"Anything else?"

"Some rice, water, an AK-47 rifle and ammo. He don't look old enough to be fighting, Sarg," Dale said.

"How's the Captain, Sarg?" Jeff asked.

"He hasn't come to yet, but Pardy removed the bullet and stitched him up. He says as long as infection doesn't set in he'll be okay."

"I didn't know we had a doctor working with us. What in the hell is he doing out here?" Chester said. "What do we do with this body?"

"I'd like to make a scarecrow with him and stake him out in the middle of the strip. But I guess that wouldn't be good. Bury it."

"Come on you guys—day ain't over with yet," Monahan said.

Back inside, "Any change with the Captain yet?"

"He's stirring a little, but he hasn't come to yet. He must have hit his head when he went down. I heard you tell the others to get back to work. I think I should stay here with the Captain."

"Sure, I'll take your machine. If there is any problem call me on the radio."

Late in the afternoon the Captain regained consciousness and started to moan and stir. "Easy, Captain. You were shot. You need to lie back and let your wound heal. If you're thirsty I'll get you some water."

"Yes." He drank a little water and then laid back down.

"Your shoulder is going to be sore for a few days, Sir, so you should remain in bed and stay calm. Your biggest worry now is infection." Raynalds lay back and fell asleep.

That night after everyone had eaten and Sarg and Kyler were sitting outside in the evening air, "Where did you get your medical training, Pardy?"

"I didn't."

"What do you mean, you didn't? Have you or haven't you ever studied medicine?"

"Not ever, except in Boy Scouts."

"Then how did you know what had to be done?"

"I don't know, Sarg. I just did." He wasn't about to say anything about the voice in his head or the blue light. "After all, it was pretty simple.

"Not to change the subject, but we are getting close to the end. The ground is getting softer and wetter."

"We'll go as far as we can," Monahan said.

* * * *

Two days later Colonel Elbridge flew in with the supplies. He was surprised to learn Captain Raynalds had been shot and

217

even more surprised that Private Pardy operated on him and saved his life. Capt. Raynalds was loaded into the helicopter and flown back to HQ at Binh Thuy.

"I'm here, Sergeant, until this project is finished," Elbridge said.

Later Col. Elbridge and Sgt. Monahan had another talk with Private Pardy. "Sit down, Private. Sergeant Monahan said you did an excellent job patching the Captain up. He also said you have never studied medicine."

"That's correct, Sir."

"Then how did you know what had to be done? Sergeant Monahan said you operated on the Captain as if you had done it before."

"I don't know, Sir, how I knew what to do. I just did."

"Well, Private, you saved his life. But because you have no medical training, in the future you probably should let a licensed surgeon do the operating. Out here was an extenuating circumstance. But, son, that was a damn real fine job."

Kyler left and Monahan said, "Colonel, there is something else about Pardy that I think you should know."

"Okay—go ahead."

"In an emergency Pardy steps up and controls the situation and delegates very easily to the others. He is a natural leader."

"Do the other men take offense?"

"No Sir."

"Do you?"

"No Sir, I know I have someone I can depend on."

"If you want him to be your Corporal, you have the authority to field promote him. From what you have told me I think you have made a good choice, Sarg."

When the helicopter landed at Binh Thuy, Capt. Raynalds was immediately carried by stretcher to the hospital. Dr. Hanely removed the bandages and saw the stitching front and back. "How long ago, Captain, were you shot?"

"Four days ago."

"From the incision on your back I'm to understand the field doctor had to go after the bullet." Hanely hummed and hummed looking at the incision. "His stitching could use a bit of polishing, but overall I'd say the doctor did a very fine job. What was the doctor's name, Captain? I wasn't aware that doctors went into the field with engineering units for a long period of time."

"His name, Dr. Hanely, is Corporal Kyler Pardy and he isn't a doctor. He operates a D-7 bulldozer."

"Well, he must have had medical training."

"None."

"I want to meet Corporal Pardy someday. I'm not going to do anything but check on you occasionally, Captain." Hanely left scratching his head.

* * * *

Kyler was promoted to Corporal and he accepted the promotion well and from the expression on the faces of the other men, Monahan knew they all agreed.

While the machines cleared the strip, Col. Elbridge patrolled along the Cambodia side of the strip with his AR-16 rifle and a string of grenades on his shoulders. He didn't want any more of his men shot. He patrolled back and forth all day, sometimes disappearing in the thick foliage then reappearing. Kyler thought this irresponsible, a lone man on foot patrolling for snipers was too risky. *Colonel Elbridge was taking too many chances.*

That night after eating they were all having a cup of coffee and sitting outside. "We'll finish up tomorrow, Colonel. Probably by mid-morning we'll come to marshes and the flagging indicates to stop."

"That'll be good. These men have earned a few days of R & R," Elbridge said.

219

Randall Probert

"Do we extract the same way we came in, Sir?"

"Surveyors have already laid out our route back with orange flagging. Is there enough fuel in the tank to get everything back?"

"There should be, Colonel. But the tank will be almost dry."

The next afternoon after they had come to the end they spent the rest of the day preparing. Col. Elbridge decided to take only the cook Quonset hut along. The two used for sleeping would be torched. "We need a quick extraction. We're well ahead of schedule, but a convoy of heavy equipment will make for an easy target still. Until we at least reach An Giang Province."

Everyone was busy greasing and checking their equipment so they would not have to do it in the morning.

The mess hall quonset hut was taking a beating. The men were all good with their machines and what Elbridge figured would take six days, only took them four and part of the fifth. As soon as they were at the Binh Thuy Army Base, Col. Elbridge left. "You're in charge Sergeant. I want to speak to the entire unit at 0900 tomorrow in the conference room."

Monahan showed them where to park their equipment. They were all dirty, tired and hungry. They wanted something besides k-rations. Monahan showed them to a quonset hut billet. They didn't have much of any personal gear. After they shaved and showered it was time for lunch. They walked tall and with pride over to the chow hall. No longer were they recruits or the new guys. And each of them to a man noticed this change in the unit and with himself. They had bonded together as brothers in the same family.

After lunch they took a pressure washer and cleaned all the machines, greased them and gave them a thorough check over.

As they were walking back Sgt. Monahan walked over and said, "Corporal Pardy, Dr. Hanely at the hospital would like you to stop by."

Kyler found the doctor in his office. "Come in, Corporal, and have a seat.

"I was quite impressed how well you took care of Captain Raynalds. In fact you did such a nice job I left it alone."

"How is the Captain now?"

"He's doing just fine. I discharged him two days ago. He'll still be sore for a while. It's to be expected. I'm to understand that you have never been to medical school, let alone surgery. If not for you, Corporal, the Captain would have died. Tell me this Pardy. How did you know what to do, and then do it so professionally? How did you know?" Dr. Hanely was almost pleading for an answer.

"I don't know, Doctor Hanely. I just did."

"How deep did you have to go to extract the bullet?"

"An inch."

"Did you have to do anything else inside?"

"The bullet never hit bone and I figured if a vein or an artery had been hit there would have been more blood. So I flushed the wound with antiseptic and stitched both wounds."

Dr. Hanely began laughing. "Instead of operating equipment, Corporal, you should be doctoring. My impression of you, I think you would make a fine doctor. Of course you'd have to practice up on your stitching though," and Dr. Hanely began laughing again.

"Thank you, Sir. I have been thinking about the medical field—but I just don't know. I like what I do now."

"Just give it some thought, Corporal. That's all I ask. You have a natural ability."

* * * *

The next morning in the conference room Captain Raynalds was able to join them. They all expressed how glad they were to see him recovering so well. "I'm here because of Private Pardy."

"Ah—Captain I promoted him to Corporal in the field under Colonel Elbridge's recommendation," Sergeant Monahan said.

"A damn good move too. I approve."

The Col. entered and sat at the head table with Capt. Raynalds and Sgt. Monahan. "Gentlemen, I wanted to congratulate you all for a job well done. For a green unit fresh from stateside you men performed well above what was expected of you. We have another detail which will require time in the jungle again but not as long. We'll meet here again four days from today after your three day pass to Saigon. You have certainly earned it after six weeks in the jungle doing the work you did and eating k-rations three times a day.

"You men are receiving a formal citation in your personal files and I have a Purple Heart for Captain Raynalds and Corporal Pardy.

"Corporal Pardy front and center." The Colonel waited until Kyler was standing in front of him before continuing.

Kyler was wondering what he had done wrong, to be singled out in front of the unit.

"At ease Corporal. Because of your audacity in chasing down six V-C snipers with your D-7, and instead of killing them, you captured them, the South Vietnamese interrogators have extracted much valuable information concerning the supply train that will soon be crossing into South Vietnam.

"Because of that and operating on Captain Raynalds which saved his life, I have been authorized to award you with a bronze star. Congratulations Corporal."

"Thank you Sir. I feel a little foolish when you compare my wound to Captain Raynalds."

"I understand that Corporal. But another inch and you wouldn't be here would you."

"I'm glad to see you are recovering okay, Captain," Kyler said.

"I never thanked you. Thank you."

"Did infection ever set in?"

"It was a little red around the incision and the bullet hole, but I don't think there ever was any infection."

* * * *

On their first day of leave the unit decided to have dinner aboard the floating houseboat restaurant that was tied up just ahead of the SS Greenbay cargo ship. The Greenbay had recently arrived as did the ship tied up behind it. Except this second ship had received a V-C rocket in the bridge. The ship was still operable but the radio operator had been killed.

The thirty-man unit occupied all but one table and to a man they ordered thick beef steaks smothered with Chinese vegetables and a baked Maine potato.

"Wow, this is the best tasting steak that I have ever eaten," Kyler said.

"We sure don't get food like this out in the jungle," Jeff said.

"It's probably a good thing. We'd be too fat and lazy to do our jobs," Kyler replied.

"Did you notice all those fishing boats tied up to the dock?"

"Yeah."

"They aren't very big, are they, Sarg told me that entire families live on those boats. Only getting off long enough to sell their fish or buy supplies," Jeff said. "They spend their entire lives on those boats."

"They don't look big enough to be able to stretch out and sleep, let alone a family. It must be pretty cramped," Kyler said.

On the wall by the check out cashier were photos of the restaurant after it had exploded. The cashier noticed Kyler's interest and said," V-C come blow up restaurant two times. Family, we rebuild. Thank you, Joe. Come again."

"Hey guys, we should have a special name for our unit," Steve suggested.

"That would be good, but what?" Jeff asked.

"How about the Caterpillar Squad?" Marvin said. He was usually so quiet, he often got left out of conversations.

Everyone nodded their head in approval. "We are the Caterpillar Squad then!" Dale shouted.

The guys were about two hundred feet away from the floating restaurant when it blew up for the third time. They stood and looked at each other, knowing how close they had all come to dying. "How do you tell a North Vietnamese from the South Vietnamese?" Jeff asked.

"I really don't know, Jeff. But I think we should be careful on the streets of Saigon."

They left and crossed the Canal Bridge and followed the Coastal Road until it intersected with Tudor St. Kyler and Jeff went first to the USO Club. They mailed letters home and then telephoned their folks. Kyler's line rang several times before anyone picked up. He had just three minutes to talk and tell them he was okay. At the three minute limit the line went dead. But it was good to hear his mother and father's voice. For the first time since leaving, hearing their voices actually made him home sick.

There was music and dancing at the USO Club and Jeff found himself a partner. In between dances, Kyler told Jeff, "I'm going for a walk around the city, Jeff."

"You be careful, Kyler. See ya in the morning back at base," Jeff said as he scooped up his girl for another dance.

Kyler went outside and started walking up the sidewalk. He passed the huge Continental Hotel. The air was really foul smelling. He saw women washing their babies in the gutter water and living in cardboard boxes on the sidewalk. One box was a Cheerios box another a Kleenex Tissue box. He wondered what they had to eat. He had never realized before now how fortunate he was and how lowly some people had to live. He turned around and gave each woman $5.00. They looked at Kyler wondering why in the world was this stranger giving them money. They couldn't even more speak English than Kyler could speak Vietnamese. The two women smiled and nodded their head several times.

He continued on walking trying to put himself in the position as these two women and wondering how in the world they survived.

The street he was following was heading to the outskirts of the city. Overhead lighting was less and the brightly lit businesses were back behind him. And there were fewer people. For some strange reason he began to think of the woman he had been with on the inner when he was only a boy. He was thinking how strange it was that he should think of her every day and now on Tudor Street in Saigon. He was wishing he could meet here in the physical.

Just then there was a loud turmoil on an empty side street across from Tudor Street. He stopped walking to look. There, three South Vietnamese soldiers were beating a fallen man with their rifle butts. When one of them noticed Kyler watching them, that one soldier hollered something in Vietnamese at Kyler and then the three dragged the body around a corner out of sight.

Kyler looked up ahead. He was at the city limit and nothing but darkness ahead of him. He decided it would be best to turn around and head back.

Back in the city lights he saw a bar/lounge on the opposite side of Tudor Street called Texas Bar. He walked in and sat down at the bar. There were a few soldiers there, but no one from his unit. There were more girls than men.

Someone dropped a quarter in the jukebox and music played and people started dancing. Kyler ordered a beer. He took a sip and then held the mug in both hands thinking about the three soldiers he had seen and then the woman he had been with in his dream years ago. He was smiling as he saw the images of her in his head.

He took another drink of his beer. Then his thoughts were back with the woman in his head, and he asked himself why of all the thousands of dreams he has had would this one particular inner experience (dream) stay with him. And what had bothered him even more all of these years—he didn't know who she was, or what she had said to him.

More than anything else in this world he wished he knew who she was. He took another drink of his beer and as he was setting it down on the bar top, he noticed another woman had just come in and was walking across the floor. It was almost as if she knew Kyler was watching her, as she turned to look at him. She was wearing an indigo blue silk dress. Her hair was black and straight. She had a square jaw and when she smiled, it illuminated the entire lounge.

Kyler was stunned. She looked so familiar, like he had known her from another place. But where would that be? But he was engulfed with her. Not just her beauty, but because he was sure he had known her somewhere.

She walked over and stood next to Kyler and said, "Hi Joe—you buy me a drink, no?"

"Sure, you want a beer?"

"Beer yes."

When she had her beer she said and stood up, "Come Joe we go sit over here," and she led him to an empty table in the corner. She sat beside him. "I called Kim Ly. What your name Joe?"

"Kyler Pardy. Hello, Kim Ly."

When she said his name it came out more like 'Kyia Pady'. But that was close enough.

Slow music was playing, "Kim Ly, would you like to dance?"

"You wish to dance with Kim Ly? Yes, I dance with you, Pady."

Kim Ly melted into Kyler's arms. They were the only ones dancing and everyone was watching them. He held her to him and lost himself with her essence, with every breath he took.

Kim Ly was enjoying herself as much as Kyler. He was different than most of the men she met at the lounge. Kyler didn't want to go immediately to bed. When the music had ended they sat back at their table. "Would you like to go get something to eat, Kim Ly?"

"You wish Kim Ly to eat at restaurant with you, Pady?"

"Yes, Kim Ly. You and me go eat at a restaurant. If you know where there is good food."

"What food you like eat, Pady?"

"Anything you like Kim Ly. Do you know a nice place?"

Two streets over was a Polynesian restaurant. The menu was in Vietnamese and Kim Ly had to order for them both.

He told Kim Ly about his unit eating earlier at the floating houseboat restaurant and blowing up when they left. "No! Do not you go to houseboats eats. Blow up too many time. Big brass go there to eat and V-C blows up boat. You no go there no more."

The meal was delicious. There was several different kinds of fish, rice sautéed with a mixture of vegetables, oil and a tangy seasoning. With a bottle of wine, Kim Ly ate as if she hadn't eaten for days.

"You like this food, Pady?"

"Yes, it was very good."

"Have you had enough?"

"You know what I would like now—a piece of apple pie."

"Apple pie. I don't know what pie is."

"Ask the waitress if they have apple pie."

Kim Ly asked and the waitress and she shook her head no. They finished the wine and talked long into the night. Finally it was time to go. They walked back to the Texas Lounge.

Before going inside, Kim Ly stopped and turned to face Kyler, "You go back to Army now?"

"No, I have three days off."

Kim Ly was so happy she jumped into Kyler's arms. Good thing he caught her. She nibbled his ear and kissed him and said, "I like you Pad, you come home with Kim Ly. I wish to bang you good, Pady, all night. Kim Ly not charge you. Okay?"

Kyler was laughing, more with her than at her and he said, "I wish to bang you to, Kim Ly. I stay with you all night."

Kim Ly hugged him and kissed him and said, "Come, you come with Kim Ly" and she took his hand and led him to her room above the Texas Lounge.

* * * *

Kim Ly never asked him what he did or what outfit he was with. If she had, Kyler might have thought she was North Vietnamese looking to extract information from American GIs. But she didn't.

He returned to base and told Kim Ly if he could, he would be back at the lounge that night. At the security gate he was stopped and asked for his identification and then told, "Corporal Pardy, you are requested to report to the conference room a.s.a.p."

Kyler was the last of the unit to arrive. He was still in civilian attire. "Take a seat, Corporal," Colonel Elbridge said.

"Your three day pass has to be cut short. The base at Tay Ninh has come under small artillery fire lately. The V-C hide their artillery in the forest out of sight of our spotters. Their infantry never expose themselves in the open clearing. If our troops try to cross the clearing and pursue the V-C, they are cut down. Colonel Hausman has requested our help to extend the clearing. We will only be taking ten dozers. Each operator will have another man from our unit riding with him in case of an attack. I expect the two to swap positions.

"Sergeant Monahan is passing out a list of operators. The operator can choose your extra man. The rest of the men, along with Colonel Hausman's troops will engage the V-C if any are spotted.

"This is going to be a fight men, not a cake walk like your last detail. Your machines have already been loaded onto trucks and we leave at 1200 hours.

There was a good dirt road all the way to Tay Ninh. This was the dry season and the road was dusty. Monahan had volunteered to buddy up with Kyler. This was serious business this time and there was little conversation on the trip out.

They arrived at the Tay Ninh base before dark. The machines were unloaded and the men not assigned to clearing joined forces with Capt. Lanley.

* * * *

It took a week, what otherwise should have only taken a couple of days. It was a constant battle every day. Kyler was engaged in his first fire fight. It didn't seem as they were gaining at all. Before the job was completed and the V-C artillery driven back, five of Monahan's unit had been killed. Jeff was one of them. Three others were wounded. But the job was finished. Kyler and the others understood now how bad the frontline infantry had it.

After each assignment the Caterpillar Squad would get a three day pass for Saigon only. And each time Kyler would go see Kim Ly.

* * * *

The Caterpillar Squad soon earned a reputation of getting the job done, no matter how difficult the situation. They rebuilt bridges that had been sabotaged by the V-C or a South Vietnamese traitor. They built schools in wayward villages. They built roads, repaired runways. Anything that needed to be built, rebuilt or cleared. As well as heavy equipment operators, carpenters and masons, the Caterpillar Squad was also a terrific frontline infantry combatant.

The day finally came when the Caterpillar Squad had earned enough rotational points to go home. There were rumors that the United States was going to offer a treaty to North

Vietnam and pull out. There was too much opposition to the war back home. Except the people in Washington would never let the military fight like it was anything but a police action. And fighting like this, the Vietnam War could go on forever. So President Nixon said to bring the boys home. Kyler and the Caterpillar Squad had returned state side before this decision and for the remainder of his enlistment Kyler was stationed at Fort Hamilton.

When his enlistment was over, he re-enlisted and was sent to a military college studying civil engineering. When he graduated he was a second Lieutenant and he chose to stay in the Northeast, the North Atlantic Division.

Col. Elbridge was now a General. Sgt. Monahan retired. Captain Raynalds after fully recovering from his shoulder wound was promoted to Major. None of the original members, except for Kyler, remained in the Caterpillar Squad, although the new squad chose to keep the name.

Kyler did a lot of work in the northeast but he also was being sent to all corners of the world. Sometimes for something as simple as building a road or school house.

By now he had been married and then divorced twice. Both wives complained about him being gone so much. Even when he was home, it seemed he was still searching for something. And he still would see that woman on the inner in that experience when he was nine years old. Every day. That experience (dream) had by now become part of him. And this was something he could never share with anyone else. Especially not his wives.

Because of his leadership abilities Kyler worked his way up the promotional gradient rather rapidly. He now was Major Kyler Pardy. And by now most of his friends and associates simply called him Pardy.

At every assignment while on his own time, he would walk around the area. He often called it his restlessness, but in actuality he was searching for something.

Much of his time and work was stateside; particularly after a devastating storm.

In mid-summer of 1990 he was sent to Saudi Arabia to construct and enlarge landing strips, bases and housing for what President Bush was calling Operation Desert Shield. Later when the troops and supplies were being stockpiled, Maj. Pardy and his regiment of Corp Engineers returned to the states.

One night while relaxing, he began thinking about his future. He had twenty-two years in and he wasn't sure if he wanted to be involved in another war. He had had his share of fighting. And he knew that all of his life since that dream with the beautiful woman that he had always been searching for something. And now after twenty-two years in the Army he wasn't any closer to finding it.

He had had a good career in the Army and he was certainly glad his choice to enlist was the right choice. But now he knew it was time to let go.

* * * *

Kyler had no home of his own. He had always lived on base, so now a civilian once again he drove to Maine to visit his folks. They were certainly happy to see him. "What will you do now, son?" his father asked.

"When I was doing some work around Caribou I drove around the county and I liked what I saw. The people were friendly and there was plenty of wilderness. Good fishing and hunting. I'd like to find some land somewhere and build a log house. I found a lumber company in Oakfield that makes log houses. When I get squared around and start building, you and Mom will have to come up."

He spent a week visiting with his folks and making sure they were ready for winter. There was only half enough firewood so he and his dad went out into the woods with chainsaws and worked up enough for the coming cold. That filled the shed.

They cut fir boughs to bank around the house and Kyler wrapped insulation around the water pipes so they would not freeze.

Every morning after breakfast Kyler took his folks down to the coffee shop. More to meet and talk with old friends than to have another cup of coffee. There were very few people that Kyler recognized anymore. It seemed like all the people he had known were gone. Either translated (passed away) or moved away. Other than his folks he found no reason to settle here.

Five years ago while doing some work in Aroostook County in Caribou and Fort Fairfield one weekend he had gone for a drive and found himself in a quaint little village along side the Aroostook River. Ox Bow. There had, maybe fifty years earlier, been many farms. He drove by the only store, called Deep in the Woods Gifts. He had stopped on the way back and had a cup of coffee with Steve and Judy Sherman—*nice people,* he thought. There was a hunting lodge beside Umcolcus Stream, The Ox Bow lodge.

The road came to an end at a closed cable across the road. Apparently you had to pay for the use of the road to use it. The Aroostook River was just over the bank by the turn around. Kyler had gotten out to stretch and look at the river. It was a beautiful piece of wilderness. Other than the gate shack there was no buildings to be seen.

When Kyler left his folks he drove to Ox Bow with the hopes of buying some land to build on. He had already drawn up a set of plans before his retirement.

It was a long drive but the scenery was well worth the drive. He stopped at the mile 247 scenic turnout adjacent to I-95. Mt. Katahdin to the west stood out in all its majesty.

As he drove through Patten he saw a sign that said *Lumberman's Museum.* "I will have to visit after I'm settled."

As he left the farmland behind, deep forests began to crowd in on the road. Rt. 11 became terrible. It was worse than when he was here five years ago. But he enjoyed the ride up through the spruce and fir forest.

His stomach was growling. Now he wished he had stopped for something to eat in Patten or Sherman.

At the bottom of Dunbar Hill in T7-R5, a pickup had pulled over to the side and stopped and someone was standing in the road with a rifle to his shoulder. Automatically images of Vietnam flashed through his head. Then he saw what the shooter was doing. There was a huge bull moose standing in the ditch about a hundred feet away looking not at the man with the rifle, but at a cow moose that was crossing the road about a hundred yards up the road. Kyler stopped and waited. He heard the report of the rifle and then the bull fell in the ditch. All three men were wearing blaze orange, so Kyler assumed this must be moose season. But he knew it was illegal to shoot from a paved road. He drove on and the men all waved. He waved back.

The Ox Bow road wasn't much better than Rt. 11. In his car he didn't feel the bumps so much. But if he was going to live in the wilderness a pickup would be more practical. He was enjoying the ride though.

He decided he would stop at Sherman's Gift Shop and see if they would have any coffee and a sandwich. As he pulled into the driveway he could see lights on inside of the store and there were two vehicles in the yard.

"Hello, Mrs. Sherman, I was here five years ago and stopped and bought coffee and a sandwich. From looking at your gift shop I'd say you no longer have food."

"You're Mr. Pardy, aren't you?" Judy asked.

"Yes Ma'am."

"You can drop the Ma'am. It's Judy. My husband Steve and I were just sitting down for lunch. Won't you join us?"

"I don't want to put you out."

"If you were going to do that I wouldn't have invited you. Come on." Kyler followed Judy to the kitchen table. Judy introduced Steve and Kyler.

After eating a ham and cheese sandwich, Steve asked, "What brings you back to Ox Bow?"

"I'm retired now and I'd like to find some land and build a log house here in Ox Bow."

"Steve, what about your Uncle Lester Junkin's old farm. Do you think he would sell some land?"

"I think he would. Would you like to ride up and talk with my uncle?"

"Yes."

They finished their coffee and rode up the road to Lester's. Lester was very agreeable. He wanted to sell and Kyler agreed to his price. The field and half the wood lot with a right of way for Lester and/or heirs. Steve showed Kyler a log camp he could rent until he had his house built.

* * * *

For the rest of that year Kyler was busy make arrangements with Katahdin Forest Products for his house (building package) to be delivered on site May 15th the following year. He traded in his car for a Silverado pickup. The cabin he was renting came furnished, so until he moved into his new house he didn't have to buy any furnishings.

The contract he had with Katahdin Forest Products included company builders to close in the house to weather and roof. He would do the inside himself.

* * * *

The next spring, on schedule, Katahdin Forest Products delivered the house package and two days later the carpentry crews started building. Their biggest problem were the blackflies.

By the end of summer the house was done, lawns graded and seeded. He went to Presque Isle and bought a truckload of furnishings for the house, and he bought a few items from Judy at the Deep in the Woods Gift Shop. He even had a wood pile all worked up for winter.

One evening in late September as he sat out on his porch late in the evening watching the northern lights dance across the skyline, he had this peculiar feeling that he was missing something. But try as hard as he could, he could not think of what. He heard coyotes off in the distance howling, an owl close by screeched. He smiled and thought, *This is home.*

That winter while he was driving south on Rt. 11 heading to Patten, in a heavy snowstorm, there was six inches of snow on the road and it had not been plowed yet. He put his pickup in four wheel drive. When he came to Deadman Pitch, a little south of the Ox Bow Road, he saw strange marks on the right side of the road. Like drag marks. He backed down to the bottom of the hill and parked off to the side and walked up. Both sides of the road dropped off about thirty feet, and on the right side, the drag marks were actually where a big rig truck had gone off the road and over the bank. It now lay upside down. It apparently couldn't make the hill and while the driver was backing down, the truck had gone out of control and off the road.

As Kyler started down the slope to check if anyone was hurt, he wondered if the leaking fuel might cause the truck to explode. Just then a blue globe of light encompassed the truck and for some reason Kyler knew it would be safe. He climbed up on the rig and looked inside the cab. The driver was not there. He looked around the truck to see if the driver had been thrown from the cab. He found where the driver had dug a hole in the snow and crawled out through the window and then he saw the filled in boot tracks in the snow leading to the bottom of the hill and then to the road. At least the driver was alright.

That night he laid awake for a long time thinking about that blue light, and the times he had seen it in Vietnam and then in Saudi Arabia and the voice. Then he thought of the woman he had experienced in the inner.

All these memories and the overturned truck brought back his restlessness—still searching for something and not knowing where to look.

He found it difficult to sit still for long. The evenings were the worst. During the daylight hours, he had a wide variety of things to do to keep his mind and body busy. He purchased a snowmobile, an ATV, he hunted, trapped and fished. But none of these activities could quiet the restlessness that was always present.

His folks both passed away within a couple of weeks of each other and this left a void for a while.

Even as active as Kyler was, he developed angina and the doctor gave him a prescription of Nitroglycerin pills. "Take one only as needed for now, Kyler. Your angina is only in its early stage. Some time we'll have to fit you with a stint. Come back in three months and let me check you. If the angina worsens then come in right away."

The only times he would feel any discomfort would be in the evening after a day of physical work. Like working on firewood. He learned that if he didn't exert himself his angina didn't bother him.

That spring an uncle from Connecticut, Ralph Gravlin, came to visit and do some fishing. Kyler borrowed a canoe from Steve and then left his uncle's car at the turn around by the Ox Bow gate and they drove to T8-R8 and put the canoe in at Moosehorn Crossing in the Millinocket Stream.

Trout fishing was good between the bridge and the Devil's Elbow and then again in a quiet pool just below the Elbow on the right. They kept two trout each that would go 2lbs apiece. They canoed down to the confluence of the Munsungan Stream. The two streams formed the headwaters of the Aroostook River. They each caught another large trout in the quick water where the streams met.

"That's a nice looking log camp up there," Ralph said.

"Yeah, Steve told me it belongs to Matt Libby. I understand he has a set of nice sporting camps on Millinocket Lake in T8-R9.

They were all day canoeing the river back to Ralph's car

and then they had to drive back to Moosehorn Crossing to get Kyler's pickup. It had been a long tiring day and Kyler had to take a glycerin pill.

After eating a late supper of brook trout, they sat out on the porch in the warm spring air sipping coffee. That evening his Uncle Ralph introduced him to Eckankar,[1] a religion that Kyler had never heard of. And he had many questions. While he listened to his uncle he began to wonder if Eckankar was what he had been searching for all of his life.

His Uncle Ralph also introduced Kyler how to chant, or sing Hu.

It was midnight before they went inside. The next morning his uncle had to leave. "I really enjoyed that fishing trip, Kyler. You have a nice place here. Maybe this winter you could come to Connecticut to an Eckankar seminar."

"I would like that Uncle Ralph. I'll keep in touch."

After his Uncle Ralph left, Kyler made himself a cup of coffee and sat out on the porch. He took a sip and it was too hot so he set it down on the railing to cool. He sat back in his rocker and began thinking about what his uncle had said about Eckankar. It was certainly a new religion to him. He had never heard of it before. But as he sat and rocked and sipping coffee he was going over and over in his mind what his uncle had said to him.

Already in a few short hours, some of life's questions had been answered, sort of. But at least clearer than any other religion that he knew anything about.

He would definitely make it a point to attend a seminar with his uncle. *Maybe there is something to this,* he was thinking.

Something had awakened on his inner, or was awakening. He was obvious of a noticeable change in the days after his uncle returned to Connecticut. He was always full of energy without requiring much sleep. Weather permitting, he would sit out on

---

1   The word Eckankar is a trademarked word and is an organized religion. *www.Eckankar.org*

the porch for hours, long after the sun had set. He worked in his garden every day. Even though there was no need, other than to keep busy.

He was going for longer walks and more often. His inner being was still searching for something. In the back of his mind he now knew how to find his answers, but he wasn't ready yet to look.

One warm day while walking along his firewood road in the woods he found a cool place to sit under a huge shade tree. He leaned back against the tree. *I wonder what is it in a past life that is affecting me in this life?*

He knew how to find the answer, but still he was hesitant to look. He was sitting on a soft cushion of moss and stayed under the shade tree for a long time before walking back to the house.

As he sat there in the cool shade of the tree, he began thinking, *I'm living alone, you know I should be lonely, but I'm not. I'm happy.* Just then he felt something like a warm gust of air surround him and he began feeling this happiness and the warming glow from his inner being out to the flesh on his body. It was almost as if someone had wrapped a warm blanket around him.

He sat there experiencing this happiness and the warm glow around him until evening when his stomach started growling.

He turned on the TV and watched the local news while he ate supper. When he had finished eating and the kitchen cleared, he made a pot of coffee, turned the T.V. off and sat in his rocker on the porch. Time just seemed better with a cup of hot coffee.

The black flies had died off for the summer and the bats were now chasing mosquitoes. They would dart down close to Kyler and he paid them no attention. Coyotes were howling down across the road. They were making so much noise they sounded like an entire pack.

When his coffee was gone he set the cup on the top of the

railing and thinking what was in his past lives that was affecting this life. It was time to discover what. He began chanting Hu. He sang or chanted Hu several times and then all was still.

He opened his eyes some time later and the sun had set. He could see images in his mind of a palace or temple like structure and a pastel colored sky. He thought he had gone to sleep and these images floating around in his head were only fragments of dreaming. He looked at his watch and couldn't believe so much time had passed. It was after midnight. He thought he had only dozed off and then awakened. But several hours had passed.

As he sat there in his rocker on the porch he began smiling. He was beginning to realize the image of the palace or temple were not mere fragments of a dream. He understood now he was there, wherever there was. Somewhere beyond the physical realm of life he was sure.

The night air was still warm and he decided to stay in his rocker for the remainder of the night basking in the warm glow that surrounded him.

All night he kept seeing images of the grand temple in his mind. The sun started to illuminate the tree tops, he was not sleepy or tired, even though he had not slept all night. For some strange reason he seemed to be filled with excitement and an expectation. Although he had no idea what that might be.

This time of the day, watching the sun rise was the best part of the day. Everything was reawakening and coming to life. Kyler too was reawakening to a new and higher level of understanding. Birds were singing now and looking for food. A red fox came out from around the corner of the garage and ran down his driveway to the road.

After eating a large breakfast he tuned up his chainsaw and went out back to work up some firewood. By noon he had hauled in four pickup loads of firewood and as he was throwing off the last piece from his pickup, suddenly images of past lives started rolling across his inner vision like a movie roll of film.

He watched someone, he presumed himself, in that

life, inside the Andersonville prison in Georgia. He watched as 12,000 soldiers died.

Then the images switched to the Revolutionary War and he saw Arnold talking to Washington and knew he was Benedict Arnold in that former life.

The images switched again to India and for some unknown reason Kyler knew the time frame was in the mid-1600s. He saw this holy man in the foothills of the Himalayan Mountains. And he understood he had become a holy man because of a broken heart.

Then he saw a splendid palace. But not like the temple he had seen earlier. And somehow he knew he had been a slave, a servant inside this palace.

He dropped the last piece of wood in the pile and stepped down out of the pickup body. There was too much energy and a sudden release of knowledge for him to go inside and sit down. And too much excitement flowing through him of his new discovery of himself.

Instead of eating lunch and relaxing, he washed up, changed his shirt and went for a walk. All the while more images coming and going through his mind. Pausing only long enough for him to identify with each image.

As he walked along the woods road more images kept flashing in his inner vision. Not complete scenes, only pictures like a post card.

There was still the need to search for something and he was very much aware of that now. He also now understood that his restlessness for all of his life was actually his need to find something. Although he now understood that, it wasn't bringing him any closer to finding out what.

As he walked along enjoying the fresh smells of the forest, he was also realizing that when his Uncle Ralph had introduced him to Eckankar he had awakened him to a whole new world of understanding.

He spent most of the day walking in the woods, all while

the images kept flashing across his inner vision. But now he was tired and hungry. He returned home and ate supper and lay down on the couch in the living room and was instantly asleep.

He slept sound even though he was on the couch. He lay on his back all night without moving. Then at the first sign of the sun the next morning, Kyler awoke. And instead of fixing breakfast, he made a cup of coffee and went out on the porch to watch as the day awakened.

Already this early in the morning there wasn't a cloud to be seen and the sky was the bluest that he could ever remember. Almost like crystal. "This is going to be a nice day," he said as he stood up and stretched and then went inside to shower. Afterwards he had a big breakfast and another cup of coffee on the porch.

He was happy just sitting there enjoying his coffee. But when the coffee was gone, he became restless and he mowed the lawn. Then he worked in the garden. And all the while he knew he had discovered something important during the night while he was in that inner world.

When he had finished with the garden, he decided to split the wood piled up in his driveway. He swung the splitting maul block after block without tiring, even though sweat was running down his face and his shirt was wet with sweat. He was feeling good. Like a young man.

By noon he had split the four loads of wood. He would wait a couple of days before he threw the wood in the basement. Let the sunshine and breeze dry the wood first.

After washing up and changing his clothes he made a pot of coffee and returned to the porch. He set the pot of coffee on the railing and sat down. Long ago while working in the Army Corp of Engineers, he began favoring a cup of hot coffee over a cold beer even on a hot day. He enjoyed a good cup of coffee.

He had just poured a second cup and had set the pot down when something had triggered a recess deep in his mind and spirit and he said out loud, "Look for me in this life." He said it again and again. "That's what she was saying to me in that dream when I was nine. Look for me in this life!" He shouted it this time.

And that memory started more images to appear and suddenly he knew who the girl was. "She was a princess and I was her servant." Then all the memories of that time came rushing back. "My name was Ekani and the Princess was Katarikari." He could remember every detail now of that life, as if he was still living it. He remembered Canda, Gopal Das, Chapal and that he had been a Hindu Holy man and why he had become a Sadhu.

There was so much excitement, happiness, and so many memories coming alive. Tears started running down his face. Not from sadness but the love that was flowing through him. He couldn't just sit there so he stood up and started walking towards the woods. His favorite passtime. He wasn't aware of anything except the love and knowledge these memories were bringing him.

He was walking right along not paying any attention to anything. Almost as if he was in a hurry to be somewhere. His angina was beginning to cause some discomfort, only slightly. He had experienced more severe moments. He checked his pockets for his Nitroglycerin pills and he had forgotten to put them in his pocket when he changed his clothes. So he slowed his pace.

By the time he found his favorite tree to sit under and lean back against the trunk, the pain in his chest was a little more severe. He tried relaxing and then a deep breath. There, that helped some. All his thoughts and images in his mind were of Katarikari, now that he understood she had been protecting him all through the different life times. He was just so happy to have all these memories and what was even better was that they all seemed to be in the moment and not three hundred and forty years ago.

The angina was back again and more severe. The pain was getting much worse. He looked up the road where he had come from and he saw someone walking towards him. Whoever it was wasn't walking like a man. He waited—no it is definitely a woman. A little closer now and she was smiling radiantly, and wearing a blueish green silk dress. His heart almost exploded with excitement as he recognized Katarikari. He had found her at last. The pain in his chest felt like an elephant sitting on him.

Ignoring the pain, he jumped up and ran to Katarikari, as he was running he was aware that his chest no longer hurt. He stopped in front of her and took both her hands in his and said, "Katarikari, I love you."

"You have had a long journey, Ekani."

And Now For The Rest Of The Story

The Afghan Mughals under the reign of Aurangzeb had moved across northern India to the Bengal Sea with the intention of a two-front war against the Maratha Empire and gaining control of all of India. Aurangzeb's greatest obstacle was Shivaji Maharaj.

Under Aurangzeb's reign, industry and agriculture began to flourish and many magnificent temples were built. But everyone had to adhere to Islamic customs and anyone found not wearing appropriate Muslim attire was punished.

Shivaji Maharaj led the Maratha Army against the invading Muslims to secure their land and preserve their way of life—The Eternal Way. But the constant fighting was becoming too expensive in both men and supplies, and Shivaji Maharaj knew if they were ever to defeat the Afghans they could no longer continue to fight the traditional Afghan way. Two opposing armies meeting on the field of battle and duking it out, man to man. So he informed his generals that if they were going to defeat the Afghans they would have to develop a guerilla style of fighting. And if his generals could not accomplish this, he would replace them with generals who could.

With the Afghans finally driven from India, in 1674, Shivaji Maharaj proclaimed himself Chhatrapati Shri Shivaji Maharaj (king) and declared Raigad as the Empire's Capital.

Shri Shivaji died in 1680 and his eldest son Sambhaji proclaimed himself king of the Empire in 1681. Sambhaji was a great warrior like his father and he was very popular among the people.

Eight years later Sambhaji was betrayed by some family members and he was killed in 1689 by Aurangzeb's army.

Rajaram, a younger brother now became the king of the Maratha Empire and moved the Capital back to Satara. In 1700 the Capital came under siege by the Afghans and Rajaram was killed. Now his wife Tarabai assumed the throne and led the

Maratha Empire in battle.

In 1705 Tarabai led her army in battle at Malwa. In 1707 Emperor Aurangzeb died and so too did his empire begin to die.

From early childhood I never believed Benedict Arnold to be a traitor. It just didn't seem plausible for someone who had fought so valiantly against the British and used his own money to fund the Quebec expedition to be a traitor. It was a gut feeling and common sense which convinced me, and not facts. But after researching his life for this book I am more convinced now than ever that Arnold was not a traitor.

Washington often praised Arnold in front of his other generals for Arnold's tenacity and his strategic abilities. This praise made the other generals jealous and I found it no wonder why the other generals wrote derogatory letters to Washington and Congress.

There is a Boot Monument at Saratoga with this inscription, "In memory of the most brilliant soldier of the Continental Army, who desperately wounded on this spot... winning for his countrymen the decisive battle of the American Revolution, and for himself the rank of Major General." [1]Arnold's name is left blank, but Arnold was in command of that decisive battle.

At the United States Military Academy at West Point there are plaques commemorating all of the generals that served in the Revolution. One plaque bears only the rank and date of birth, but no name (Major General—born 1740).

There is a historical marker in Danvers, Massachusetts commemorating his Quebec expedition in 1775. There are also historical markers to Benedict Arnold in Moscow, Maine, on the shore of Lake Champlain in New York and two in Skowhegan, Maine.

I honestly do not believe that the people of the United States would commemorate a traitor. I believe Arnold fought

---

1   *Wikipedia*

the last of the war the only way he knew how, even though his actions would be misinterpreted by Washington's generals and members of the Continental Congress.

The Union prisoners of war were taken to Camp Sumter, the Confederate prisoner of war camp near Andersonville, Georgia, about the same time Maj. Gen. Sherman was making his way through Georgia.

The Commandant of Andersonville was a Swiss-born Confederate, Captain Henrich Hartmann (Henry) Wriz. It is conceivable that Wriz took out his hatred and frustration of Sherman's march through Georgia to justify his treatment of the Union Prisoners.

Of the 30,000 men encamped in the crowded compound some 12,000 men died. When the Confederates lost the war Wriz was arrested and taken to Washington to stand trial. The most serious charges he was found guilty of: 11 counts of 13 charges of murder. On November 10, 1865, Wriz was found guilty of all charges and was hanged.

Wirz claimed that because of the effects of Sherman's burning of Georgia, he was unable to attain proper medical supplies and food. He had the option to release the prisoners, as in their condition they were no threat to anyone. But he made the choice to continue their imprisonment.

Acknowledgments

Most of the research was done with Wikipedia. I would like to thank Laura Ashton for your help formatting this for publishing and I would also like to thank Amy Henley for your help typing, suggestions and rewrites.

Author, Randall Probert

Randall Probert lived and was raised in Strong, Maine, a small town in the western mountains of Maine. Six months after graduating from high school, he left the small town behind for Baltimore, Maryland and a Marine Engineering School, situated downtown near what was then called "The Block". Because of bad weather, the flight from Portland to New York was canceled and this made him late for the connecting flight to Baltimore. A young kid, alone, from the backwoods of Maine finally found his way to Washington DC and boarded a bus from there to Baltimore. After leaving the Merchant Marines, he went to an aviation school in Lexington, Massachusetts.

During his interview for Maine Game Warden he was asked, "You have gone from the high seas to the air. . .are you sure you want to be a Game Warden?" Mr. Probert retired from Warden Service in 1997 and started writing historical novels about the history in the areas where he patrolled as a game warden, with his own experiences as a game warden as those of the wardens in his books. Mr. Probert has since expanded his purview and has written two science fiction books, *PARADIGM* and *PARADIGM II,* and has written a mystical adventure, *AN ESOTERIC JOURNEY,* and now *EKANI'S JOURNEY.*

Other Books by Randall Probert

A Forgotten Legacy

An Eloquent Caper

Courier de Bois

Katrina's Valley

Mysteries at Matagamon Lake

A Warden's Worry

A Quandry at Knowles Corner

Paradigm

Trial at Norway Dam

A Grafton Tale

Paradigm II

Train to Barnjum

A Trapper's Legacy

An Esoteric Journey

The Three Day Club

Eben McNinch

Lucien Jandreau